"The trouble is, I *want* to kill," Pete said. "I want to make them pay for what they did to me, to Janice, to Simone. That's why I'm bothered. I'm angry, and I'm scared. Because I killed two men, and maybe next time it will be easier."

Andrews didn't move. He just kept staring. With assessment, new awareness. When he spoke at last, his voice was respectful. "Then maybe you've got a chance."

"ACTION GALORE . . . *BLOOD OATH* IS WAITING FOR THE MOVIES."
Pittsburgh Post-Gazette

Another Fawcett Crest Book

by David Morrell

FIRST BLOOD

BLOOD OATH

David Morrell

FAWCETT CREST • NEW YORK

A Fawcett Crest Book
Published by Ballantine Books
Copyright © 1982 by David Morrell

No part of this book may be used or reproduced in any manner whatsoever
without written permission except in the case of brief quotations embodied
in critical articles or reviews.

All rights reserved. Published in the United States by Ballantine Books,
a division of Random House, Inc., New York, and simultaneously in
Canada by Random House of Canada Limited, Toronto.

Library of Congress Catalog Card Number: 82-5615

ISBN 0-449-20391-3

This edition published by arrangement with St. Martin's/Marek

Manufactured in the United States of America

First Ballantine Books Edition: September 1983
Second Printing: February 1985

for George Morrell
born: ?, died: 1943
in memoriam
the father I never knew

They reached a place where an old man was rowing a boat over a stretch of water. The ferryman was Charon and those he would not admit to his boat were the unfortunates who had not been duly buried. They were doomed to wander aimlessly for a hundred years, with never a place to rest in.

EDITH HAMILTON

Part 1

1

The stark white rows of crosses stretched forever. They were perfectly aligned, each cross and each row an equal distance from the other. Horizontal, vertical—the lines were laid out in a grid of balanced, reasoned order.

Houston felt a sudden chill that made him tremble. Just the wind across this hill, he told himself without believing. His rented Citroen was parked on the highest point of land around here. He leaned against it and stared down at the military grave-yard half a mile below him. Gusts tugged at his hair and numbed his cheeks. He had to squint. A tear stung his right eye. Just the wind, he thought again but still did not believe. Sure, just the wind.

The crosses gleamed, as if each morning squads of grieving soldiers passed among them wiping dust and polishing. Their brilliance bothered Houston. Their calm order was disturbing. Thirty-seven years ago, ten thousand soldiers died down there. He wondered if a general had stood where he now leaned against the Citroen. The valley would have been a seething hellhole: flames, explosions, smoke and craters, bodies strewn across the savaged landscape, chaos rumbling. His imagination startled him. The wind played tricks. It shrieked, and Houston thought he heard the crack of far-off rifles. He was sure that he heard high-pitched wails and frightened moans and . . .

Houston shuddered. As he blinked another tear away, the valley was again that neat, sane grid of crosses, stark against the lush thick grass, so dark a green that it was almost olive black—the hair of graves—while in the distance churning clouds effaced a sky as deeply blue as he had ever seen.

"There'll be a storm soon," Janice said beside him.

Houston nodded, turning. Janice clutched her brown tweed blazer tightly to her chest and shivered. Her long auburn hair was blowing straight back in the wind. Her cheeks were raw and red. Her green eyes, narrowed and moistened like his own, implored him. "Can't we watch from in the car? I'm frozen."

Houston smiled at her. "I guess I was off somewhere."

"Hey, take your time. You've waited thirty-seven years for this. But good Lord, aren't you cold?"

"We'll put the heater on. We may as well go down there."

Now he turned the other way and opened the driver's door to climb inside the Citroen. His jogging shoes felt hard against the pedals. Janice slid in on the other side. They shut their doors. His cheeks were numb. His hands were cold. The wind shrieked, muffled, past his window.

"I feel . . . hollow . . . feel uneasy," Houston said.

"It's natural. To be expected. After all, he's your father."

"Was."

Houston started the engine, pulled out from the "scenic tourist stop" (the sign had said in French), and angled down the curving two-lane blacktop toward the rendezvous he'd spent his whole life waiting for.

"It's strange," he said. "As a kid, I wondered what this place would look like. I imagined graveyards like we have at home. But this is . . . I don't know."

"It's sanitized, homogenized, anesthetized, and packed in cellophane."

He laughed. "You never left the sixties. If I close my eyes, I'll see you making speeches on the front steps of the student union. 'Burn your draft cards! Seize the administration building!' "

Janice hid her face. "I wasn't that bad."

"Hell, no, you were good. But I have to tell the truth. I didn't burn my card."

"I saw you."

"Parking ticket."

"You deceitful . . . ! All you wanted was to—"

"Get inside your pants. I may as well fess up."

"You horny hypocrite."

"A horny pragmatist. Let's speak precisely."

They kept laughing as the rows of crosses magnified before them. It's like whistling when a hearse goes past, he thought.

"You're really spooked," she said.

"There are no trees. You noticed that?"

"A bunch of trees would ruin the design. The Army likes things neat and trim. In shipshape."

"That's the Navy."

"Come on, you know what I mean. The military kills, and then it glamorizes death."

"Wrong war for that rhetoric. This wasn't Vietnam."

"I grant you. Necessary war. No question. But from standing up there staring at those crosses, you'd never know the pain they represent."

"I'm not sure I want to be reminded."

He felt Janice study him. "I'm sorry," she said. "I guess I wasn't thinking."

"Thirty-seven years." He shook his head from side to side. He clenched the steering wheel. "Did you know I never saw a picture of him?"

Janice was astonished. "What? You're kidding."

"Mom burned every photograph. She said she couldn't bear to be reminded. Then she wished she hadn't done that. But there wasn't any way to bring the pictures back."

"She must have loved him enormously."

"I only know she had chances to remarry, but she didn't take them. And I still remember—this must have been years later— how she'd cry herself to sleep. I'd wake up, and I'd hear her. I'd go in and ask her what was wrong. 'Just thinking, Peter,' she'd tell me, eyes red, sniffling. 'Just remembering your father.' "

"Jesus."

"All those crosses. Which one is he buried under?"

Janice put her hand on his knee and squeezed with reassurance. Then she fumbled in her burlap purse and found the pack of cigarettes. She lit one and handed it to him.

He nodded, drawing deeply on the cigarette. American. Low tar and nicotine. He'd had some trouble finding that kind over here, and he had paid four times the stateside value. But the French brands he had tried had made him cough. Besides, he hoped that hard-to-find expensive cigarettes would help to keep his habit in control.

The Citroen filled with smoke. He rolled his window down and felt the wind push at him. Smoke rushed out the window. Houston watched the tall seed-tasseled grass bend flat on each side of the road. The blacktop angled left along the slope. From this perspective, he stared ahead toward wide rich orchards on the west side of the valley. But the wind cast clouds that hid the sun. A shadow swept across the valley. Houston swung around a curve. His view was to the right now, eastward, and the cemetery filled his windshield—close, intense, and vivid—crosses white against the sudden shadow, endless.

Houston watched the stone fence loom larger, more distinct. He drove through an open ornate iron gate and stopped at a parking lot. They got out from the Citroen and shivered in the wind before the sprawling low white building that reminded Houston of administration centers in the big state parks back home, all glass and metal. Impersonal. The word is "institutional," he thought. The shrubs seemed made of plastic, and the lawn reminded him of astroturf.

"It's crazy," Houston said. "This isn't going to make a difference. Nothing's going to change because I came here. Hell, I didn't even know the man." His voice was strident.

"Want to turn around?"

He shook his head. "I can't. I haven't thought about my dad in years. But I remember when I was a kid I made a promise to myself that one day I would see his grave. And now my mother's dead. We came to France to take my mind off her. But I keep thinking of her. Maybe if I visit *this* grave, I'll accept her own. Or maybe I just want to tell him that his wife is dead."

6

Jan put her hand in his and clutched it. Houston's throat felt tight.

"Let's keep your promise."

Houston nodded. He walked past a sign—AMERICAN BATTLE MONUMENT—and up the hedge-lined sidewalk toward the glass doors at the entrance. Pushing through, he smelled stuffy air and heard the echo of his footsteps off the imitation marble. There were wall displays around the long narrow room: photographs and maps that dramatized the progress of the battle, rifles, helmets, uniforms, and mess kits; models, dioramas, paintings, flags. The room was headache-bright. He heard the door hiss shut behind him. He felt Janice close beside him.

But he concentrated on the counter straight across from him. A lean-faced clerk with short hair, thin lips, and a dark suit braced his shoulders, waiting. Houston walked across to him.

"Sir, may I help?"

Houston saw the clerk's American Legion pin on his lapel. "I'm not sure how. . . . My father died here," Houston said. "I don't know how to find his grave. They're alphabetic?" His voice was hollow in the mausoleum echo of the room.

"No, sir." The clerk leaned forward, so solicitous that Houston was reminded of a funeral director. "They're arranged by regiments and companies. If I could have his name, I'll find the grave for you."

"It's Stephen Houston."

"Do you know his middle name? In case of repetition."

"Pardon me?"

"There might be several Stephen Houstons."

"Oh, I see. It's Samuel."

The clerk, whose voice was Southern, looked at him with interest. "You're from Texas, sir?" he drawled.

"No, what would make you think that?"

"Sorry, sir. It's just the middle name. Sam Houston."

"Sure, of course. No, we're from Indiana."

"If you'll wait a moment, please." The clerk turned toward a console underneath the counter.

7

Houston glanced at Jan. The bright fluorescent lights hummed. He felt throbbing in his temples. "I could use another cigarette," he said.

Behind him, fingers tapped the keyboard of the console. Jan fumbled in her purse. Houston heard the puzzled Texan voice.

"That's Stephen Samuel Houston, sir?"

"That's right." He took the cigarette from Jan. He lit it, and he turned to face the clerk.

He didn't like the frown he saw. His heart raced. "What's the matter?"

"If you'd tell me how the name is spelled, sir."

"H-o-u—"

"No. 'Houston' I'm familiar with. The first name, sir. I'm spelling it with 'ph' in the middle. Sometimes there's a 'v' instead."

"You're right the first time." Houston's stomach burned.

"You're certain that he's buried here?"

"I'm absolutely positive."

"Perhaps another cemetery?"

"This one."

"Just a moment, sir."

The clerk walked stiffly toward a door. He knocked. A muffled voice inside responded. Houston watched the clerk go in and shut the door.

"Now what the hell was that about?" he said to Jan.

Her puzzled eyes moved nervously. "I guess their fool computer isn't working."

Houston turned abruptly as the door came open. He stared at a square-jawed older man, dark-eyed, wearing a navy blazer. Houston listened to the echo of his footsteps.

"Mr. Houston, I'm Superintendent Andrews." Nervous, Houston shook hands reluctantly. "My assistant informs me you're here to see your father's grave."

"That's right."

"He can't find any record that your father was interred here."

Houston gaped.

"He double-checked, and no one by that name shows up in our computer."

"That's impossible."

"Not quite, sir. When we programmed our old records, we were careful. But we're human, and apparently mistakes were made."

"Mistakes? This happened before?"

"Regrettably. Last year. And then again last month." Andrews seemed disturbed. "Our former records are downstairs. I'll check them. It won't take me fifteen minutes."

"Wait. Those other graves. You found them?"

But the superintendent didn't answer.

2

Houston paced, bewildered. First the superintendent took much longer than the fifteen minutes he had promised. Ninety minutes. Then when he at last came back, he asked them if they'd step inside his office. He was frowning.

Houston frowned as well. He glanced at Jan, stubbed out another cigarette, and followed her inside the office.

It constricted Houston. Small, severe, and windowless. A metal desk with nothing on it. Three steel chairs. A telephone on the wall. Bright lights, aggravating Houston's headache.

"Probably you've guessed," Andrews said.

Houston stiffened in the chair. "But—"

"Please, before you get upset, there might be several explanations. Perhaps he was buried in the cemetery north of here. It's fifty miles away."

"No, he was killed here in this battle."

"So your natural assumption is that since he died here he was also buried here." Andrews waited.

Houston thought about it angrily. He calmed himself, relenting. "Yes, I was assuming."

"But the military, in particular in wartime, isn't always organized or logical." Andrews pursed his lips. "You know the meaning of the acronym SNAFU?"

"Of course."

"Well, it could easily apply here. Rather than do things the easy way, the paper pushers could have had your father buried somewhere else."

"Then"—Houston strained to hide his fierce impatience—"phone that other cemetery."

"I already did that. What we're doing now is waiting for a callback."

But the call, when it came through, was not what Houston hoped for. Andrews hung the phone back on the wall. He shook his head, tapping a pencil on his desk.

"Look, this is crazy," Houston said.

"I'd be dishonest if I didn't mention one more possibility."

"What is it?"

'I hate to say it. It'll only make you angry."

Houston squinted. "You mean *angrier*."

"There's a chance—I have to emphasize a *small* one—that your father was identified as someone else."

"Another name?"

"Exactly. If his dogtags were misplaced—"

"He's buried out there, but his name is Smith or Jones?" Houston's voice rose.

"Or John Doe, an unknown, unidentified. In battle, dogtags sometimes are destroyed, and bodies sometimes are so—"

"*Please*," Jan begged.

"Mrs. Houston, sorry. It's not something I enjoy discussing. There's another possibility—that when the cemetery plots were catalogued an error of omission—"

"Please speak English," Houston said.

10

"Your father possibly was buried but not listed in our records."

"Are you telling me you lost his body?"

"I'm not telling you *I* lost his body, sir." The superintendent's face changed color, red, then gray. His jaw seemed squarer, cheekbones harder. "I was stationed here five years ago. I don't know what my predecessors might have done. But I assure you I do my job well."

Houston felt the anger, like the smell of ozone, in the stifling office.

"Pete, Mr. Andrews wants to help us," Jan said anxiously.

Houston shifted in the chair. He rubbed his throbbing forehead, nodding awkwardly, embarrassed. "I don't mean you," he said. "I mean, well, someone . . . *anybody.*"

Houston watched the superintendent glare at him. "I'm sorry," Houston told him. "I'm a teacher. I should speak with more precision. I apologize."

Andrews' glare became a thoughtful gaze. Past his dark eyes, his bright intelligence considered the apology. He sighed. "I'm too damn serious—excuse my language, ma'am. I used to be in the Army. A sergeant. Now I work for the Department of Defense. I'm loyal to the service. You don't know how much I hate to admit the foul-ups the military sometimes makes. The jokes people tell." He shook his head. "I do my best, believe me. I felt bad the other times this happened. I feel twice as bad now. Whatever stupid error happened here, it wasn't mine. I shouldn't blame myself. I do, though. . . . Mr. Houston, what's the matter with your forehead?"

"Rotten headache." Houston squinted in the blinding lights. Their humming was a dentist's drill.

"Here, wait a second," Jan said, searching through her purse. She found a metal tin of aspirins and pried at the lid. "I've got some coffee left."

He swallowed tepid bitter coffee with three pills. He set the cup down, closed his eyes, and waited, hoping for the pain to shrink.

"I promise satisfaction, Mr. Houston. I'll find out what happened."

Houston raised his eyelids, peering through the sharp light toward the superintendent.

'You're a teacher, Mr. Houston. Did you say that?"

Had he? He could not remember. "Yes. In Indiana."

"High school?"

"College. Dunston College. It's a private school near Evansville."

"That's almost in Kentucky."

Houston's interest rose. "That's—how did you know?"

"I was raised in Louisville. I haven't been back home since—well, since I was stationed here. They tell me the smog is worse."

"Believe it."

"Progress. Lord preserve us. You teach . . . ?"

"Creative writing."

"You're a writer?" Andrews seemed impressed.

"I've had four novels published."

"Which is how you could afford to travel overseas?"

Houston felt his spine begin to tingle. Something fluttered in his stomach. "You're not asking questions for the hell of it. You've got a reason." He glared at Andrews. "If you think I'm imagining all this, that just because I write, I'd make this up—"

"No, Mr. Houston, I'm not thinking that at all. But please bear with me for a moment. I'm assuming you've never been to France before."

"If I had, I'd have come to see my father's grave."

"But coming to your father's grave was not the reason for your trip to France."

"I've lost you."

"When the two of you sat down to plan your trip, your major purpose wasn't—"

"Coming to this cemetery? No, my mother died. After the funeral I had to get away."

"And then you figured that since you were here in France you'd pay respects."

12

"Death was on my mind. I don't see what all of this—"

"You didn't come prepared. You don't have any details that would help me. For example, your father's serial number. Do you even know his rank?"

"Corporal."

"That helps. When you get home, search through your family's records. Make a copy of the War Department's letter to your mother, any other documents that you can find."

"They don't exist."

"I beg your pardon." Andrews blinked, astonished.

"My mother burned them all, the letters my father sent, his photographs, the notice from the War Department. Everything. She loved him very much. I guess she broke down. She tried to cancel every memory. Whatever could remind her of him was destroyed."

"I hear you, but I'm having trouble understanding."

"I just told you she loved him."

"No." Andrews said it firmly. "I don't understand how you can be so positive he was buried here."

"She told me."

"When?"

"As I grew up. When I began to ask her why I didn't have a father."

"You're relying on your childhood memory?" The superintendent's face contorted in bewilderment.

"She told me often. See, by then she'd regretted what she'd done. She wished she had his pictures and his letters. He became a kind of legend for us. She repeated tales about him, word for word. She made me promise to remember all the details. 'Peter,' I can still recall her saying. 'Peter, though your father's dead, he still exists as long as we remember him.' "

Andrews tapped a pencil on the desk.

3

"He thinks I'm crazy!" Houston said.

He stood with Janice near the Citroen. The wind had died. The clouds had disappeared. The sun glared.

"No, he doesn't," Janice told him, staring at him, troubled. "But in *his* place what would *you* do? Did the military screw things up, or did you simply misremember?"

"Hey, I told you—"

"I believe you. You don't need to prove to me how well you can remember things. I've seen the way you don't need lecture notes in class. I don't need convincing. But the superintendent does. To him, a fact isn't a fact unless it's written down and doublechecked. As far as he's concerned, he did the best he could for you, considering the nature of your evidence.

"Which means he thinks I'm crazy."

"No. Mistaken."

Houston pushed his fingers through his hair. He faced the oppressive white building in confusion. "Fine, I'll grant him that much. Possibly I'm wrong." He turned abruptly toward her. "Not because I misremember. But my mother could have misremembered."

"We can't ask her."

"Is that it then?" Houston asked, in pain, reluctant, unaccepting. "We simply leave it like this?"

"We can write the War Department when we're home."

"We're here, though. Within walking distance, somewhere close, my father's buried."

"If you find some evidence, Andrews can at least locate the

14

grave in case we come back. And anyway, you said it earlier: What difference does it make?'' She blinked, as if she suddenly considered what her words meant. ''Forget that last part.''

Houston stared at her. ''To me, a man in middle age, I guess it doesn't make a bit of difference. Hell, my life won't change because I stand before his grave. But to that boy who grew up haunted by the father . . . Dammit, what's the matter with me?''

''Nothing. You're sentimental. It's attractive.''

Houston smiled at her. ''You do know what to say.''

''I ought to. We've been married long enough.''

He kissed her.

Glancing once more toward the building, he saw someone watching far back from a window.

''It's not me who's wrong,'' he told the distant shadow.

''What?''

''I just . . . This damn headache. Why don't *you* drive?''

Houston climbed inside the Citroen. They'd left the windows closed. The seat was hot, air stale and cloying. As he rolled the window down, he felt a thought uncurl.

Jan drove through the iron gate. She angled up the curving blacktop toward the summit.

Though he sensed the graves behind him, Houston didn't turn to look. He had this other thing to occupy him, this persistent nagging thought that there was something he had not remembered.

''There was a Frenchman,'' he said.

''Where? I didn't see him. You don't mean I almost hit him.''

''No. Not here. There was a Frenchman. I remember now,''

''Remember what?''

''A Frenchman. Then. In nineteen forty-four. My mother said she got some letters from him.''

Now his mind was clear. The deep black corner of his recollection was illuminated. Houston's stomach burned excitedly.

''Do the letters still exist?'' Jan said.

''I doubt it. If she burned the other things, she would have burned those letters too. It doesn't matter. I remember what she said about them.'' His exhilaration rose. ''The Frenchman said his people felt obliged to all those soldiers who had died to liberate his country. Every member of this village had selected a different grave. They vowed to tend the graves, to see there were flowers planted. Each fallen soldier seemed a brother or a son to them.''

Jan frowned. She reached the top and concentrated on the road.

''This Frenchman chose my father's grave.''

''I don't see how that helps us.''

''He'd remember. We can ask him where the grave is.''

''If he's still alive, and if—There isn't any sense to this. We don't know who he is.''

''I do know who he is.''

''You can't expect me to believe—''

''Pierre. That was his first name. That's why I remember it. Pierre de St. Laurent.''

''The village where we're staying. St. Laurent. But why would you remember that his first name—'' She stared at him.

''Of course. My mother said to me, 'And Peter, if it's any consolation, just remember that the man in France who tends your father's grave is Peter. *Just like you. Pierre.*' ''

4

The village stretched on both sides of a languid river. In the middle of the afternoon, the sleepy sunshine settled on the shops and houses, making Houston feel he'd returned to normalcy. He smiled at flower sellers, fruit vendors, old men smoking pipes in cottage doorways. If it hadn't been for traffic, phone poles, and electric cables, he'd have been convinced that he was in the seventeenth century.

Jan drove across an old stone bridge. Beneath it, two boats drifted lazily. In one, a man and boy were fishing. Straight ahead he saw the village square, where tall expansive trees contrasted with a slender rigid obelisk—the monument for World War Two. He brooded past a group of children toward the bleak plaque on the obelisk—the roster of the village war dead.

"Aren't you getting out?" Jan asked him.

Houston roused himself. She'd stopped beside their hotel, which faced toward the park and then the river.

"I can read a menu over here," he said. "And I can find the men's room. But I don't think I can trust myself to ask the proper questions, let alone translate the answers."

They walked toward the entrance to the hotel. Years before, the place had been a manor. Now the tourists ate and slept where nobles once had ruled the land. "Europe puts things in perspective," Janice had remarked when they arrived. "This place was built before America was founded."

In the high-beamed lobby, they approached the counter. Houston used his halting French to ask the manager if an interpreter could be employed.

The man responded slowly that monsieur should take advantage of this visit to perfect his knowledge of the language. An interpreter would make him lazy. Pardon the impertinence. The manager continued smiling.

Houston laughed. The manager relaxed.

"*D'accord. Je sais. Mais nous. . .*" Houston faltered. "We have business to conduct. I need to understand precisely. *Précisement.*"

That was a different matter altogether. If monsieur would kindly wait . . .

"I'm starving," Janice said.

Pete told the manager where they'd be waiting.

In the dining room, they sat beside a window that looked toward the huge trees in the park. They ordered dry white wine, cold chicken, a salad.

Pete felt a shadow. Glancing up, he saw a woman standing by him at the table.

"Mr. Houston?"

She was thirty, maybe less but certainly no more. A tall, thin, dark- and long-haired woman with attractive eyes; a full curved mouth, a smooth deep voice.

"My father is the manager. He says you need someone to interpret."

Her arrival was so unexpected that for several moments Houston failed to realize she spoke English without any trace of foreign accent.

"Yes, that's right."

"If I can be of help to you."

"Sit down please. Would you like some wine?"

"No, thank you." When she sat, she tucked her skirt beneath her. She wore sandals and a yellow sweater with the sleeves pulled up. She crossed her hands on her lap and waited.

"This is Janice," Houston said. "My name is Peter." They shook hands.

"Simone," she said.

"Your English is remarkable."

"I studied hotel management at Berkeley. In the sixties. When the campus riots started, I came back to France."

So I was wrong, he thought. She isn't thirty. More like thirty-five. You'd never know it. He explained what he wanted, though he avoided mentioning what had happened at the cemetery.

"So you want to thank this man," Simone rephrased. "For tending to your father's grave."

"We're in the neighborhood. I figure it's the least I can do."

Simone frowned. "Thirty-seven years."

"I know. He must be dead."

"It's not just that. If he's alive, he might be hard to locate. Many people in this village come from families so old that their last name is St. Laurent. Descendants of the St. Laurents who

18

settled here. You might as well be looking for a certain Smith or Jones back in America.''

"But *Pierre* de St. Laurent. That helps to narrow things.''

She thought about it. "Please wait here a moment.'' She stood smoothly, with aristocratic poise, and left the room.

"Attractive,'' Janice said.

"Oh, really? I didn't notice.''

"Fool, you'd better eat your lunch before you get yourself in trouble.''

He grinned. They finished drinking coffee by the time Simone came back.

"I checked the village phone book,'' she said. "Remarkably, there's no St. Laurent with such a common given name. If we were in the States, we could consult a local census list. But here in St. Laurent we have none.''

"Then there isn't any way?''

Simone seemed troubled.

"What then?'' Houston asked.

"One man possibly can help you.''

Houston frowned at her reluctance.

"He's old. He isn't well. But he knows everything about this village.''

Houston stood. "Let's find him.''

5

Houston's nostrils flared from camphor fumes. The drapes were closed. The room was dark except for glowing embers from a smoking log inside the hearth.

The ancient priest sat in a chair before the fireplace. His

name was Father Devereaux. He was frail and wrinkled, almost shrunken, his wispy hair reminding Houston of a spiderweb. He coughed from deep inside his chest; he did so often, and each time the effort gave him pain. He raised a crushed but ample handkerchief from underneath the blanket that he clutched around him, wiping at his mouth. He could only muster strength for short, slow phrases, but his voice was soft and thin and almost soundless, so that Houston—though he didn't understand the language—found that he was leaning close.

"So long ago. So much has happened." Turning from the priest. Simone translated for them.

"Tell him I appreciate his effort. Tell him anything he remembers might be useful," Houston said.

Simone spoke French. The priest responded.

"He recalls the man you're looking for."

Now Houston glanced toward Janice, trying to subdue his quick excitement.

"But he's sorry. He can't help you."

"Why?" Houston said. "If he remembers."

"He apologizes. But the man you seek was young then. He himself was young. Too much has happened."

Houston stiffened. "There's something wrong. You're sure he understands?"

"Oh, perfectly."

"Then why . . . ? Look, ask him this. The man I'm searching for, does he still live here in this village?"

Simone explained. The priest slowly shook his head.

"Now what does that mean?" Houston said. "He either doesn't know, or else he isn't telling."

Father Devereaux coughed. He wiped the bulky handkerchief across his mouth and closed his eyes. Houston shuddered sympathetically. Simone spoke briefly and received what, from the priest, was an elaborate answer.

"Some of that I understood," Jan said. But Houston waited, anxious for Simone's translation.

"He is ignorant, he says. He doesn't know where this man lives or even *if* he lives. What's more, he doesn't care. He says he knows that in this matter he has not fulfilled his obligations, but he asks the Lord to make allowance. As a pastor, he is duty-bound to watch each member of his flock, but in this case he is indifferent. He must love a God-created soul but does not have to like the man who harbors it.'' A spark cracked in the fireplace.

''I don't understand,'' Houston said.

The priest began to speak again. His voice dimmed. Then he coughed so deeply that the rattle clawed through Houston's stomach.

''He must rest, he says. He can't answer any more questions.''

''But—''

''There's something else. He says that everything he knows about this man was learned in the confessional. Many years ago; so much has changed. He still recalls when meat on Friday was a mortal sin. And failing to attend a mass on Sunday. And divorce.'' She paused. ''He still recalls when he could say a mass in Latin. He is grateful to be dying before further changes weary him. But this much, for himself at least, has not changed. He will not reveal the secrets that he heard as a confessor.''

Houston concentrated on the priest by the fireplace. The wizened face stared toward him, ghost eyes glowing. Houston sighed and slowly nodded.

Father Devereaux turned toward Simone and with more energy spoke to her privately. The tone was like a parent's. Although Houston tried to follow what the priest had to say to her, the sick-sweet camphor fumes distracted him. He finally gave up the effort.

Jan gaped, shocked, confused, discouraged, it was difficult to tell.

The priest stopped. Simone leaned down to kiss his hand. He blessed her. She helped him stand. Pete thanked him, though for what he wasn't sure.

''God help you,'' Father Devereaux replied in French. He

21

gripped a sofa, then a chair, and shuffled coughing from the room.

Outside the camphor of the rectory, Houston breathed the freshness of a garden in late afternoon. "What now?" he said.

"The village clerk," Simone suggested. They walked toward the iron gate set in the garden's wall.

'That last part. You didn't translate," Houston said.

"No, it was private."

"At the hotel you were hesitant to bring us here."

She nodded. Houston pulled the gate and let her through.

"You heard him speak about divorce," she said.

Now it was Houston's turn to nod.

"Well, when I went to Berkeley, I got married. He was wrong for me. It didn't work."

So it had not been campus riots that had driven her back home to France. It was a ruined marriage and divorce.

"He says that I should take confession, and he says that he will pray for me."

6

The basement of the village courthouse was near the river. Moisture permeated everything. The wooden floor felt soft, the dingy counter sticky, Papers, stored in wooden boxes stacked on rows of shelves throughout the room, gave off a dank and fetid odor.

Houston watched the clerk, who stared back with narrowed eyes and shook his head emphatically, reminding Houston of the sergeant and the priest, repeating, "*Non, monsieur.*" The man was in his fifties, overweight and apprehensive. For his lunch he'd eaten sausage. Houston smelled the garlic wafting from him, mixed with pipe smoke and stale wine.

Houston understood his apprehension. They had been here for an hour now. They'd asked the clerk to check the village tax roll for Pierre de St. Laurent, but no such name had been discovered. Then they'd asked him to check the list of people who owned neighboring land. Again the name had not been present.

"Est-il mort?" the clerk had wondered, then had instantly regretted what he'd said. He seemed to want to bite his tongue, for his suggestion would mean further work, a search through all the death files, going backward through the years. He sighed and started bringing boxes to the counter. Although Houston understood that only clerks could touch the boxes, this man gratefully accepted help.

In fact, the clerk let Houston, Janice, and Simone do all the work. He snapped his suspenders, hands pressed to his striped shirt, rocking back and forth on his heels. He glanced repeatedly past Houston toward a dusty clock on the wall.

Pete could read the language, even if he couldn't speak it, but he had trouble with the papers. The documents were often stuck together, and a careless flick of hand could tear them easily. The ink was fainter as he worked back through the years, and different hands had their secret scrawls. Both he and Janice often asked Simone for her interpretation. Nineteen eighties, then the seventies, the sixties. Each box had been arranged alphabetically, but all the St. Laurents were bunched together randomly, their first names in no special order. In this moldy basement without windows and with a few pale dangling light bulbs, Houston's headache started throbbing once again. He found that he was squinting.

"I could use a drink," Jan said.

"A lot of them," Pete answered. "We're half done at least. Lord, more than half." He was mistaken. There were only three boxes they had not investigated. He had 1953. Simone had 1952, and Jan had 1951.

"Where's nineteen fifty?" Houston asked.

The clerk was puzzled. *"Qu'est-ce que c'est?"*

Simone translated. The clerk began a lengthy explanation.

"That's the last of them," Simone told Houston.

"What?"

"The records stop in nineteen fifty-one. He's right. I totally forgot."

"But why?"

"There was a fire. I remember now. In nineteen fifty. I was just a child, but I remember that my mother brought me down to watch. The blaze made night seem day."

"*The courthouse?*"

"It was old but elegant, a proper courthouse. Not like this converted warehouse. Who knows how it happened? Someone left a cigarette? Perhaps a faulty fuse box? Who can say? The damage, though, was total. Mother let me watch until I got so sleepy she had to take me home. But in the morning I came back with her, and there was nothing left except the shell. For months I tasted smoke when I walked past."

"But surely *something* could be saved."

She merely looked at him.

7

They walked along the cobbled street. The sky was orange, but here the buildings blocked the sunset, casting early dusk. Houston squinted through the shadows toward the river's mist that hung above the trees beyond the far end of the street.

"At least we tried," Jan said.

Hand in hand with her, he nodded listlessly, preoccupied by Pierre St. Laurent. "It's like the man just disappeared."

"In America, you'd say you tried a long shot," Simone said, "but too many factors were against you."

"*Someone* must remember him," he said, his voice taut with frustration.

"No, not necessarily," Simone replied.

Houston glanced at her.

"When the war was over, many villages had been so shattered that the memory of what had happened was unbearable," she told him. "People who had lost their homes, who grieved for parents, spouses, children, they decided to make a fresh start somewhere else. As an American, you don't understand these things. You've been fortunate to have few wars on your land. But here in France it's rare when we have peace. Entire centuries have been occupied by war." She paused, her eyes sad. "Dislocation. It's hard to explain. Imagine your Civil War. Georgia after Sherman had razed it. Not a farmhouse left standing. Not a blade of grass left growing. Absolute ruin. Now imagine that you visit Georgia thirty-seven years later. You're looking for a man whose name is common, who lived in a certain village during Sherman's march. Would you expect to find that man? Would it seem strange to you that no one now remembered him?"

"There has to be a way."

"Your sense of obligation is that great? Your need to thank him?"

Houston almost told her his real motive. But abruptly something closed within him. His reluctance disturbed him. He explained it to himself by guessing that he didn't have the strength to voice his memories. His deep emotions, held in check for so long, were potentially too painful. "It's a point of honor, I suppose."

Simone frowned, puzzled. "We can go to the police tomorrow."

Jan was startled. "Why?"

"Since you're determined."

Houston felt exhausted. He was grateful when they left the narrow cobbled street and came out on the level sidewalk that

was opposite the park. The shadows had disappeared. He stood
in brilliant sunset. Past the calmness of the park the river's mist
was pastel orange.

"It's like a Cézanne," Jan said.

So why let boyhood sorrows taint the present? Houston
thought. I'm here. The country's beautiful. The food is great,
the people friendly. Why let something from another time destroy my peace of mind? The here and now—that's all that matters. And the wine, he thought. Oh, yes, the wine. "Let's have
that drink," he said. "Simone, would you have supper with
us?"

"Thank you, but my father needs me. I've been away too
long. Perhaps another time before you leave."

"Tomorrow then."

"And the police?"

"No, I think not. I doubt they'd be much help." Jan's hand
remained in his. He felt a tension leave her. "I'll pay you. I
don't know your rates."

"My English needed practice. There's no charge."

He understood she hoped he wouldn't try to argue. His ex-
haustion muted his determination to find his father's grave. After all, he'd done his best, he told himself. What difference did
his failure make? No difference. None at all. To see the grave
would have resulted only in self-pity.

They went into the hotel, where he turned to thank Simone.
He never got the chance. Her father, dressed impeccably, a
golden watch chain dangling from his vest, approached. Trim,
aristocratic, he had kindly, cheerful eyes. Simone explained
where she had been.

The old man's face went pale. "*Comment?*" He turned to
Houston, started. "*Quoi?*" His voice was wary, troubled.

Houston's stomach burned. "*Pardon?*"

"Pierre de St. Laurent?" The old man's eyes were shocked,
his voice astonished.

"*Oui.*"

The old man spoke to Simone. He rattled phrases off so fast
that Houston couldn't understand a word. Simone frowned.

26

"What?"

"My father wishes he had known. He could have helped you, warned you, saved you lots of trouble, maybe trouble yet to come."

8

They had to wait. Although the old man was profoundly anxious to explain to them, he had to pay attention to his duties at the hotel, supervising dinner. With extreme reluctance, he took leave of Jan and Houston.

"Later," the old man said in French. "We must speak about this later." He began to walk away, but then, distressed, he quickly turned to them. "At length," he said and then repeated, "*longuement*. For there is much that you don't understand."

The lobby's spaciousness made Pete feel small. His skin began to tingle. He felt conscious of his back. Simone was leaving. "Wait," Pete said.

"I have to help my father."

Then Pete and Janice were alone. The muffled noises from the dining room seemed ghostly. He felt isolated, somehow separated from the polished wooden beams and paneled walls.

The elevator hummed. The cage descended, and the metal gate was pushed aside. A guest in black tie and dinner jacket stepped out, passing them from right to left to reach the dining room. The guest came close enough for Houston to breathe talcum powder—lilac-scented. At the same time, Houston seemed to see him from a distance, through the wrong end of a telescope.

Unreal, he thought. "What's going on?" he said to Janice.

"Peter Lorre."

"What?"

"The travel agent didn't mention foreign intrigue when he gave us our itinerary."

"We must have stirred up some local scandal."

"We've stirred up something, that's for sure. So what do we do now?"

They glanced at one another's jeans, no more inclined to change their clothes than they were to eat. But they forced themselves to go upstairs and put on something more formal, then to come back down to the dining room. The quiche was excellent, but Houston didn't give it the attention it deserved. His stomach tensed as if he expected an urgent phone call that was always postponed. Preoccupied, they lingered over coffee, but the manager did not appear. Simone remained invisible. They left the hotel for a walk, passing yellow streetlights, breathing the chill mist from the river. The constellations hovered above them, coldly crystalline.

When they returned to the hotel, Simone was waiting with her father at the counter. Both were stiff, intense, as Houston walked with Janice toward them. Till this moment, the relationship between the manager and Houston was of host and paying guest. But now the manager became a confidant, a personal acquaintance. "Jacques Monsard," his daughter introduced him. The first name seemed much too common for a small aging man of such aristocratic features. Houston shook his hand and was invited gravely to take brandy in the old man's living quarters.

These were two rooms on the ground floor, down a hallway toward the back, beyond a sign that said in French that no admittance was permitted. Houston never saw what, past a closed door, he assumed would be the bedroom. But the sitting room was large and well appointed—few but carefully selected antique chairs, lamps, and tables. Simple, elegant, expensive. Houston's main impression was of gentle textures and soft shadows.

The brandy was the best he'd ever tasted. As he swirled the liquor in the fragile snifter, he heard clock chimes from the mantel, ten and soon ten-thirty.

". . . He was evil." Monsard's voice was hypnotizing. He spoke French; Simone translated. "No, it's important to be accurate," Monsard went on. "No man, no true adult, would have behaved the way he did. He was a boy of twenty-one. But youth cannot excuse his actions. He was evil." Monsard enunciated carefully. "Nineteen forty-four. You are too young for an appreciation." He used *vous* not merely as a gesture of respect but also to include Simone and Janice. "You cannot envision, as I still can, what times were like. This hotel was a base of operations for the Nazis. In this very room the German general conducted staff meetings, preparing tactics to fight off the Allies."

Monsard paused. He saw that Houston's glass was empty and leaned forward, pouring. Houston lit a cigarette, but he kept his eyes on Monsard's face.

"The German officers were fed here, in the dining room that now is my responsibility. They confiscated all the better homes along the river to billet their staff. The soldiers camped along the river, in the park, and in the fields. For every villager, there were three dozen Germans. Everywhere you looked, you saw their uniforms, their helmets. And their tanks, their cannons, their . . . gun oil, that was what you smelled. Exhaust fumes. Sweat. And something rancid, indefinable, which I in time became aware was fear, both from the Germans and the villagers."

The old man's mouth pursed at the memory. He drew a breath. "There was not food enough to feed the village, and the Germans were not well supplied. They had to eat to fight, and so they searched our homes. They took our secret stores. They left us nothing. People starved. We lost the strength to serve the German officers with the efficiency they demanded."

For the first time, Monsard drank. He held the brandy on his tongue and gazed with bitter eyes toward images of long ago. "Pierre de St. Laurent," the old man said.

The hair rose on Pete's neck.

"We went to school together. We were friends. We played together often, and we wished that we were brothers. He was tall and strong, good-looking, idolized by every young girl in the village. I became aware of the advantages he took. The many girls he tricked by promising to marry them. The anger of the fathers. How I'd wasted my devotion."

So it *is* a local scandal, Houston thought. The village lecher. It's no wonder that the priest was disenchanted. Houston listened nonetheless. Again his glass was empty, and again Monsard refilled it. Now the room was smoky.

"There were rumors that a cache of food was hidden somewhere in the village. Late at night—the Germans loved to terrorize when people slept—they ransacked a château. They found the cache behind a hidden cellar door, and in the morning, on the bridge, with all the village forced to watch, they shot each member of that household, even two babies. Then they threw the bodies from the bridge and let them drift along the river. It was obvious that someone had informed, for otherwise how could the food have been discovered so precisely? The informer was Pierre, although I did not know this at the time. The action was so vile that I could not imagine who would do it. Never mind that those who hid the food were selfish and unsharing. That's a different sin, another matter. The informer, by cooperating with the Germans, had committed a much greater sin.

"The Allies came," the old man continued. "They feinted toward the north and tricked the Germans, who became convinced that in this village they were undetected. So the Germans tried to catch the Allies by surprise, to intercept them. What the Germans didn't know was that the Allies had been warned. The Germans lost the battle, though the losses on both sides were gross, unthinkable."

"The Allies? But who warned them?" Houston's voice rose.

"Yes," the old man said. "You understand."

"Pierre?"

"He snuck through German lines at night. He risked the Allied sentries. But he reached his goal. He told his story. Undetected he came back.''

Jan broke her silence. "Why?" The old man frowned. "If he collaborated with the Germans. Why?" Jan said. "It makes no sense for him to risk his life to help the Allies."

"*Qu'est-ce que c'est?*" the old man asked Simone.

She told him, and he nodded gravely. "*Oui. C'est illogique.*" Simone's translation filled the gap as if intruding from a parallel dimension. "But the lack of logic is apparent only. Not in fact or actual. Since we did not suspect him as a traitor to us, we interpreted the risk he took as bravery, as loyalty. Oh, he was celebrated. He was feted. He became our hero, and he had his pick of girls.''

The old man sipped his brandy, concentrating on a window, on the blackness of the night, as if the darkness were a screen upon which images now flickered. Houston heard an animal's sharp cry outside and suspected that a night bird was successful in its hunting. He felt cold abruptly, and a further sip of brandy did not warm him.

"Oh, Pierre was clever," Monsard said. "He must have feared that we suspected him and were planning our revenge. Whatever, to protect himself, he had to make himself immune from accusation, had to demonstrate his loyalty beyond a doubt. Perhaps the Germans were not generous enough. Perhaps he thought the Allies would pay more. From greed, he sought a more rewarding master. But I don't believe the Allies paid him. The Americans respected altruistic motives. They maintained that Frenchmen should betray the Germans for the sake of liberation only. I imagine that Pierre was disappointed. But a part of me imagines something else." The old man's eyes appeared to darken, as if sickened and appalled.

"An altogether different explanation. Evil. Disgusting. It has always puzzled me how he crept through the German lines so easily, and with the same apparent ease snuck back. Suppose the Germans paid him to take information to the Allies. In a second battle, fifty miles north of here, the Allies were defeated. The Americans were beaten because of information that the Germans had beforehand, information that was secret, that was crucial to the Allied tactics. You must know about the Underground. I was a member, as Pierre was. When the Allies won this hotel, when Americans made plans inside this room, the members of the Underground were called in to give help. It was important, we were told, for us to infiltrate the German lines and make assessments of their strength. We did so, our great moment, but our information was in error. When the Allies mustered their attack, they found that they had been expected. They faced reinforcements. I feel certain that Pierre was the informer. Either he switched sides again, or else he was a German agent all the time. To me, the blood of thousands stained the fields because of him. He was completely selfish, of no worth or consequence. He looked out only for himself.''

''I mean no disrespect,'' Pete said, ''but where's your proof?''

Simone translated.

''Proof?'' The old man's face contorted with disgust. ''He disappeared the morning of the fight in which the Allies were defeated. He packed his belongings, and he vanished. There could be only one reason. Only something truly hideous would make him so afraid of our reprisals that he ran away.''

9

Pete glanced out toward the lobby as the elevator took them up. He felt so numb, so drained, that for a moment he imagined he was not ascending, but that the lobby floor was dropping away. Houston closed his eyes. Disoriented, he pressed hard against the elevator's wall. But then the second's vertigo was gone. The dizziness had passed, though he noticed with alarm that he was sweating.

"Did you drink too much?" Jan asked. "You really killed that brandy."

Houston mustered strength to blink. He saw a corridor appear. His stomach settled while the elevator smoothly stopped. He drew a breath and pushed off from the wall. "I need some sleep," he said. "I should have eaten more."

He pulled the cage door open, heard the scrape of metal, paused, and glanced at her in pained confusion. "Well, we listened for two hours. He was totally convincing, don't you think? But if you asked me now, I'd say the only thing we know for sure is that his friend dropped out of sight one day. We don't know *why* he disappeared. Monsard is simply guessing."

"No, we do know something else," Jan said. "Before he disappeared, St. Laurent went to the priest. He took confession."

Houston's mind relaxed. Then weariness set in again. "If his confession and his disappearance are related, I don't see the link," he said. "We can't prove a connection."

"But it's clear to me."

"Because you're not a Catholic. Sure, to us as Protestant Americans, confession seems unusual. But not to Catholics here in France, and not in nineteen forty-four. These people ask the priest to hear confession all the time. In World War Two, with so much death around them, they'd have used confession *twice* as often." Houston realized that he still gripped the cage-door handle. He let go and stepped back so that Janice could walk out first.

But she stayed in the elevator. "That's not what I mean," she said.

He frowned at her. "What is it then?"

"St. Laurent wasn't some altar boy. He liked the girls. He got himself and them in trouble. You remember, Monsard mentioned several scandals?" Houston nodded. "Do you think he would confess that kind of sin?" Jan asked.

"If what he'd done was common knowledge, then he'd realize he couldn't hide it from the priest. It wouldn't hurt him to confess that he was lustful.''

''Right. The priest might give him hell. But what's the point of going to confession and not telling every sin, especially a sin the priest knew all about already. Would lust have shocked Father Devereaux?''

''Hardly. Priests are specialists in human nature. They expect to hear the sin of lust.''

''All right then,'' Jan said, eyes severe. ''Explain to me what so disgusted Father Devereaux that to this day he still remembers that confession and despises the young man who came to him for absolution.''

Houston felt as if the elevator were dropping. He had to reach the hallway. Janice followed, clutching at his arm. ''And something else,'' she said. ''The way Monsard describes him, I don't think Pierre was terribly religious to begin with. I'm just guessing, but I doubt he made a habit of confession. This time, though, he saw the priest, and he told everything.''

''But why?''

''Because Pierre de St. Laurent was scared to death. He asked for absolution before something awful happened to him.'' In the silence of the corridor they stared at one another. ''Father Devereaux's the only man who knows the secret,'' Jan continued. ''And for sure it isn't lust, and it's for damn sure he's not telling.''

Houston blinked at her. The sound of the elevator bell startled him. Someone down below them had pressed a button. But the elevator didn't move. Houston pulled the metal grill until the catch snapped into place. As cables creaked, a motor hummed and the cage descended.

''We'll wake everybody up,'' he said. They walked along the hallway. Houston heard the elevator reach the lobby and the motor stop. He heard the grill as it was opened down there, its sound like that of a fingernail scraped along a blackboard. Then the motor started again.

''This is foolish,'' Houston said. ''Why should I be worried?

That's just someone who was out late, coming back to get some sleep.''

''You're scaring *me* now,'' Jan said.

As they reached their door, the elevator halted on their level. Houston fumbled in his pocket for the key. The elevator's door was yanked abruptly open. Houston stared along the hall. And almost laughed.

The guest in black tie and dinner jacket, who had reeked of lilac talcum as he'd walked past Houston in the lobby, stumbled from the elevator, blearily looked down the hall toward Jan and Houston, lost his balance as he shut the grill, and staggered down the far end of the hallway.

''So much for imagination.'' Houston laughed and kissed Jan.

''Want to fool around?''

He grinned and turned the key. They stepped inside their room. The place was dark except for the dim light from the hall that cast their silhouettes across the floor.

''The thing is, I don't care what St. Laurent was up to. All I want to know is where—''

He flicked the lights, and in mid-sentence Houston halted.

10

They stared toward the bed. A man lay propped against the pillows glaring at them.

In his middle thirties, square-jawed, with a thin nose and short dark hair combed straight from right to left, the man looked sick, perhaps because his stubble made his face seem gray. His clothes were dark—crew sweater, wool pants, crepe-soled shoes.

Astonished, Houston felt a scalding panic. He received too many messages at once. Jan's sharp grip on his arm transmitted fright. Conflicting instincts prompted him to shout for help, to flee with Jan, to grab the phone, to storm in and confront this man. His will became a flywheel. Then the flywheel caught and jammed and froze, and he stood paralyzed.

"Please shut the door," the man said in a deep, calm voice. The words were English, but the accent was distinctly foreign, though not French.

Too many details. Houston was conscious that he hadn't moved, that he was gaping, that while blood roared in his head he wasn't breathing.

"Please," the man repeated. "Shut the door."

"No," Jan said.

Adrenaline insisted. Forced to act but with no other clear directive, Houston shut the door before he understood what he was doing.

"Pete!" Jan said and tried to grab the door.

But Houston raised a hand to stop her. He glared toward the man. "All right, I closed it."

From the bed, the man considered him, then breathed out slowly. "You'd better have a damn good reason," Houston said.

"I'm calling the police," Jan said. She stalked across the room.

"I wouldn't do that Mrs. Houston."

As she grabbed the phone, the man jumped off the bed. Jan's eyes enlarged with fear. She recoiled hard against the wall. The man pressed the cradle down and yanked the phone away from her.

Pete lunged. "God damn it, get your hands away from her! I'll ram that fucking phone—"

The man swung toward him, the phone raised as a bludgeon. Houston stared in horror at the coldest, most unfeeling eyes he'd ever seen. He stopped abruptly. Frantically he stumbled back.

"Don't make this complicated," the man said.

"Tell me what the hell you want."

The man set down the phone. "I should have thought it was obvious. The same as you. Pierre de St. Laurent."

The name was like a coin that rattled in an empty metal cup, or like a diamond's screeching over glass. Instantly it shut all other thoughts from Houston's mind. "You know we're looking for him?"

"Everybody does," the man replied.

"But how . . . ?"

"The clerk whose records you went through. His life is dull. He sharpens it with gossip. Two Americans inconvenienced him. The name Pierre de St. Laurent means nothing to him. But the older folks remember. After thirty-seven years, the sudden mention of the name is news. It's not surprising that I know about your search."

"That doesn't give you any right to—"

"Mrs. Houston, you look uncomfortable. Please sit down, why don't you? While we chat." The man had earlier used "folks." Now "chat" confirmed it, Houston thought. The idiom was less American than British.

Houston glanced toward Jan, whose eyes were more wary than frightened now. She kept her distance as she circled toward a chair. For one tense instant, she appeared about to yank open the door. But then she sat.

"Are you some kind of cop?" Pete said. "A— '

"—person with some interest in this matter. Nothing more. Don't make this more mysterious than necessary. I too have been looking for him."

"Why?"

"I can't tell you, It's delicate. A private motive."

"You won't tell us? But you're asking us for help?"

The man began to laugh, but without mirth or relaxation. The sound was like a consumptive's cough.

"You don't understand. No, it is I who offer you help. You

have reached a blank wall in your search. But I can help you past it.''

''How and why?''

The man squinted. ''Why? Because my efforts aren't successful. It's possible that with your fresh view you may notice a detail I've missed. And how? With this address. The city known as Roncevaux. Rue Gabriel. One hundred and thirteen.''

''He lives there?''

''No more questions. You have all you need to know.''

''And if I find him?''

''You tell me.''

''But how will I find *you?*''

''You don't. I'll come to you.''

The man moved smoothly toward the door.

''Remember. Roncevaux. Rue Gabriel. One hundred and thirteen.'' He gripped the doorknob. ''Mr. Houston. Mrs. Houston.''

Nodding, he slipped out.

The door clicked shut. Pete glanced at Jan. Exploding into motion, he ran toward the door. He yanked it open.

The hall was empty.

11

''Pete, let's stop this.''

''What?''

''I'm scared.''

Houston, concentrating on the curve he was approaching, couldn't take the time to look at her. The Citroen took the curve smartly, then sped down a straightaway. He had his window low. He smelled the cool, fresh morning dampness. As he glanced away from fields and fences, Houston saw that Jan was ashen. "I'm scared too," he said "That doesn't mean I'll back away."

"You're being stubborn."

"You're damn right I am. What's more, I'm angry. I woke up yesterday expecting I'd see my father's grave. But everywhere I went I got the runaround. I heard all kinds of reasons why I couldn't find that grave. At the cemetery, Andrews as much as said I was crazy. I met a priest who wouldn't talk to me. A clerk whose records don't go farther back than nineteen fifty-one. Monsard who spins fantastic stories about nineteen forty-four. And then that creep who takes a catnap on our bed and thinks he's the midnight messenger."

"I still say we should go to the police."

"Think about it. We went over this last night. The cops might never find that guy. Suppose they did. The most they could charge him with is trespass. There's no sign he broke in. We checked our stuff, and nothing's missing. So the cops would want to know what he was doing there. They'd want to know what we discussed with him. Imagine their reaction if we told the truth. A disappearing grave. A villager who vanished back in nineteen forty-four. They'd treat me like the superintendent did. They'd think I'm crazy."

"I'd feel safer if we spoke to them."

"Who says we're in danger? No one's threatened us. Besides, we'd have to stay in town while they investigated. But ten days from now, we fly back home. I'd like to get this fool thing settled and enjoy what's left of our vacation."

"No, there's more than that."

The Citroen droned smoothly down the two-lane road. The sun was warmer, higher. Houston glanced at fields on either side and saw farmers at their work. He shrugged. "What makes you think there's more?"

"You just admitted you're scared."

"Because of something nagging in my head. A thought that

isn't clear yet. If Pierre de St. Laurent was even half as selfish as Monsard believes, you tell me why he took the time to write a letter to my mother, why he promised to maintain my father's grave. And then abruptly disappeared. I'm sure the answer to that question's simple. But I won't sleep easy till I hear it. And I'm terrified that there won't *be* a simple answer, even *any* answer.''

"All right, promise me."

He studied her.

"I won't complain," she said. "I'll shut my mouth and go along with you on this. In Roncevaux, I'll wait while you go off and ask your questions. But if you can't find anything, you have to promise that you'll stop this, that you'll whisk me off—''

"—to passionate, exciting places." Houston laughed. "That's what I'm doing. Hey, I'm taking you on an adventure."

"You're a con man." Janice laughed.

Then suddenly, in sick, hot, squirming fear, he heard her scream. His foot kicked spastically on the accelerator. The Citroen surged forward with a rush that pressed him back against the seat. His startled hands torqued the steering wheel. The car swerved sharply right, then left, before he had control.

He stared at Jan as quickly as he could. Her eyes were panicked, huge and black and bottomless. Her face was twisted, stark and white. Her scream became a hopeless moan.

He had to watch where he steered. As the girders of an ancient bridge loomed closer, Houston heard the roar beside him. On his left. He had been hearing it behind him. In his rearview mirror he had seen the van dart close, its visor down so that he couldn't see the driver's face.

But now relentlessly it rushed beside him, black, immense, its din so loud that Houston barely heard Jan's screaming. Nonetheless he felt her panic. They raced toward the bridge.

The bridge was narrow, one-lane, girders hulking on each side. As Houston squinted horror-stricken toward it, he felt oddly as if he were speeding through a tunnel, his perspective lengthened. Hurtling past a road sign, Houston didn't need to read the French to know that its equivalent in English was NO PASSING.

"What the hell is wrong with—" But he never had the chance to finish, for the van veered toward the Citroen to squeeze it off the road. Except there *wasn't* any road. A line of pine trees stopped abruptly on the right. Beyond them, an abyss dropped to the river.

"Pete!"

The van collided with the Citroen, a harsh, metallic thud that shuddered through the car. Houston thought too late about the brakes. The bottleneck was petrifying. All he managed was to steer. Again the van struck the Citroen. He felt the jolt. His door bulged inward. If he didn't steer away, he'd hit the bridge. He had a vision of the car's disintegration, of himself and Janice bursting through the windshield.

Houston didn't know he'd veered. The van raced forward through the bottleneck, and weightless, Houston stared at open sky. The falling car began to tilt. He saw the far bank of the river. Then the car upended, plummeting. He gaped at churning water.

Vacuum. Soundlessness. The rush of empty air. He didn't have a chance to brace himself. Perversely, Houston felt a vague euphoria, a hush, a silent peace.

Although the water's froth looked soft, the car hit as if it had struck cement. The impact parted Houston's jaws. The recoil snapped them back together, cutting his tongue. He shot out a hand to cushion Jan.

Then he was gagging, choking. He couldn't see. He couldn't breathe. He couldn't move. His sense of balance was reversed. And then he realized that he was upside down. His lungs revolted from the water he'd inhaled. The more he coughed, the more he felt the spurt of water down his throat. His eyes were open, but the muddy water in his eyes was worse than blindness. Drowning, Houston thought that he would lose his mind.

He fumbled with the seatbelt. He had never fastened it. He grappled with the door, but it was frozen. He felt Jan move beside him. He lunged through the window—it was open, he remembered—as if the sky above was every goal he'd ever wanted. His belt caught on the window frame. He wedged a foot against the steering wheel. He kicked and suddenly was free. His shoulder scraped against a rock. The current caught him. He surged upward as his chest exploded and the darkness seemed to thicken. He heard murky, hollow echoes roaring in his ears.

He had to breathe at last. It was that simple. It was necessary and instinctive. And precisely at that moment, as he breathed, he broke the surface. He emerged in brilliant sunshine to the cool, sweet, pure, refreshing air.

He filled his lungs, thrashing to keep his head above the current. He pivoted to look for Jan. Oh, Jesus, she was down there!

Houston waited, He kept waiting. As the current sped him farther downriver, he couldn't wait any longer. Drawing breath, denying weakness, he dove, clawing down.

His stomach cramped. He jackknifed inward, head colliding with his knees. At once the coldness of the water numbed and soothed him. He was sleepy. Then he saw a haloed figure, and he knew it was his father.

12

Death was not at all what he'd expected. Neither dark, nor terrifying, it was soft and calm and gentle. With his father here to guide him, Houston felt no fear at all. He had so many questions for his father. Weeping, Houston found that he was looking upward as if he were once again a boy. His loving father stood above him, but the haloed face was indistinct. There were no features. As Houston stretched to see more clearly, frantic for the vision, straining on his tiptoes, he was angered by the hand that fell across his shoulder from behind. The hand was dragging him away. He yanked the hand off. But the hand gripped even stronger. "Let me go!" he shouted, raging. Houston stumbled forward toward his father. But now other hands were grabbing at him, pulling at his shoulders, clutching at his waist. He struggled, flailing. "Let me go!" He screamed hysterically. His sight was blurred. His eyes were thick with tears. "He's my father! Don't you understand!" But the hands would not allow it. They kept yanking at him, jerking hard to drag him backward. "Help me!" Houston shouted, begging to his father. But his father gazed at him with passive, formless features. "Not again! Don't let it happen!" Houston wailed. Instead his father, eyeless, studied him. Then with a shrug, his father raised his right hand, waved it slowly once in mute farewell, and smoothly turned and walked away. His father's back receded toward the distance, swallowed by the mist. "You've got to help me!" Houston shouted. "You're my father!" But he didn't blame his father. Houston blamed the hands that clutched him, and he spun in total livid rage to strangle those who held him.

Light stabbed at him. Noises flooded over him. He tried to shield his eyes, to plug his ears. But someone held him, pinned his hands. "You bastards!" Houston shouted.

Then he understood that it was Jan, and he remembered how he'd tried to save her, and his grief for his lost father was replaced by thanks that she had lived. "You made it," he was saying. "Christ, you can't imagine how I was afraid!" She stood close, leaning toward him.

"Jan, I love you."

But her hair had darkened, and her face was now more slender, but with sadder eyes. This woman wasn't Jan, and yet he knew her. "Please, you have to rest," the woman said.

He saw that she was pinning down his hands. He squirmed to free himself.

"You must relax," she told him. "You'll disturb your bandages. You'll strain your ribs." He felt a pressure on his fore-head, felt a stabbing in his chest. Pain swarmed through him like the sting of hornets.

"Jesus." In agony he looked, and there were doctors, there were nurses. But he couldn't understand what they were say-ing. French. That's right. They're speaking French.

"Where's Jan?"

The room was silent.

Houston peered from one face to another. Then he settled on the woman whom he knew, who wasn't Jan. "Simone?"

She nodded, sad-eyed. Houston swallowed. "Jan?" She shook her head regretfully.

"She isn't!" Houston shouted. "No! She can't be!" She kept staring at him. Freezing terror gripped his heart. A raging panic swelled within him. He thrashed from the bed. "Tell me where she is!"

The room exploded into motion. Doctors and nurses scram-bled toward him. Houston struggled with them, straining to get past them. "Jan! Where?"

Pinprick. No, a needle. To his left, a nurse. A hypodermic pierced his arm. He felt the spurt of liquid reach his blood.

"No! Jan! I have to—"

He felt dizzy. He clutched at his skull. He fell back on the bed. Simone leaned down. She pulled the sheet up beneath his chin. Her face distorted, lengthened, wavered, as if she were under water. "I'll be with you," she said.

But in Houston's mind he saw the water rushing toward him. He heard a distant anguished scream. The darkness took him, and he drowned.

Part 2

13

His grief consumed him. He did not care where he was or how long he had been unconscious or how badly he'd been injured. For desperate days he convinced himself that none of it was real, that Jan was still alive, that he had suffered through a nightmare. But his memory insisted, and his grief was unendurable. He was certain that his mind would crack. He couldn't bear the agony. Then something ruptured. Sorrow numbed him, sapping strength and hope and will to live. His tears distorted everything. The ceiling seemed to ripple.

He was on a bed in darkness. He heard water rushing. Rumbling?

Thunder.

It was night. A streetlight showed the rain streaming down the window, casting its mosaic shadow on the ceiling.

Houston, groggy to begin with, felt that he was under water. At the same time, he, vertiginous, appeared to stare down from a great height. His mind could not sustain the contradictory perspectives. Bile rushed scalding from his stomach; he fought back vomit.

Lightning flickered, and he saw the room: the ornate woodwork on the walls, the hulking ancient bureau, the huge brooding sofa.

Thunder rumbled. To his right, a scrollwork door came open. Light spilled in. A woman's shadow filled the doorway. But she wasn't any nurse, and this not a hospital. He heard a fire crackling from a hearth in the other room.

The woman approached him. Silhouetted, she was featureless. Reminded of his dream, he felt disoriented, frightened by the way she seemed to float.

He stared at her. His stomach burned. My God, yes, she was Jan! His heart raced uncontrollably. Abruptly it convulsed. She turned in profile toward the window. In another flash of lightning Houston recognized her face.

"Simone?" His voice was tortured.

She spun, startled, peering toward him in the darkness.

Choking, he wiped his swollen eyes. "I thought you were—" He couldn't say Jan's name. In agony his throat seized shut.

She stared at him, concerned. She flicked on a corner lamp. Its glow was warm, reflecting off a mirror that was clear and deep beyond belief, with gold flecks gleaming from its frame.

He blinked, confused. His throat was raw. "Where am I?"

"The hotel. My father's room."

She came across to him. She broke the seal on bottled water, poured, and held his hand to help him drink. The water tingled, sweet and cool. He felt his swollen tongue absorb it.

"Not too much at once," she said. His lips now felt sensation, sharp and stinging.

"I was in the hospital." He slumped back on his pillow. But his statement was also a question. He was not sure if he actually had been there or had dreamed it.

"There was nothing more the doctors could do for you, except to watch. My father said that we could watch you here. He feels the obligation. He is still ashamed."

"Because that man was in our room?"

"This is my father's home. His guests are his responsibility."

"There wasn't any way he could have known. He's not to blame. . . . But thank him for me." Rain lashed at the window. "Tell me everything that happened."

"We were hoping you'd tell us," she said. "A farmer found you on the riverbank. He gave you up for dead, but when the ambulance arrived, a doctor managed to revive you. The police searched up the river, and they found where you had crashed the guardrail at the bridge. A team of scuba divers swam down to your car.'' She rubbed her shoulder, glancing toward the window.

''And?''

''I'm sorry. Your wife was still inside.''

He closed his eyes.

''On the radio, we heard the news about your accident. My father couldn't leave, but he insisted that I go to you. The rest you know. As soon as it was feasible, I brought you here. A doctor visits you. Your head was injured. You sustained a small concussion, and your ribs were fractured. You can feel the tape that binds them.''

''Someone ran us off the road,'' he said, remembering. She stared. ''A van. A big black square-faced van. The bridge was one-lane, and the bastard tried to pass us.''

''The police have asked to speak with you.''

''They won't do any good. I didn't get the license number. They won't find the van.''

''Somebody drunk or in a hurry.''

''No. It was intentional.'' She stiffened.

''Someone *meant* to do it.'' Houston glared.

''You're still confused. Your mind's fooling you.''

''A stranger hid inside our room. He could have phoned or sent a message. But he came to us in secret. I can't prove he was even there. When I described the man, your father didn't recognize him. Did your father ask around the village?''

''No one knew the man.''

''All right then. So the stranger sent us to a town a hundred miles away, and on the road we had an accident. If I had died, you never would have known the way it happened. But I lived, and I can tell you it wasn't an accident. That driver *meant* to push us off the road. It was *deliberate*. There wasn't any reason for that van to try to pass us.''

''But it makes no sense. Who'd want to kill you? Why?''

''Pierre de St. Laurent.'' Houston watched the way she studied him, as if she thought he was crazy. ''Yes, I know,'' he said. "It's thirty-seven years ago. Who cares what happened then? Someone does. A lot."

"You need to rest."

"No, listen. Promise me. You have to take me there. To Roncevaux. I want to see who lives at that address."

"I can't encourage you to—"

"Promise me."

"We'll talk about it later." She stared, troubled, toward the window.

"What's the matter?" Houston said.

"It's not the right time."

"Go on and say it."

"There's a question I have to ask. I wish I didn't." Houston frowned at her. "You have to make arrangements." Houston didn't understand. "Your embassy made inquiries. Your wife, yourself, you have no parents and no children. There was no one who could sign the documents."

"For what?"

"I have to ask you where you want her buried."

"Jesus." Houston couldn't hold the tears back. He was crying. He kept on. He thought he'd never stop.

14

The coffin slowly sank beneath the floor. He shuddered. Something rumbled underneath him. Then the coffin disappeared. The trap door eased up, whirring, to the level of the floor. It snapped into place. The rumbling stopped. The room was still.

He told himself, Don't think about what's going to happen

next. But then he heard, or thought he heard, a different noise, more ominous, below him: something roaring like a furnace.

Houston had to get away. He turned from purple velvet drapes, from waist-high posts joined by ropes that surrounded the place where the coffin had been set. His shoes scraped on the floor.

Simone, in black, was close behind him, standing with her father, who was dressed in mourning. Houston squinted at them, muscles tensing in his cheeks. The man in charge stepped near to Houston, soberly consoling. If monsieur would come back in the morning . . .

Houston, nodding, murmured, "Thank you." But his throat was so grief-swollen that his voice cracked. His eyesight dimmed. The room turned gray. He feared he was going to faint. He listed, reaching toward Simone. She grabbed his arm. Monsard quickly took his other arm. They helped him toward the exit.

He was vaguely aware of walking down a hallway. Then a door came open, and the sunlight glared on him. Dizzy, he peered down to shield his eyes. The steps, the sidewalk, then the grass. He slumped on a concrete bench, his head between his knees. "I'll be okay," he told them.

But his grief came racking out of him. He thought for sure his heart would break.

Then someone held him tightly. Houston blinked up through his tears. Simone sat with her arm around him. Houston's sobs tore through him. "You have to understand. That's how Jan wanted it."

"There's no need to explain."

"She made me promise. What else could I do? I had to honor what she wanted. Cremation." Houston clenched his fists and moaned. "If I'd buried her in France, then what would I have done when I was home? I'd want to see her grave. I'd have to come to France to see it." He pawed at his eyes.

"And what if I'd buried her at home? I would have flown home with the body, and it's possible I never would return here." He strained to breathe.

Simone leaned back from him. Her voice was gentle. "That's so bad? Considering what happened here, I wouldn't think you'd want to see this place again."

"I have to stay," he told her.

"Why?"

"Because somebody wants to stop me asking questions. If I leave, then he accomplishes what he intended. I won't let him have that satisfaction."

She frowned at him. "Then you still believe—"

"That Jan was murdered? Absolutely."

"But the police investigated. There's no proof. They checked the address you gave them. No one named St. Laurent was ever there. They searched for the van. They even went to body shops in case its side was being repaired. They didn't find it."

"I bet they wonder if it exists. You saw the way they looked at me. They think I'm hysterical, or maybe I was drunk, or I simply lost control of the car and I'm lying about the van to hide my mistake."

She shook her head. "They believe you. It was hit-and-run."

"It was more than that. I know it. I'm not leaving till I find out why my wife died. She was fine and good. I loved her. And some bastard's going to pay for what he did to her." The steel edge of his voice surprised him. Rage shut out his grief. He didn't want that. Rage felt ugly. But his anger had complete control.

Monsard spoke in French. Simone responded. Then she looked at Houston. "My father's right. I don't see what . . ."

She was reluctant to continue. Houston stared at her. "Go on," he said.

"If you won't count on the police, if you don't think they're trying hard enough, I don't see what you think you can accomplish on your own. You're just one person, and forgive me, but you don't know what you're doing."

Houston smiled bitterly. "But apparently I'm managing just fine, or else whoever drove that van would not have tried to kill me. I'll keep doing what I was. I'll ask more questions, follow where the answers take me. I'm damn close. That much is certain.''

"If you're right—I won't insult you by pretending to believe you—if you're right, though, then you'll put yourself in danger. Maybe next time you won't be so lucky.''

Houston clenched his teeth. "You want to know the truth? I should be scared. Except I feel so Goddamned empty, and I feel so Goddamned angry that I'm not afraid at all. I'm hoping he'll try for me again. That way he'll show himself. I'll have a chance to get my hands around his throat.''

She winced.

"My wife is dead. I've only got two choices. Either I go home and grieve forever, or I tell myself she was murdered and I try to find out why. What would you do? If I go back home, if I don't try—" His eyes implored her. *"Help me.''*

15

Though the buildings were older and the architecture was distinctly European, Roncevaux reminded Houston of the mill towns he had known in western Pennsylvania. Even the topography was similar. The thickly wooded lumpy hills through which a dirty dying river flowed—and in the middle of a narrow valley, Roncevaux, industrial pollution capping it from hill to hill with haze. This was a part of France he would have preferred to avoid; but since Jan had died, his memory of pristine countrysides was tainted, and this underside of France was now in keeping with his feelings.

He'd been told that the main product here was paper, and he

smelled the rancid, bitter mash. He squinted toward the buildings, stone façades caked ashen gray. His eyes began to water, irritated by the grit that settled from the sky. He closed his window and turned toward Simone.

She drove her recent-model white Renault. She'd asked him at the start if he wanted to do the driving, but his ribs still ached if he raised his arms or turned abruptly. What was more, he now felt nervous about driving—"gun shy," if she understood the slang. Instead, he navigated from a map while she maneuvered through the busy traffic. Even major streets were narrow, and the somber buildings seemed to squeeze him as he studied street sign after street sign. Noon, and yet the dense haze shut the sun out.

"Imagine what it's like to live here," Houston said.

"What's worse, they don't have any choice. You're sorry you came?"

Instead of answering, he pointed toward an intersection. "Left here. Do you see it?"

She nodded toward the sign: RUE GABRIEL.

His anger quickened. Soon, he thought.

She turned the corner into an ancient part of town. The buildings seemed to list. Exhausted. Wooden, parched, and peeling.

Houston shuddered. Old men on the street looked decadent, diseased. There weren't many numbers on the buildings. Fifty-five. Then eighty-three, and ninety, ninety-six. Those figures hung fatigued on top of doors. But his heart beat faster when he saw one hundred and thirteen.

Simone drove by it.

"Wait."

"I have to find a parking space," she said.

He glanced back, trying to determine if the building had apartments. There were old stone steps and then a wooden arch. The windows on the four stories seemed to have been painted over. Either that or they'd never been washed. Ahead, a truck pulled sharply from the curb. It narrowly avoided scraping the Renault's front fender. As he flinched, Simone braked quickly, jerked hard on the steering wheel, and slid the car neatly into the parking space the truck had left.

He marveled at her skill. She made an obscene gesture toward the truck. Despite himself, he had to laugh. She glanced at him in surprise, and then she had to laugh as well. "I learned to drive in San Francisco," she explained.

"I'd have thought you'd learned on stock car tracks. I'm glad I'm not behind the wheel."

"We'd better lock it. In this district, we'll be lucky if it isn't stripped when we get back."

"I feel like I'm back home." And then he wished he was back home, had never come to France, had never taken Jan here.

"You turned pale," Simone said, worried.

"Just a thought I wasn't ready for." He stepped from the Renault and locked it. "Let's check out the building. Settle this."

Impatiently he waited while she came around to join him. Then they walked along the littered street. They passed three toughs who snickered toward Simone. They reached one hundred and thirteen.

Houston stared up at the opaque windows, squinted toward the darkness of the splintered wooden archway, drew a breath, and climbed the steps.

There was a dusty door beyond the archway. He turned the knob. It opened, creaking. They entered an unlit corridor. He smelled the must, the mildew, and if he was not mistaken, urine. A door came open to his right. A bald unshaven man zipped up his pants as he stepped out. Beyond him, Houston saw two pull-chain urinals.

The man stopped in surprise. He grinned, embarrassed. "*Pardonnez, madame.*" And Houston understood. "I did not hear you."

"*J'accepte.*" She spoke rapidly in French then. The unshaven man replied as quickly.

Houston waited in suspense.

Simone turned. "It's an office building. He's the janitor, he says. So many offices are vacant, he's afraid the place will soon be sold. He'll lose his job." The bald, unshaven man kept grinning nervously. "He thinks we're here to buy the place," Simone continued.

"Ask him."

"St. Laurent?" Simone told the man. "Pierre de St. Laurent?"

"*Ah, oui. Je le connais.*"

Abruptly Houston felt a scalding in his stomach. "Did he say he knows him?" He tried to keep his voice controlled. "But the police claimed St. Laurent wasn't here."

"*Le nom. Je connais le nom. Quarante et un.*" The man nodded cooperatively, pointing toward the wooden stairs in back. "*Il a loué quarante et un.*"

"Simone, quick tell me."

"St. Laurent. He rented number forty-one. Upstairs."

"My God, he's seen him?" Houston didn't know which impulse he should follow first—to hurry up the stairs, or wait and get more information.

"*Avez-vous lui vu?*" Simone asked. The janitor replied. Simone turned back to Houston. "No. He says he gets instructions from the rental agent. He received a note directing him to leave the office open and to put the keys on the desk. He then received another note directing him to change the name on the office door. The mailman comes with parcels for him."

"Is he up there?" Houston asked. "*Est-il ici?*"

"*Jamais,*" the janitor responded, then elaborated.

"What?"

Simone explained. "He says that St. Laurent is never here. Each night the office needs no cleaning. And the parcels are unopened."

"What the hell?" abruptly Houston started toward the stairwell. He trembled.

"Peter?"

He heard footsteps from behind him but didn't bother turning. Clutching the rail, he went up two steps at a time. The stairway creaked. The railing wobbled. At the top, a dangling yellow light bulb lit the second hallway.

"Peter?"

Finally he turned. Simone hurried behind him. "The police came here," he said to her, "and they learned nothing. I don't understand it. But this proves I had a visitor that night."

"I never doubted it."

"But you're my witness when we go back to the cops. I never could have linked this place with St. Laurent unless somebody told me where to look. You came here with me, and you know how hard it is to find. I had to have directions. Someone had to point me here."

"I said I believed you."

They climbed higher as they talked. They reached the third floor, but no light hung from the ceiling; the darkness troubled Houston.

Then the fourth. They reached the fourth.

16

He paused. There was no sound here, though he did hear muffled traffic noises coming from the street. He smelled the mildew and the must. His apprehension made the corridor appear to lengthen. But his anger took the place of his uneasiness, and he continued down the hallway.

Forty-one was at the far end of the corridor. He squinted toward the letters—IMPORTATIONS, ST. LAURENT—stenciled on the frosted window.

Houston knocked. No answer. Houston knocked again, and this time when he got no answer he tensed to grip the doorknob.

Simone reached for his hand. "You're sure?" she said. "If what you think is true, you'll be in danger."

"Both of us," he said. "I wasn't thinking. Look, you'd better wait out here."

"You must be joking. If you think I'm going to stay out here alone . . ."

"I have to do this. I owe it to Jan." Houston pushed the door. It scraped on rusty hinges and revealed a one-room office—there were no doors to provide a second exit—and two frosted windows.

Houston stepped inside. He felt Simone clutch at his arm but didn't look at her. He concentrated on the office. To his left the room was barren. To his right he saw a dingy wooden cabinet. He searched the drawers; they were empty.

Straight ahead, a battered desk showed liquid stains from bottles and glasses. On the desk there was a phone. And three small packages with canceled stamps on them.

Houston walked around the desk and stared down at the packages. They were addressed in type: PIERRE DE ST. LAURENT. He picked one up. "It's heavy." Houston shook it. "Doesn't rattle. Wonder what it is."

He set the package down and raised the phone, nodding when he heard the dial tone. "Well, it's working. *Someone* must be using it." And that was all. Except for one parched leather chair, there was nothing else inside the room.

"What do we do now?" she said.

"I'd like to know what's in these packages."

"You mean you're going to open them?"

"No, I don't want to show that we've been here. The door says imports. But I doubt it. Not unless he's starving. This place isn't used for business."

"What then?"

"I don't know. A drop perhaps. A place where you can leave and pick up messages."

"Or packages?"

"Could be. Except these postmarks are from several days ago. If what's inside is valuable, I wonder why nobody came to get them." Houston shook another package. "Could be heroin or money. Hell, it could just be books." He pursed his lips. "Maybe nothing's wrong here."

"And the office wasn't locked," she said.

"Suggesting that these packages are worthless. Dammit," Houston said, "we don't know any more than what we learned downstairs."

"I have a thought." He studied her. "You're still determined?" she asked.

Houston nodded.

"We can wait in an empty office down the hall. If someone comes to get the packages, we'll follow him. He might be St. Laurent. Or he might go to St. Laurent."

He grinned. "Simone, that's—" Houston stopped his sentence short. His grin dissolved. On guard, he turned abruptly toward the door. Footsteps creaked in the hall outside.

They hadn't closed the door. Simone stepped backward. Houston swung around the desk. The janitor peered at them from the corridor. "*Ça va bien?*" His eyes were nervous.

Houston breathed out, understanding. Sure, this guy's supposed to watch the building. Now he's worried that we're in here. He's afraid he'll lose his job. "Explain that we're importers," he told Simone, "that we'll come back when someone's here."

She translated, and they started out. The janitor started past them toward the office.

"*Merci,*" Houston said.

They walked along the hallway. "Later," Houston told the man. "*Plus tard.*" They reached the stairs.

"We can't wait in an empty office now," he said to her. "We'll have to find another way." They started down the stairs.

The janitor went in the office as if making sure that nothing had been touched. The phone rang from behind them in the office. Houston paused and turned. "Simone, wait. Listen. Translate what he says."

"He might not answer it."

The phone stopped. Silence. Houston waited tensely.

Out of sight, the janitor said, "*Oui?*"

The blast disintegrated walls. The roof collapsed. The hallway disappeared. The shock wave toppled Houston backward, slamming him against the wall.

He dropped, weightless, groaning when he hit the stairs. Simone screamed. He smelled smoke and something acrid, sharp, and pungent. He felt heat. A portion of a wall crashed near him.

Something landed on him, squirming. In a panic, Houston saw it was Simone. In the fierce light of the flames, he saw the blood on her, on both of them.

He screamed. The scorching heat was closer. He had fallen down the stairway to the third floor. Glancing upward, he saw flames envelop everything above him.

Coughing from the smoke, he felt the heat press onto him. His clothes were warm. His vision swirled.

"We've got to—" But he breathed in smoke and, choking, couldn't finish.

He stumbled with her down the wreckage of the stairway. Once they lost their balance. Once they fell back as a flaming chunk of ceiling dropped before them. Clutching the banister, they climbed down to a different section of the stairs.

Or tried to. For the banister, which had been wobbly to begin with, gave way, and they fell hard on the next floor's landing. Houston moaned from the pain that jolted through his body. But the flames were high above them now. "Are you okay?" he asked.

Simone was white-faced, shaking. She had strength to stand. They continued downward. In a minute they lurched coughing from the building. At the curb they slumped across the fender of a car. A crowd had gathered. People rushed to help. And through the roar of flames above him, Houston heard the strident wail of fast-approaching sirens.

17

"In the morning, we'll start sorting through the wreckage," the inspector said, "though from the scope of the destruction, I suspect we won't find much."

They were in a narrow room with seven desks. Near Houston, two policemen hurriedly made phone calls. Houston rubbed his shoulder, glancing toward them.

"Feeling any better?" the inspector asked.

"Sore."

"I'll bet you are."

The ambulance attendants had rushed Simone and Houston to Emergency. Slight burns. Contusions. Shock. Simone had sprained a wrist; Houston had dislocated a shoulder. The bandages around his injured ribs had minimized the impact. Houston was nonetheless sore from head to feet.

And dizzy from the medication he'd been given. He did not recall when day had turned to evening, and he had no recollection of his trip from the hospital to the police station. Indeed, he'd been so groggy that he hadn't thought it strange when the inspector, who had said his name was Alfred Bellay, introduced himself in English.

But the startled look that crossed Simone's face made him wonder. Suddenly alert, he studied this tall, slim, good-looking, well-dressed man. "Did you speak English?" he said.

"That's why I've been assigned to you. As soon as the firemen discovered you were American, they called to ask for my help. Years ago, in Paris, I had dealings with the British, and I had to learn the language."

Houston's thoughts became more clear. This man seemed in his middle thirties. If, when younger, he had started his career in Paris, then he must have stepped on someone's toes to be forced to work in Roncevaux. Lord, who would want to live here?

Alfred Bellay said, "Then you assume it was a bomb?"

"I can't imagine what else."

"Leaking gas perhaps."

"I smelled none."

"Mademoiselle?"

She shook her head.

"Then you suspect those packages contained explosives?"

"We checked everything inside the room, but we didn't open the packages. Where else could the bomb have been?"

"The phone rang."

"Yes."

"The janitor went in the room to answer it."

"That's right."

"He picked the phone up, spoke, and . . ." Bellay raised his hands to mime an explosion.

"That's right."

"Then we have two possibilities. The bomb went off by accident, at random, for no special reason at that time. That's one. Or else the bomb went off exactly when it should have, detonated by remote control. The phone itself would not have detonated the device. If so, the first ring would have been sufficient. I recall you said the phone rang twice."

Pete nodded.

"Then whoever called was waiting to make certain there was someone in the office. When he heard a voice, he pressed a button, and a shortwave signal tripped the bomb."

Houston had already thought of that, reluctant to suggest the possibility, suspicious of how Bellay would react.

"You haven't told me what the two of you were doing there," Bellay said.

"We went to see a man."

"Please, Mr. Houston," Bellay said. "You're making this

tedious. I ask a question, and you answer no more than you have to. Someone uninvolved would willingly elaborate. You know more than you're volunteering."

"Go on. Tell him," Simone said.

Bellay glanced at her, his eyebrows raised. "So you speak English too."

She nodded.

"Then if nothing else, at least the three of us have *that* in common. Tell me what? Go on and finish."

"Someone wants to kill us," Houston said.

"That seems apparent. Why?"

"We're looking for a man. Pierre de St. Laurent. He disappeared in nineteen forty-four. A man suggested we could find him in that office."

"What man? Who suggested?"

"We don't know. He didn't give his name. He left a message and was gone."

"So you came here."

"The first time I was with my wife. There was a traffic accident. My wife was killed."

Bellay looked at him, startled. "Deliberate, you think, considering what's happened?"

"I'm certain."

"I was doubtful, though," Simone intruded. "I agree with Peter now. Somebody tried to kill him. To prevent him from locating St. Laurent."

"And why is St. Laurent important to you?" Bellay asked. His eyes were hard on Houston.

"That's the strange part," Houston said. "My father was a soldier. He was killed in nineteen forty-four. This St. Laurent maintained his grave. I merely felt like thanking him."

As Houston finished, he glanced toward the checkered floor. He didn't know why he still lied, why he did not admit that he'd been searching for his father's grave. Too personal, too complicated, he thought. No, something else. And you're afraid of it. You won't face up to it.

"Commendable," Bellay said dryly. "But apparently he

63

wants no thanks. You say St. Laurent disappeared in nineteen forty-four?''

''Yes, and the more dead ends I found, the more I was determined to find him. Then that stranger sent us here, and—''

Bellay frowned. ''There's something else.''

''I'm telling you the truth.''

''But all of it? Surely you can see my point. This incident is senseless. Why would St. Laurent try to kill you?''

''That's what's driving me crazy. I don't know.''

''Alfred?''

Bellay swung to face the two policemen who had been making phone calls in the background througout this conversation. One of them had spoken to him.

''*Oui?*'' he answered.

The conversation was in French. Simone seemed agitated as she listened.

Bellay turned to Houston. ''That entire block of buildings has a manager, a rental agent. He checked through his records. Verlaine Enterprises owns that building, but they never heard of St. Laurent. The rental agent verifies that St. Laurent did lease the office, though.''

''Then he can give us a description of the man.''

''I wish it were that simple. St. Laurent conducted all of his transactions by phone and through the mail. He paid in cash by letter.''

Houston groaned, in part because the sedatives had worn off and his back was aching fiercely, but in part as well because he'd reached another impasse. Once again Pierre de St. Laurent had managed to evade him.

''When?'' he asked.

''Excuse me?'' Bellay said.

''The office. What day was it leased?''

''This month. The eleventh.''

''That's three days ago.''

''And why is that important?''

Houston shivered, raging. "Jan was dead by then. The bastards!"

"Peter, there's your proof." Simone sat bolt-upright in her chair.

"Of *what?*" Bellay said.

Houston's voice was angry. "When that stranger sent us here, there wasn't any way he could have known that St. Laurent was in that office. The office wasn't even rented yet. It didn't *have* to be. They never meant for us to get here. When they found out I had lived, they hoped I'd follow through on what I started. So they waited until the cops had checked the building—then they leased the office, and they waited. Goddamned bastards. They watched me go in the building. They called the office, confident I'd answer the phone. They had to make sure I was in the room."

18

Houston drove at random, constantly checking his rearview mirror. He turned left, then right for no apparent reason. On occasion, he went all the way around a block. He sped up. He slowed down. And when at last he had been satisfied that there was no one following, he darted toward the main road out of Roncevaux and pressed his foot on the accelerator.

"This road takes us out of town," Simone said, surprised.

"I know it."

"But the hotel Bellay sent us to is back the other way."

"That's why I'm going *this* way."

"Then you didn't lose direction back there? All those wrong streets you were taking? Oh, my God."

"You understand now. They won't think we'll leave town this soon. We're hurt. It's natural for us to spend the night here. How long would it take for someone to discover where we're staying?"

"We could check in under different names."

"That only makes it harder for them. Not impossible. If we stayed here, eventually they'd find us."

"We could ask Bellay for a guard."

"Would you trust a guard? We wouldn't know him, wouldn't know if someone made a switch and wore a uniform to fool us. Even if we trusted him, a man who wants to kill us bad enough can find a way to do it. We don't have another choice. We've got to leave. While we've been hunting St. Laurent, somebody's hunted us. The next time he'll make extra sure. He'll fix it so no one ever finds us."

She shuddered. "Don't talk like that."

"I have to make you understand. We're fighting for our lives."

The high beams on the headlights showed the empty tree-lined road ahead. Pete squinted toward a road sign. "Do you know that town?"

"I've never even heard of it," she said.

"Well, maybe no one else has. Ten kilometers. Let's try it. I can't drive much longer. My shoulder's in agony."

"My wrist is swollen. I can't drive at all," she said.

He geared down into second. Fighting not to groan, he turned the steering wheel. His throbbing arm resisted. The Renault slipped past a ditch and headed east along a gravel road, its headlights probing through the dark.

"Simone, I'm sorry."

"Why?"

"For getting you involved."

"I didn't have to come along. You told me Jan was murdered, but I thought you were imagining. I humored you."

"But I knew it was not imagination. I knew there was risk. I was so caught up in my rage I didn't realize I was putting you in danger too. I never should have asked for help."

"It doesn't make a difference now. I'm here. I made my choice. Let's say we both were wrong. It doesn't change a thing."

"Look, I could take my chances. You could leave me in this town. But when you got back home . . . I'm worried. Maybe he'll come after *you*," he said.

She didn't speak, but he could hear her draw in her breath.

"You see? It's maybe not just for tonight while you're with me. He might decide that you're involved. He might be worried you're a danger to him. Do we separate, or do we face this thing together?" Houston waited, but she didn't answer.

He kept staring past the headlights. All at once he saw some cottages, a café, a service station. Lights were few. He saw no people. One lone car was parked along the street. Before he knew it, he was through the town, the darkened countryside before him once again. He made a U-turn, tensing from the painful effort, and went back the way he'd come.

"Simone, you didn't answer me."

"I'm furious."

"I told you I was sorry."

"Not at you. I'm angry, and I'm frightened, and I don't like being threatened. In the States, when I was married, that's the way my husband was. He wanted to control me. When I left him, he chased after me. He terrorized me. Twice he tried to kill me."

"Jesus."

"I came back to France. I made a promise to myself. I'd never live in fear again. I won't submit to always wondering if someone's hiding in the bushes. I won't sacrifice my freedom, flinching every time I hear a footstep. This is my fight now. I want that bastard stopped."

19

HOTEL, *the sign said, but the place seemed the equivalent* of a boarding house in the States. A stark old home, a block away from the main intersection. Here the neighborhood was absolutely dark. He parked the car behind some bushes down a lane. As cats snarled, they walked toward the street.

The house was dark and quiet. Houston knocked on the door. No answer.

Houston knocked again. He shivered from fatigue, the aftermath of shock. Simone stepped deeper in the shadows as the headlights of a car went past.

A third knock, and at last a light came on inside. A shadow hobbled down a hallway toward the entrance. An old woman in a bulky robe and baggy nightcap peered through a narrow window. Then she pulled the door open a crack and frowned suspiciously at them.

Simone did all the talking, quite a lot, it seemed to Houston, just to rent a room. But this aged woman was annoyed that she'd been wakened, and she seemed to recognize that Houston and Simone were different nationalities, which raised the question of whether they were married.

Houston nodded his assurance.

If they weren't, the woman said, she'd have to rent them separate rooms.

Pete understood. She isn't bothered if we live in sin, but if she rents two rooms, then she gets twice the money.

They couldn't risk the night in separate rooms. At last Simone resolved the issue by agreeing to pay double for one room, and now the aged woman, satisfied, nodded.

They had brought their bags. They stepped inside. Houston paid. The woman gestured without ceremony toward the stairs and a door that faced them at the top. They went up wearily.

"She missed her calling," Houston said. "She should be selling cars."

"She told me breakfast is at six."

"Which means she figures we'll sleep through it, so she won't be bothered making it. I take it back. She ought to be a politician."

They went inside. The room was neat and clean but small. A brass bed had a too-soft mattress, sagging in the middle. Houston set the bags down, testing it. Simone had shut the door.

"I hope you're not embarrassed," Houston said. "There isn't any other way. We have to share the room."

"I've seen a man asleep before. The question is, Who gets the bed, who gets the chair?"

"You want to toss a coin?"

"I think I'll exercise my womanly prerogative and offer you the chair."

"I was afraid of that." He glanced around. "There isn't any bathroom."

"Twice the price, and you expect to get a bathroom? You're a dreamer."

Houston pulled the door and peered out. "Down the hall. Well, since I'm sleeping in the chair—"

"You get the bathroom first. I was afraid of that."

They grinned at one another. Then the circumstances that had forced them here occurred to them, and instantly they sobered.

"I won't take too long," he said.

He grabbed his bag and left the room. When he came back, wearing pajamas and a robe, he discovered that Simone had already undressed and put on her own robe. While she went out, he found a blanket in the bureau, and he nestled in the chair. But something nagged at him. A puzzling detail he was certain he had missed.

Simone returned. She set her bag down. But instead of getting into bed, she sat on its edge and stared at him. "Bellay was right."

"About what?"

"You haven't told the truth," she said.

"You're wrong."

"Not all of it." Her face was tense. "I felt suspicious from the start. You seemed too eager to find St. Laurent and thank him."

"He maintained my father's grave. I owed him. What's so strange about—"

"He didn't do it."

"What?"

"He disappeared in nineteen forty-four. He never kept his promise to your mother. You don't owe him anything."

Pete felt his face blanch. Something swelled within him, at the same time sinking, burning.

"But I let the contradiction pass," she said. "I figured you must have a reason not to tell me your real motive. It was none of my concern, I thought. I liked you. I was curious, I went along."

"Simone, I never meant to—"

"Let me finish. Then your wife died, and I sympathized with what you'd been through. Unlike some of my compatriots, I feel a fondness for Americans. I pushed away my doubts. I helped you further. But now someone wants to kill me. I'm not blaming you for that. As I said, I made my choice, and even if I made it blindly, it was my choice. I'll stand by it. But as long as I'm involved in this, please be honest with me. All the way here I was waiting for an explanation, but you wouldn't trust me, wouldn't honor me by telling me the truth. I can't wait any longer. What the hell is this about?"

Pete concentrated on her. He felt nervous, bothered not just by the danger they were in, but by a different kind of fear, a lurking hidden threat to peace of mind and sanity. The threat was like a vicious animal that stalked in secret. He'd been trying to ignore it, to pretend it wasn't there, to make believe that his suspicions had no basis in reality.

But now the time had come. The animal was snarling from the darkness. "In my bag," he said. "I've got some brandy." Houston pushed the blanket from him, leaned out from the chair, and reached his bag. He opened it and found the brandy bottle. When he looked around, he saw no glasses.

"Guess we'll have to rough it." He twisted the top off and raised the bottle to his lips. Then, blinking, he offered her the bottle.

She surprised him by accepting. She peered at the label, raised the bottle, and drank deeply. Houston watched her throat move as she swallowed. Then she set the bottle on the floor between them.

"The truth," she said. "You're just postponing it."

He studied her, reluctant to talk. Then, as if his fierce restraint had snapped, his mind stumbled forward. "It's my father. I can't find his grave." The words hung in the air.

He fumbled through his jacket, found the pack, and lit a cigarette.

Simone was baffled. "What's that got to do with—"

"My mother always told me he was buried in the military cemetery near your town." Despite the pressure in his chest, he forced himself on. "As long as I was in France, I figured I should pay my respects. But dammit, there's no record of his being buried there. I didn't understand. Then I remembered that Pierre de St. Laurent had written to my mother, saying he'd maintained the grave. I figured if I talked to St. Laurent, then he would tell me where the grave is."

She was totally bewildered. "And that's . . . ? You believe your wife died and that janitor and nearly you and I because somebody wants to stop you from locating where your father's buried?"

"No. You put it that way, it sounds foolish."

71

"What then?"

Houston drew on his cigarette. "It's not easy. Every time the thought suggests itself, I smother it. I mean, it's so insane that if I found out it was true I'd—"

"Peter." Her eyes appealed to him. "It can't be any more insane than what's already happened. Tell me," she said. "Trust me."

Houston nodded. "You have to understand. I never knew my father. He was killed about the same time I was born. My mother glorified him. She told me how smart he was, how handsome, how he loved us. He was tall and strong, and he was good at fixing cars, and he could sing like an opera star. He was a saint to us. But all the time I was growing up, I saw the fathers my friends had, and I envied them. I knew those fathers couldn't be as wonderful as mine had been, but they were living, and I wished with all my heart that one of them was mine. I asked my mother if she ever planned on marrying again. She told me, 'I'll never find a man to match your father.' And she didn't. To her death, she stayed unmarried."

He blew smoke. Simone picked up the bottle and drank. Her brow was furrowed.

"Kids are so inventive," Houston said. "Let's call it fantasy, a child's suspicion based on insecurity. Or maybe we should call it hope." He shook his head. "But I began to have this daydream. Soon it came to me when I was sleeping. I invited it. I analyzed it. I imagined different—I don't know—scenarios I guess adults would call them. What if he had never died? Supposing he had lost his memory and didn't know he had a wife and son. Or let's try this. Supposing he'd been mutilated, scarred so badly that he couldn't bring himself to let us see his ugliness. Or worse, the blackest possibility. Supposing he was perfectly all right, but he'd decided that he didn't want to come back home. That he'd abandoned us, that he had turned his back on me and left me to grow up alone."

Houston felt his sudden tears. His throat was bitter. He

pinched off his cigarette as if to crush his sorrow, hoping that the pain of his burned fingers would distract him.

"Peter," she said softly. She stood and moved close to him. She put her hands on his shoulders.

But he was shaking, and though he smelled her perfume, Houston couldn't make himself look up at her. "It's like I said," he told her, eyes shut. "Kids can be inventive."

Now her hands were tight on his shoulders. "You suspect your father's still alive?" Her voice was taut with incredulity. And something else—an eerie terror.

"In time, the boy put away his fantasies. He finally grew up. But now I find out that my father isn't buried where my mother said he was, and that Pierre de St. Laurent dropped out of sight, and Christ, I want to know what's going on! If what my mother said about his grave isn't true, then what else isn't? How many other things I took for granted won't be what I thought they were? The only man who knows for sure is St. Laurent, and someone's so uptight about us finding him that so far he's tried twice to kill me. And he killed my wife, and—"

Houston's voice broke. She pulled him toward her, pressed his face against her stomach, held him, soothed him.

They both stiffened at a knock on the door.

They turned uneasily. A louder knock.

Simone went over. Wiping his tears, Houston watched her pull the door ajar. He braced himself, on guard.

He heard the aged woman's voice.

Simone replied. The woman answered. The woman's footsteps shuffled down the stairs.

Simone closed the door. "She says we're keeping her awake."

He nodded. "It's just as well. If I keep on like this, I'll be a basket case."

She came across, studying him. She leaned down and kissed him on the cheek. "We'll find Pierre de St. Laurent," she said. "One way or another, we'll find all your answers."

Sleep came sooner than he had expected. When Simone

73

turned off the light, he heard her slippered feet pad toward the bed. He heard the sound of her robe as she removed it, then the rustle of the sheets as she crawled beneath the covers.

He drifted, and he dreamed, and in his dream, he once again was at 113 Rue Gabriel. He left the office with Simone. He watched the janitor go in. Once again he heard the phone ring. The explosion threw him down the stairs. He felt Simone land hard on him. He lifted her. But then he saw the way her head was twisted at a grotesque angle, saw the fist-sized chunk of wood imbedded in her forehead. She was dead. My God, he'd killed her! First Jan, then Simone. Not once, but twice. He screamed as Simone's dead eyes peered toward him. He kept screaming. He was running in a panic.

"Peter!"

He struggled with the hands that grabbed him.

"Pete, it's nothing! It's a nightmare!"

He blinked, trembling, staring at Simone who'd grabbed him as he struggled from the chair.

"Not once, but twice," he said.

"Pete, it's over. You were dreaming."

"Once, then twice."

His skin was gooseflesh. He fumbled toward the light switch and turned toward her in the sudden glare. "It happened twice," he told her, breathless.

"Yes, I know. The car wreck, then the bomb. What is it?"

"That's not what I mean." His understanding jolted him as if he'd been shocked. Because at last he recalled that nagging detail. "Twice. It happened twice before. The cemetery. Last month someone else came looking for his father's grave. The sergeant couldn't find it. And last year. The sergeant said it happened then as well."

Houston watched Simone's eyes widen.

"Oh, my God," she said. *"There are other missing graves?"*

20

He yanked the gearshift into second. The Renault whined up the hill, then swooped across the summit. He switched into third. "There it is."

She gasped.

"You've never seen it?"

"Didn't want to be reminded. Lord, how many mother's sons?"

"Ten thousand."

"*Oh*," she said. "*The waste.*"

He slowed down at the iron gate, then raced across the parking lot. His brakes squealed as he skidded to a stop before the AMERICAN BATTLE MONUMENT sign.

They rushed toward the wide low building. Houston pushed through, held the door for her, then turned. Past the dioramas in the middle of the room, he saw the lean, tall clerk behind the counter.

The clerk was like a robot, triggered by the clatter of approaching footsteps. He stood straighter. "Yes, sir? Mr. . . . Houston? How are you today?"

"The superintendent."

"Sir, he's busy in his office."

"Get him."

"If you've found more information, you should talk to me."

"I told you I want Andrews."

Now the clerk appeared offended. Shrugging, he turned toward the superintendent's door.

He didn't have to knock. It opened.

Shoulders braced, Andrews stepped out, rolling down his sleeves. His muscles swelled his crisp, clean shirt. "I'm sorry, Mr. Houston." He shook hands. "I've learned nothing."

"But I have," Houston said.

Andrews studied him. He glanced puzzled toward Simone.

"My wife . . ." Houston swallowed. "She's dead. This woman's helping me."

Andrews stiffened. "Dead? But that's . . ."

"I don't want to talk about it." Houston's voice was angry, cracking. "It's too painful. Somehow, without wanting to, I've stumbled into something. Look, I've got to ask a question."

"Anything," Andrews told him.

"When my wife and I were here, you told us mistakes can sometimes happen."

"Yes, that's true. The military isn't perfect."

"Then you gave me two examples."

"I don't—"

"Last year someone else came looking for his father's grave but couldn't find it."

"True."

"The same thing happened last month, you said. I need their names."

"But why?" The superintendent's forehead furrowed deeply. He leaned forward. "You're suggesting—"

"Please. I need the names."

"—that there's a link, that if we find one grave we'll find the others."

"I don't know. I'm only guessing. But I can't help feeling something's wrong. Coincidence? Well, maybe. But I—"

"Just a moment."

Houston watched the superintendent disappear into his office. For a brutal instant he was so reminded of the first time he had been here, Jan beside him, that he hoped insanely if he turned his head he'd see her.

Instead Simone was facing him. His grief swelled, aching.

"Jeffrey Hutchinson." Andrews returned with a piece of paper in his hand. "I couldn't find the other name. Last month he left his number and address in case I found out where the grave is."

Houston took out his wallet. "I can pay for you to make the call, or I can try to find a public phone."

"What? I don't—"

"If he was here last month, then he's had time to get back home. I have to talk to him."

"But why? He told me everything he knows."

"I think there's something he forgot."

Andrews frowned at him. "You're that convinced that something's wrong, that all of this has some connection?"

"There's just one way to find out."

Andrews thought a moment. "Transatlantic. It's still night back in the States."

"Then probably he's sleeping. There's a good chance he'll be home."

Andrews stared at him. "I'll tell you what. I'll make a deal with you. If this turns out to be a huge mistake, you pay the Department of Defense for the phone call. If you're right, then put your money in your pocket."

"I don't care about the money. All I want to do is talk to him."

Andrews nodded. "In my office."

Houston was again reminded of the first time he had been here. He had followed Janice into the superintendent's office. This time he followed Simone, and in the interval between these visits, everything had changed. He felt his anger, felt his grief again.

The fluorescent lights still hummed in the narrow office. Andrews picked up the wall phone; he pointed toward the hard steel chairs. "This takes some time."

But Houston stopped him. "Wait."

Andrews' hand was just about to punch a number. "Why?"

"Before you start . . . Here, let me have this sheet of paper.'' Houston took a pencil from the desk and wrote on the paper. Then he folded it and set it on the desk.

"What was *that* about?" the superintendent said.

"I have to prove this to you."

Andrews didn't understand. His eyes were focused hard on Houston. Doubt burned far behind them. Then he punched a number on the phone. "This had better make some sense," he said. He spoke into the phone.

Houston marveled at his flawless French. "If the lines aren't all tied up," Andrews said in English, explaining to Houston. He tapped his fingers on the wall. He switched to French again. "*Oui? . . . Ah, merci.*" To Houston: "We're in luck."

Houston waited.

"Yes? Mr. Hutchinson?" Andrews said. "I know it's somewhat early to be calling, but. . . . Superintendent Andrews, sir. I'm at the military cemetery north of St. Laurent in France. . . . That's right. . . . No, sir , I don't have any news. . . . I'm well aware, sir. I apologize for waking you. . . . Please, just a moment. There's a man who'd like to speak with you."

Despite the distance, Houston heard the growling from the receiver. With a wince, Andrews offered it to Houston. "Glad it's you who has to talk to him."

Pete held the phone. The voice had stopped. He heard the crackling of the transatlantic line. He heard a murky overlap of voices from a conversation on a different line. He spoke distinctly.

"Mr. Hutchinson, my name is Peter Houston. You don't know me, so don't try to think of where we've met."

"Christ, do you realize what time it is?" The voice was husky.

"Yes. Near five, I think, where you are."

"Quarter to! You woke my wife and kids! I don't mind if you've got news! The sergeant said there wasn't any! What the hell? Do you guys get a kick from phoning people overseas and waking them? For God's sake, what's this all—''

"I'm sorry we caused you any trouble. But I have to ask a question, Mr. Hutchinson. The answer might mean nothing. But it might locate your father's grave. I had to get in touch with you at once."

"And who the hell are you? You're with the army?"

"No. I can't explain right now. Please, let me ask the question."

"Anything to get some sleep! I work two jobs you know! I—"

"Mr. Hutchinson, did your mother ever get a letter from a Frenchman? Back in nineteen forty-four. The Frenchman would have said that he was grateful to the men who died to liberate his homeland. In exchange, he would have promised to maintain your father's grave."

"That's your question? Who remembers that far back?"

Just me, Pete thought. I guess you really have to want a father. "Then you don't remember?"

"No, of course not! I was just a baby!"

Houston's throat-tight fierce excitement started weakening.

"Now, Christ, you woke my mother!" Hutchinson continued. "Here she comes! You've got the whole damned house up!"

"Mr. Hutchinson, please ask her." Houston's heart beat fast again.

"Ask what?"

"About the Frenchman."

"Oh, for . . . Hang on! Just a minute!"

Houston heard the muffled rattle of the phone as it was set on something hard. He heard a young child crying and the garble of a far-off conversation.

Hutchinson spoke unexpectedly. "She got a letter. Does that satisfy you?"

"No, I need to know the Frenchman's name."

"Oh, for the love of—"

"Please. She's there. It only takes a second. Ask her."

Once again the muffled conversation.

Then the young child wasn't weeping any more. The garbled conversation stopped. All Houston heard was that dim static from the transatlantic line.

"I think he walked away and left me," Houston said to Andrews and Simone. "He's getting even, running up the charges."

Houston glanced down at his watch. A minute passed. "He's playing games. I'll hang up and try again."

But as he reached to hang the phone up, Hutchinson came back.

"Pierre de St. Laurent. She kept the letters. Does that satisfy you?"

"Mr. Hutchinson, you can't imagine. Thank you." Houston almost laughed with joy. "I'm going to put Superintendent Andrews back on. Tell him what you told me."

"This is crazy."

"Just a minute longer." Houston's hand shook with excitement; he gestured toward Andrews. "Take the phone."

Simone leaned forward, anxious.

"Can you guess" he asked her.

But Andrews was already speaking. "Mr. Hutchinson? Yes, let me have that name please." Andrews frowned as though the name he heard was gibberish. "Yes, thank you," he said and glanced at Houston angrily. "I'm not sure if it's important. If it helps, though, you can bet I'll soon get back to you."

Andrews hung up, staring at Houston. "Let's pretend that I'm not quick today," he said, "that I've been stupid since I crawled from bed. The way you got excited, evidently you discovered something. If you did, I missed it. That name is of absolutely no significance to me."

"What was it?"

"St. Laurent. Pierre de St. Laurent."

"All right." Houston's voice was tight, triumphant. "Open up that sheet of paper."

"I was wondering—" Andrews stopped what he was saying and picked up the paper.

Houston heard Simone breathe out. Then he turned to watch

Andrews' stunned, bewildered face peer up from what was on the page: PIERRE DE ST LAURENT.

"But how did—how could you have known?"

"I hope you've got time," Peter said.

"For what?"

"The damnedest story you ever heard."

21

It took an hour. As the clerk brought coffee refills and the ashtray filled up with stubbed cigarettes; as Houston's voice grew weary and Simone supplied additional details, Houston watched the superintendent's eyes and took his cues from them. The eyes at first were disbelieving. Shortly they were curious. The intrigue they displayed changed quickly to astonishment, then shock, and finally a startled understanding of the implications.

"If you're right . . ." He looked as if his ordered world could not bear this insanity. "It can't be true. It isn't possible. Christ, how could such a thing have happened?"

"How and what?" Pete said. "We've got to check your records."

"What you're looking for won't be in them. It can't be. Not if this is true."

"You've got a teletype?"

Andrews nodded. "With the radio in the communications room."

"Well, what we're looking for must be in *someone's* records."

Houston's hands were on the desk. He leaned toward Andrews, who was blank-faced for a moment. Andrews pursed his lips, determined. He pushed back his chair and got up quickly. "Let's get to it."

They went from the office and walked along the counter, nearing *No Admittance,* both in French and English, on a door down at the far end of the massive room.

Andrews pushed through, let them enter. They were in a pure white hall with fluorescent lights in the ceiling. One door: washroom. Next door: maintenance equipment. Third door: communications. They entered.

Houston saw a radio, a teletype, and several bulky instruments he didn't recognize. A clerk sat at the radio.

"I'm almost finished."

"Why so much equipment at a cemetery?" Houston asked.

"All this stuff gets sent to us so we're prepared for World War Three. It makes no sense."

"For once you'll get to use it."

Despite himself, Andrews grinned. "I hope I still remember how." But Houston sensed the fear with which Andrews sat down to experiment.

Andrews tapped some letters, and the teletype responded, printing what appeared to be a code. "This teletype is linked with our main European office." Andrews explained. "The other operator just acknowledged he's receiving me."

Andrews tapped more letters. "I'm requesting clearance to the States."

The teletype printed, YOUR REQUEST ACKNOWLEDGED. PURPOSE. Pause. Then a question mark.

"I'd better make it good."

As Houston wondered nervously, Andrews tapped more letters: CEMETERY RECORDS INCOMPLETE. REQUIRE INFORMATION TO LOCATE GRAVE OF MISSING SOLDIER.

"That'll make them scratch their heads. If they don't understand it, then they'll pass the buck to someone else."

A pause. The teletype clattered: REQUEST AFFIRMED. STATE DESTINATION.

Andrews rubbed his chin. "A damn good question."

"Start with World War Two assignment records. Who was in what unit," Houston said.

Andrews nodded, sitting straighter, tapping on the keyboard. The machine responded.

"We're through," Andrews said. "We're talking to the States."

Houston's breathing quickened.

"They'll reroute us back and forth across the country. Different offices. In time, we'll find those records."

It took half an hour. Houston felt a shock when the search concluded at an Army installation near the town where he taught in Indiana. "All my years there, and I had to come to France to learn the purpose of that base."

Andrews braced himself. "Here goes. Begin with basics."

Houston's throat felt bitter, swollen, as he saw the name Andrews started typing: STEPHEN SAMUEL HOUSTON. STATUS. WORLD WAR TWO. Andrews finished typing.

The answer came: SEARCHING RECORDS.

They waited. Fifteen minutes. Twenty-five. Houston's throat felt raw from cigarettes. "What's taking them so long?" he said.

"Big war," Andrews told him, shrugging.

The clatter of the teletype began: REPLY TO STATUS QUERY. STEPHEN SAMUEL HOUSTON. Pause. THIRD ARMY.

"Patton," Houston said and didn't understand his growing excitement.

SECOND INFANTRY DIVISION. THIRTEENTH REGIMENT. SECOND BATTALION. D COMPANY. Pause. FIFTH PLATOON.

"Strike one. Let's try for two," Andrews said and resumed typing: MUCH OBLIGED. HAVE SECOND QUERY. STATUS. WORLD WAR TWO.

Andrews glanced down at the sheet of paper on which Hutchinson had left his father's name. He typed, PAUL ANDREW HUTCHINSON.

They waited. This time, the wait was shorter. THIRD ARMY. SECOND INFANTRY DIVISION. THIRTEENTH REGIMENT. SECOND BATTALION. D COMPANY. Pause. FIFTH PLATOON.

The skin on Houston's neck went cold. "They're the same."

"You figured they wouldn't be?" Andrews said.

"I figured I was crazy! I hoped I was wrong! Two missing graves! Pierre de St. Laurent is linked to both of them! And now we find out that my father and this Hutchinson were both in the same company! Hell, in the same platoon!"

"Too much coincidence. You're right," Andrews said. "I don't like it. What do we do now, though? Should I sign off? Have you got some other questions?"

"Mr. Andrews?" Simone said. Startled, they turned to her. "Please ask if they'll wait," she said.

They studied her. Her smooth, curved face, her strong, high cheekbones seemed more elegant than ever. Houston watched her full lips purse in thought.

"What is it?" Andrews asked.

"I don't understand the military," she replied. "Explain it to me. All those categories. That's the breakdown?"

"That's right. Army, then division, regiment, battalion, company, and finally platoon."

"How large is a platoon?"

Andrews shrugged. "It varies. About fifty men."

"In wartime?"

"It depends on the number of casualties. But even with replacements, we can bet they weren't at total strength. Let's be conservative and guess at thirty. Could be less, but let's say thirty. There's a further subdivision into squads. An even split. Let's say there were fifteen men in each."

"Then I suggest we do two things. First, we determine which squad Peter's father and this Hutchinson were in." The room was absolutely silent.

"And?"

"We get in touch with the relatives of the other men in the squad and learn how many of those soldiers died at St. Laurent."

"But don't have graves," Pete said. And suddenly was frightened.

22

They worked all day. Since the communications room had no windows, they failed to realize that dusk had come. Houston had the sense that he was held in stasis, that day and night were parts of a forgotten, lost, irrelevant dimension.

Finally his tension was too much. He stepped outside.

The dusk was lovely. Standing by Simone's Renault, he heard her walk up close beside him. He kept staring at the hills, the fields, the golden grain, the orchards studding the horizon.

He turned to face her.

"You know, I tell myself that if I wish with all my might, I'll blink and see Andrews showing me my father's grave. I'll thank Andrews, and I'll pay respects to my dead father. Then my life will go on as it should have. Back home. Back to teaching, writing. Living to a ripe old age with Janice. It's as if I only need to concentrate, to think of how things could have been."

He breathed with frustration and nostalgia. Simone did not reply. She only looked at him as if until this moment she had never truly seen him. Then she slowly moved her lips in what was possibly a mournful smile. She shrugged with little movement, and at last she took his hand, squeezing it gently. They returned to the building.

"It's all here," Andrews said when they came back inside the claustrophobic room. He swung to face them, pointing toward the sheets of print across the table. But his voice contained no hint of victory.

Houston braced himself. The weary lines on the superintendent's face communicated everything he soon would know. "Show me," he said.

Andrews pointed. "On this sheet are the names of all the men in that platoon. I've drawn a line across it. Below are the members of the second squad. It turns out my guess was on the nose. Fifteen men."

"My father. And there's Hutchinson." Although the other names had no significance to Houston, he read down the list. "All right, go on," he said.

"Now this bottom list, that's where I had some trouble. Tracking down the relatives, for one thing. So many transatlantic calls would have been questioned by my superiors. I've got a buddy in the States. He owes me several favors, so I phoned him, and he did the job. I had to promise I'd pay his phone bill. I don't care about the cost. The main thing is he did it."

Houston didn't rush him. They were each adjusting in their different ways to what they'd learned. For now, it was the superintendent's story. Let him tell it his way.

"The fifteen men in the second squad," Andrews said. "You understand, we're just talking now about the men who were alive before the battle here."

"I follow. What about them?"

"Hell, they died."

"What? Every one of them?" Simone said.

"To a man. The whole damn squad."

"Jesus Christ," Pete said.

"I'm no expert in statistics, but I can't believe the fighting was so bad here that not one of them survived. Oh, sure, I read the pamphlets we hand out. This battle wasn't any picnic, but it wasn't D-Day either. Just to check, though, I went through the regiment's report about the battle. All that stuff is here so we can answer questions from the visitors. The casualties averaged thirty percent. Some units had it rough, while others got away with just a scratch. Okay, an average. Thirty percent. So was this squad so damned unlucky that not only four or five of them went down but *all* of them? A hundred percent mortality rate?"

Houston had trouble breathing. "Finish it."

"I checked our burial records, and I found exactly what I should have if the situation had been normal. Of those fifteen men, I learned that six of them are out there in the cemetery."

"And the others?"

"You tell me. Your guess would be as good as mine. I phoned the cemetery fifty miles north of here. No dice. The bodies simply disappeared. Now here's the clincher. I had someone check the disposition on each name here. Those six soldiers buried out there are described as killed in action. The remaining nine are *missing* in action. It was never proven that they died."

"Deserters? You think they ran off?" Simone asked.

"What else *can* I think?"

"But wouldn't there have been investigations?"

"You can bet there were," Andrews said. "But here in wartime France, so much to do, too little time to do it, the investigators would have quickly been distracted. Lord, just think about that summer. D-Day was in June, and by September most of France was liberated. There were mop-up operations, armies moving everywhere. In all of the confusion, anything could happen. If they deserted, where would they have gone? And why? They would have had a better chance if they'd stayed with their unit. That's what the investigators would have thought, and they'd have dropped the issue. You can bet, though, if your father showed up on your doorstep, he'd have been arrested very shortly. I'll lay odds that, for a while at least, your mother and yourself were under military watch."

In Houston's mind, he saw the house where he had lived. He saw his mother and himself come out the door and down the porch, and as that tiny version of himself walked down the street beside his mother, Houston stepped out from another house and followed. He had never understood the youthful world in which he lived. Its innocence was tainted.

"That still leaves us with a question," Houston said. "If they deserted, where in God's name did they go? And why?" He thought his mind would crack. "We really haven't proven anything."

"You're wrong," Andrews said. "The families of those missing men each received a letter."

"From the War Department?"

Andrews grimaced. "From Pierre de St. Laurent."

23

They heard the church bell in the darkness. They had not yet reached St. Laurent, but the periodic far-off tolling echoed through the night. The stars were brilliant. Houston's headache persisted. He had rolled the driver's window down. The cool air flowed over him; the bell notes resonated even at this distance.

"Services this late?" he said and glanced down at the luminous dial on his watch. "A midnight mass?"

"It's not a special feast day," Simone said.

Houston counted silently from one to four. On five, he heard the low vibration tolling once more. Then he counted again and this time murmured, "Five," precisely as the bell struck.

She had heard him. "What's the matter?"

"The bell hits every five seconds. Consistent, regular. Maybe it's not from the church. Is there a village clock with a bell that sounds the time?"

"No. Anyway, the people in the village don't stay up late. They'd be wakened by the bell. They wouldn't want it."

"Then there's got to be a reason, something so important that it justifies the nuisance."

"Some emergency?"

"But what would—"

"A fire?"

Houston shoved his foot on the accelerator. The Renault lunged forward. Wrist still swollen, Simone was not yet capable of driving. Houston's shoulder had been stiff all day, and his ribs ached, but he ignored his pain as he steered around a corkscrew curve, his headlights piercing the darkness. He drove so fast that the black of night was like a wall he hurtled toward. He searched the star-specked sky. He saw no red, no glow above the black horizon.

"We should see it," Houston said. "We're almost there."

"If it's not a fire, what else could it be?"

"We'll know damn soon."

The bell kept tolling, louder now as the Renault surged past the first signs of the village—cottages, then shops. Lights were on in many houses.

"One thing's in our favor," Houston said. "If that bell woke all these people, then it had to wake the priest. I don't intend to go to him tomorrow. I want to see him *now*. He can't refuse us this time. We've got too much evidence. He has to understand that this is more important than his silence."

"You're not a Catholic," Simone said. "You still don't understand."

"I understand that something crazy happened thirty-seven years ago. I understand my wife is dead. That priest is going to tell me what Pierre de St. Laurent confessed. I don't know how, but I'll make him tell me. He's got to!"

"His vow of secrecy is too important. If he told, the villagers would never trust him in confession."

"There has to be a way! The answer's close, and he's the only man who knows it!" He aimed the car across the old stone bridge, smelling the night mist from the river, seeing it shimmer among the trees in the park.

Straight ahead he saw the hotel, its every window lit as if a celebration were in progress.

She was stunned. "I've never seen it like this. What on earth has happened?"

He didn't bother parking at the side, but stopped abruptly at the hotel's entrance and rushed from the car, ignoring how his ribs and shoulder tortured him.

Simone preceded him. She hurried up the ancient steps. The wide oak doors were open. Guests peered toward the bell that sounded from the darkness.

Monsard stood among the guests, still dressed in evening clothes, his wrinkled face drawn tight. Simone embraced him.

Houston paused, discreetly silent near them. He strained to decipher what Monsard told her.

The impact of her father's words made her stiffen. She turned to Houston. "Not a celebration."

In the hotel's spotlights, Houston saw how white her face became.

"A wake," she said. "A vigil. All the villagers are paying their respects."

"To whom?" Pete's curiosity became unbearable.

"Père Devereaux. *Il mourut*," Monsard continued.

"What? Did he say Devereaux? The priest?"

"The priest is *dead*," Simone wailed.

Houston shook his head in absolute incomprehension. "No. No, that can't be." He blinked down at the smooth, worn steps. "We were so close," he moaned.

"*Vieux*," he heard Monsard explaining, pity in his voice. The next few sentences were garbled. Then, "*Malade*," he heard.

Simone pivoted. "The priest was old. The priest was sick," she said, her eyes stunned. "No man as more loved, respected. He'll be sorely missed."

"But how?"

"A young priest found him in the sanctuary. He'd fallen on the floor. The authorities suspect a heart attack. You saw how weak he was, how hard it was for him to breathe."

"Another day. We only needed one more day." Pete rubbed a hand across his eyes. "Forget I said that. Sure, another day. I bet he wanted many other days."

"He was so tired. In a way, it was a blessing."

"Not for him, and not for us." Pete's energy had now completely drained from him. The hotel's steps seemed to tremble. "So damn close."

He started toward the lights beyond the hotel's entrance, so accustomed to the measured cadence of the tolling that unconsciously his mind continued counting one through five. But this time, on the beat of five, no vibration resonated through the night. The echo of the final bell note dimmed, diminished, died. Except for muffled voices from the guests, from villagers who'd gathered in the misty park, the night was silent.

"God have mercy on him," Houston said. He swallowed dryly and entered the hotel.

Simone followed. "I have to speak with you."

He didn't understand. He followed her beyond the counter and the elevator toward the hallway that led toward her father's rooms in back.

She stopped so shortly that he almost bumped against her. They were at a closed door near Monsard's. "You don't sense it? You don't understand?" she said.

"Sense what?"

"The priest is dead, and all you feel is disappointment? Why aren't you suspicious? I am. Didn't we agree there was far too much coincidence? The priest was our last hope, and just as we determine to confront him, we discover we're too late. He dies. I can't believe our timing. I won't accept bad luck."

"But he was sick."

"Which made it easy."

Houston felt an eerie chill.

"The sanctuary. By himself. A pillow on his face. A sudden fright. A little pressure on his chest. Too many ways. No evidence. Pete, who would ever know?"

"The inquest—"

"This isn't a city. Things are done the old way here. No autopsy. A simple medical report. A decent burial."

"But we can't prove—"

"I feel it. I can sense it. After everything that's happened. I don't have another choice. I have to act as if that priest was murdered. Don't you see it's obvious? Whoever's after us is coming back to clean up the details.''

"It never ends. Simone, you can't stay here alone.''

"And you can't either. But my father is a greater man to fear than any enemy. He'd never let us share a room. His moral sense would be offended. He won't tolerate dishonor.''

"We can talk to him, explain to him.''

She shook her head emphatically.

"Then he can chaperon,'' Pete said.

"And put him in our danger?''

Houston's stomach seemed to drop. He tried to think. From down the hallway he heard footsteps in the lobby as the guests came back inside. "We can't speak here,'' he said.

"In my room. We can leave the door ajar to satisfy my father.'' She reached quickly for the doorknob and went in. He followed, smelling perfume and the freshness of her hair. He felt again as if he was with Janice, not Simone, and seemed to topple through a hole in time and land ten days ago, upstairs, when having listened to Monsard explain about Pierre de St. Laurent they'd gone back to their room . . . and found the steely whisker-stubbled stranger waiting for them.

It was happening again. No, Houston told himself. No, I'm not seeing this. I've lost my mind.

Because the same man was now waiting for them. With the same square jaw, the same thin nose and short dark hair combed straight from right to left. The same black clothes—crew sweater, wool pants, crepe-soled shoes. He lay on the bed exactly as he had before.

But with the difference that his chest was blood from neck to belt. The sheeny velvet spread was pooled with scarlet. Blood streaked down the ground-floor windowsill where he had crawled in, falling, leaving streaks of gore across the rug.

Simone began to scream.

Part 3

24

Her scream was like a sharp steel spike that shattered Hous-
ton's skull. He recoiled from the force. She'd put her hands up
to her face, her shriek escaping through her fingers. From behind her, Houston grabbed her shoulders, spinning her to face
him. "No," he said.

She kept on screaming.

"No," he said again. He shook her. He was conscious of too
much. The shouts, the running footsteps in the hall. The rigid
fine-boned flesh beneath the sweatered shoulders he was gripping. And the absolutely panicked look on her face as she took
down her hands, her features wild, contorted.

Now he felt the guests surge in. He heard their gasps. But he
concentrated on Simone. He pulled her toward him, hugged
her, felt her tremble against his chest. He glanced once more
beyond her toward the horror on the bed, and shock gave way to
anger. He would find the man who'd done this. He would make
him scream the way that *she* had screamed.

Monsard was near him. "Someone get a doctor!" Houston
shouted. But they didn't understand him.

"*Un médecin!*" Monsard blurted.

Several guests ran out. Houston moved Simone, giving her to
Monsard. He faced the room, the bloody figure on the bed, and
feeling nauseated, mouth sour, he moved forward.

He felt stunned. The man was breathing—not much, chest in
shallow motion. Houston watched the eyelids flicker. He'd assumed the man was dead, but now he heard the wheezing gasps,
the air that whistled weakly past drawn lips, a mucous death rattle.

Houston approached cautiously, not wanting to touch the blood that pooled across the velvet spread. He leaned down toward the injured man. The sweater had been sliced straight up the middle; Houston saw the bloody shirt. He saw the obscene mangled flesh and had to face the wall. His vision swirled. He gripped the headboard to prevent himself from falling. "A doctor's coming," he said to the man.

There was no response.

"Hang on. We'll get some help for you."

The nod was almost imperceptible.

"You can hear me?"

Now the eyelids trembled in response.

"Who did this to you?"

Houston strained to listen, but the words were slurred. "Who?" Houston said again.

"Find Charon."

Houston paled. The man had bled so much he was babbling. "I don't know what you mean. A man named Charon did this?"

"Verlaine. Find Verlaine."

It made no sense. Pete shook his head, dismayed. Switching from classic myth, the man now raved about a nineteenth-century poet. "You know someone called Verlaine?"

"No, you don't . . ." Blood foamed from his lips. His eyes were frantic.

"Where's the doctor?" Houston shouted to the crowd inside the door. They stared at him, uncomprehending. Then he saw Monsard push through them, leaving with Simone.

Pete swung to face the dying man. "You've got to help me. What about—"

"*Le blanc*," the man blurted.

Houston didn't understand why he had switched to French. "The white?"

The man writhed in delirium. "Not white. *Le blanc*. Had to kill me."

"Stab you? Why?"

"I killed the priest. I smothered him."

"But—"

"Knew too much. He might have told."

The man coughed hard. His wound gaped wider. Houston gagged.

"Betrayed me."

Houston strained to hear the liquid sounds.

"I'd seen you, talked with you. I was the link."

"With who?"

"With all of them. Verlaine and Charon."

Madness.

"They didn't trust me. Charon didn't trust me. Listen to me!" The demand was so intense that Houston shuddered from the unexpected force. The man had pushed his elbows against the bed to raise himself. His back was arched. "Listen to me!"

Houston was appalled. The man's face drained, became the color of cement. "*Le blanc.* Verlaine, Find Charon."

"Save your strength."

"No time." The voice was weak again. The breath was sibilant, like wind. "He used me one last time. But he feared that you would find me."

Houston heard voices from the hall. "*Vous en allez! Vous en allez!*"

A dark-haired man entered carrying a doctor's bag. He was followed by the town policeman.

Houston's heart beat faster. He turned quickly to the injured man. "I told you," he said. "Hang on. The doctor's here."

But Houston only needed one quick look. The face had changed again, assuming an awful stillness. "No, wait. You haven't told me," Houston pleaded. "There's too much to know."

The room was hushed.

Pete shook the man. "The doctor's here. Wake up." He leaned so close that blood soaked through his clothes. "Don't die!"

He was pushing at the ribcage when a hand settled on his own. He saw bristled hairs, and turned, beseeching, but the doctor's eyes contained no hope.

Pete's arms went slack. He nodded slowly. The doctor felt the dead man's wrist. He pulled an unresisting eyelid. The doctor's sigh said everything.

Pete groaned in answer, blinking in a daze toward where the guests who crowded in the room appeared to waver, blend together. "You heard him," he blurted to the crowd. "You heard him tell me. Charon. Something white. Verlaine. Do they mean *anything* to you?"

But ill at ease, they simply stared at him. They seemed to back away.

25

They told him later how he'd fallen on the rug, and Houston, feeling gently at the friction burn across his forehead, didn't doubt them. All the punishment his body had received had finally caught up to him. He slept for eighteen hours. He was groggy and uncoordinated when he woke, again in Monsard's bedroom and again with Simone beside him, this time with Monsard there as well.

The basic human needs came first. He stumbled toward the bathroom. His dark stubble made his face seem pale. He shut his mind off, taking simple pleasure in the sharp, clean feeling of the razor on his skin. He loved the hot shower and the luxury of fresh socks and new underwear, of soft jeans and a sweater.

He came out. The bed was made. The room was empty. Wobbly, Houston peered out through the open bedroom door to where the fireplace crackled warmly in the sitting room. The mantel clock said quarter after eight.

At night. He still could not believe that he had slept so long, that he had lost a day. Simone stood smiling. She had pulled her hair back in a ponytail. She wore a trim blue belted dress that made her eyes seem darker.

"Feeling better?" she asked.

"Rested. Groggy. What about you? When I last saw you . . ."

"I'm all right now. I apologize," she said.

"For what? For screaming? I almost screamed myself."

"The doctor gave me pills. I'm angry now, not shocked. There are some things you need to know."

"I've got some news for you as well."

Monsard sat in a deep chair by the fireplace. He leaned forward and listened, evidently guessing from their tone what they were discussing.

Houston watched Simone subdue her feelings and order her thoughts. "That man last night," she said. "His blood was on the windowsill and in the flower bed outside. The trail came through the grounds in back. It started in a stand of pine near town. There was a car. And tire tracks from someone else's car."

Pete sat down, gripping the sides of his chair. "That's what I've got to tell you. The man had strength to speak before he died. He told me he'd killed the priest."

Her face paled. "I was right."

"He wasn't clear. He mentioned Charon and then something white."

"That makes no sense," she said.

"I know it. He kept babbling. From as much as I can figure, once he'd killed the priest, he met the man who'd hired him."

"And he was stabbed."

"Exactly. He didn't say what happened next. There must have been a struggle. He escaped. He knew the layout of this place. He crawled inside your room to hide."

"If he was dying, wouldn't he have tried to find a doctor?"

"A doctor would have called the cops. Besides, he must have hoped he'd live. He didn't want to go to jail. But this way, we might help him."

"And get even for him."

Houston nodded. "But it didn't end the way he planned. Look, I don't know. He might have been delirious. He might have crawled inside your room and not been conscious of it. But he talked. He said that Charon used him one last time, then killed him to prevent my finding him and talking to him."

"What I said last night—somebody's cleaning house, removing all the details."

"And succeeding. Right now, you and I are . . ." Houston didn't want to finish.

"His last details."

Houston bit his lip.

Monsard asked a question. She explained to him. The old man glanced disturbed from her to Houston.

"Andrews is probably in danger too," Houston said.

"He called," she said.

He straightened. "When?"

"This afternoon. He did more checking. That platoon's lieutenant wasn't with the men who disappeared."

"Then the lieutenant's still alive?"

"The sergeant phoned him. The lieutenant still remembers those nine missing men. He always wondered what had happened to them. You know there were two battles. One was here, the other fifty miles north of here."

He nodded.

"The *second* battle. That was when they disappeared," she said.

"Then why pretend that they were killed and buried here in St. Laurent?"

"To draw attention from the truth, from where it happened."

"What the hell is 'it,' though?"

She just peered at him. Monsard began to ask more questions. Houston didn't pay attention. "Charon," he said. "Something white. Verlaine."

She stopped abruptly in her explanation to her father. "What?"

"It's something I forgot. Last night before he died, the man said, 'Find Verlaine,' It's useless. Who's Verlaine? And how in God's name do we find him?''

"Not a him. An *it*.'' The startled look on her face frightened him.

"You know him?''

"You don't remember? Back in Roncevaux. Bellay. When we were in his office. Those policemen in the background—they were making phone calls.''

Houston struggled to remember. "He was speaking with them.''

"And they said that block of office buildings—''

"—had a rental agent.''

"And the rental agent—''

"—said that Verlaine Enterprises owns that building.'' Houston shuddered.

"Not a him. An it. That man last night meant Verlaine Enterprises.''

Houston stood abruptly. "Get your coat. We're leaving.''

"Where?''

"To Roncevaux.''

Monsard said firmly, "*Non.*''

The room was hushed as Houston spun, surprised.

Gesturing for emphasis, the old man spoke insistently.

"What's wrong?'' Houston asked.

"My father senses your intention. He insists you stay. You need to eat, to rest, he says.''

"There's no time.''

"He says one night won't make any difference. I think he's right. We'd get there after midnight. What could we accomplish? Bellay won't be in his office.''

"We could wake him.''

"With assumptions. A sleepy man would not be sympathetic.''

Houston gripped the chair. His urgency compelled him, but his common sense dissuaded him.

"My father's afraid for us. He thinks we ought to hide.''

"And live in fear they'll find us? This way, even though we're still afraid, at least we're doing something."

"You can go back to the States."

"Is that what *you* want?"

"I'm explaining what my father said. He thinks if you went home they might feel safe and not come after us."

"But you'd be here. You'd be in danger."

"No, my father thinks I'm safe without you."

Houston stared at her in anguish. He felt torn, confused. His grief conflicted with the guilt he'd feel if Simone were injured. "I can't go home. I've got a debt to pay. My wife."

As if he understood, the old man sighed. Again he spoke. Simone translated. "Then he asks for you to compromise."

"How?"

"He offers hospitality for one last night. And then he asks you to respect his wishes as a father. To be on your way, to let me be, to seek your own death but not mine."

"Simone, you know I don't want you killed."

"It's what he said."

"But what do *you* say? Tell me what you want. I'll do it. I'll go now if it's a help to you."

"That man last night. My father says—"

A fist knocked on the door. The sound shook through the room. She stopped, alarmed.

"No, tell me," Houston said.

Her father interrupted him. "*Entrez!*"

The door came open. A young waiter, spotless, wheeled in a cart. Sweet steam escaped beneath the silver lids on the trays. The fresh French bread was in a basket covered by a napkin. Red wine glinted in a bottle.

"I'm not hungry," Houston said. He began to cry.

26

He stared out from this top-floor room. Monsard had chosen it, he was convinced, to keep Simone as far away from him as possible. Monsard had eaten dinner with them, making clear his role as wary father. There had been no chance for private conversation. Fifteen seconds after bringing Houston to this room, the old man and Simone had left, and Houston hadn't seen her after that.

Three hours had elapsed since then. It now was one o'clock, and Houston stood beside his window frowning toward the park below him, toward the mist that drifted through the trees. The hotel's spotlights were shut off. He kept the room dark lest he make himself a target at the window. But he wasn't frowning from the danger he was in. He frowned because he didn't understand Simone's change of mind, the way she had abandoned him. He hadn't realized how much he'd grown dependent on her.

Now that dependency was denied him; he was alone again. He faced the uncertain future by himself. The possibility of death. He leaned against the window frame and told himself that she was right. It made no sense for her to risk her life.

Am I so selfish that I want Simone to share my risk so I won't feel alone? he thought. Let her try to save her life. She's earned her safety.

He felt hollow. Maybe what the old man said was true. I ought to leave, he told himself. I ought to go back home and mind my business and thank God I wasn't killed.

Except this *was* his business, and no matter how he looked at

103

it, he only had one choice. To find the man who'd killed his wife. Tomorrow he would start again. Alone.

He jerked upright and realized he'd dozed against the window frame. The luminous dial on his watch showed two o'clock. Outside, the night was peaceful, still, appropriate to this idyllic village. Houston snorted at the irony. He stayed beside the window long enough to see a man come through the misty trees in the park. The man who wore the lilac-scented talcum, Houston realized, dressed formally again, returning late again. The man did not seem drunk this time, and Houston wondered idly where he'd been that he was coming back this late. But despite his eighteen-hour sleep, he still felt wearied by his disappointment, and he let the man slip from his consciousness. He stumbled toward the bed.

The sheets were cool and crisp. He slipped his clothes off and crawled under the covers. His head sank on the pillow, and he snuggled on the welcome mattress, soft yet firm, so different from the chair on which he'd slept two nights ago. The memory disturbed him. It brought back the pain Simone's decision caused, the loneliness she made him feel. He fought to shut her from his mind. He counted backward from one hundred, never reaching seventy-five.

An instinct wakened him, a premonition. He blinked in the darkness. He'd been dreaming of the man with lilac-scented talcum powder, and he realized that what had wakened him had been a noise.

A scraping. Metal scratching metal. Houston didn't move. From where he lay, he scanned the blackness of the room.

The door first. He had locked it. Someone might be picking it. No, he was wrong. The sound was somewhere else. A killer wouldn't risk discovery picking at a hallway lock. Most guests would be asleep, but one of them returning late—the man with lilac talcum—might ask questions.

The man with lilac talcum. Houston's mind began to race. The man had been here every time that trouble happened. Consistently he was in the pattern.

Houston sat up, straining toward the window. But there

wasn't any balcony. No ledge gave access to the window. Where then? Where the hell was that faint scraping sound coming from?

His stomach cramped. His hands began to shake. And then he realized—the door between this room and the adjacent one! Not one door! Two of them! The door on that side could be opened easily. But Houston had locked his own side, and now someone in the other room was picking at the lock. No late-returning guest would interrupt. The killer would have all the secrecy he needed.

The shadow of the door began to move. Houston had no weapon. He was naked, helpless in the dark. He had no chance. He breathed in, preparing to shout.

And stopped himself. A shout wouldn't bring help in time. It would only alarm the killer, forcing him to act quickly. Houston pressed his head down on the pillow. If the killer used a knife, he'd have to come up close, and Houston could grab him.

And do what? The man was surely trained, while Houston wasn't used to fighting. His hands were paralyzed with fear. His arms felt numb.

He squinted, confident that from this distance, in the dark, the killer couldn't see or know that Houston was awake. The door was fully open now, but the adjacent room was dark. Houston saw only a shadow stalking toward him. Crouching. Cautious. Taking care to do this properly. No gunshot to alarm the guests. A knife would do the trick. Or maybe Houston would be smothered like the priest.

The figure crept up to the bed. It studied Houston. Though his lungs burned, aching, Houston kept his stomach rigid, breathing slowly, feigning sleep.

A hand reached toward him.

Now! And Houston lunged. He landed on top of the figure, pushing down, trailing sheets, entangling both of them. They struggled on the floor. He cursed and fought to grab the knife. A knee jabbed sharply at his groin. He moaned and strained to keep from doubling up. He gripped the killer's throat.

"Pete, stop it!" He kept strangling. "No, Pete!" In the dark, the voice was hoarse, grotesque. "No! You're hurting me!"

He froze, grasping. Instantly, he released his hands. "Simone!"

"My throat."

"Oh, Jesus." Houston stumbled to his feet and helped her stand. He groped to turn the bedlight on. She swallowed, massaging her welted throat. She wore a shirt and jeans now. Her left cheek was swollen. She blinked rapidly, in pain.

"My God, I nearly killed you!" Houston said.

She slumped across the bed, rubbing at her neck. The sheets were on the floor.

Houston suddenly felt cold.

And naked. He was standing close before her with no clothes on. Fumbling, he picked up the sheets and wrapped them over him. He draped a long end past his shoulder.

She laughed.

"What?" he said.

"You look so foolish," she said. "So ridiculous."

"You scared me half to death."

"My father took the other key. I couldn't get in through the hallway door."

"You could have knocked, for Christ's sake."

"Suppose somebody saw me? Or my father? No, I found the key that fit the room next door."

He clutched the sheets around him. Once again, she laughed. "The key got stuck in the connecting door."

"You could have knocked on *that* door."

"That's the joke. I didn't want to wake you. Hey, I'm laughing at the both of us, not you alone. This whole thing's ridiculous. Those sheets." She pointed, giggling. "You look so undignified." Tears rolled down her cheeks.

He couldn't stop himself. He glanced down at the rumpled sheets and imagined what he looked like—his embarrassment, his indignation. Laughter grew within him. Relieved, he let it out. He slumped across the bed, laughing until his stomach ached. Tears streamed down his own face.

"Jesus, what a pair," he groaned. "And why was it so urgent, so important that you couldn't wait, that you decided to break in here?"

She stopped laughing. Now her face was childlike, her eyes afraid.

Abruptly Houston understood. "No."

"Pete, I—"

"No," he told her.

She looked shamed. "I'm sorry."

"There's no need."

"I thought . . . Forget it."

"Tell me."

"If I went to bed with you, I thought you'd understand how much I want to be with you. I told you what my father said. That doesn't mean I agree with him. I had to translate for him, had to let him have his say."

"You didn't argue with him."

"Not in front of you. He would have been insulted."

"You're not giving up?"

She firmly shook her head.

"You're going back with me?" He sat up straight. "To Roncevaux?"

"To anywhere. I couldn't let you go. I *need* you. Dammit, I'm in love with you."

"Don't say that."

She looked stunned.

"Don't say it. No."

He closed his eyes. He shook.

27

They left at dawn. She slipped a note beneath her father's door to tell him not to worry, that she'd phone him and explain, but that she couldn't hide forever. She and Houston had no other choice.

But as they drove—Pete used a different route and kept looking at his rearview mirror—they were strangely quiet. As their silence lengthened, as the narrow road curved sharply through the tree-lined hilly countryside, they fidgeted self-consciously, were strained and ill at ease.

"There's something wrong," she said. "What is it?"

Houston shook his head from side to side, avoiding her.

"That isn't fair," she said. "Be honest with me."

Houston clenched the steering wheel. "It's not your problem."

"Anything involving you concerns me. Please, don't shut me out. I don't deserve that."

Houston bit his lip until it hurt. "I'll be fine. I have to think things through."

"Last night?" she asked.

He nodded.

"What I tried to do with you?" she said.

Again he nodded. "My wife . . . Look, let's not talk about it. I don't want to hurt you."

"And you won't. I wasn't lying. I meant it when I said I love you." She held up a hand. "Let me finish. I was rushing things. I knew that. And I knew there'd be complications. But I took the risk. I had to. It was always on my mind. I had to show you."

"I'm not blaming you."

"But let me ask a question. Did you love your wife?"

"Isn't it obvious?"

"That's not a good enough answer. Tell me. Were you in love with her, or was your marriage just a habit?"

Houston's voice was strained. "I loved her."

"Would she have expected you to spend your whole life grieving for her? To be always loyal to the point where you behaved as if you still were married? To avoid another woman?"

"No. She'd probably be angry."

"Then be loyal to her memory. Respect it. Cherish what you had with her. Believe me, I'm not in competition with her. I don't want you to forget her. I want to share you."

Houston sighed. His eyes ached with tears.

"Pete, we could die today, tonight, tomorrow. But at least we'd be together. We'd have shared the moments that were given to us."

"Don't you understand? I *am* attracted to you. I don't want to be. I only want to mourn for Jan."

She stared at him.

"All I want to do is find her killer. I don't have a *right* to be attracted to you."

In response she simply touched his hand.

28

They'd never been to Bellay's office, having met him in the squad room, so when they walked inside that room but didn't see him they went over to the first of seven desks to ask an overweight policeman where Bellay was.

The policeman's response in French was so disturbing that Simone faced Houston in alarm. "He doesn't have an office," she said. "He's not even stationed here."

"That's wrong. He said he was assigned to us because he'd understand my English."

"He's from Paris."

"Yes, he told us that. He said some years ago in Paris he had dealings with the British."

"But it wasn't several years ago," she said. "This cop says Bellay arrived from Paris on the day of the explosion. You remember? We were taken to Emergency. We waited. We were brought here, and we waited some more. Then Bellay showed up. There was an interval of several hours."

Houston's temples throbbed.

"That gave him time to hurry here from Paris. He was *sent* here, Pete. He came because of us, because of the explosion. He knew more than what he told us. He was *testing* us."

The policemen in the room turned to stare at them. Everyone was silent.

Houston glanced at them. Simone raised a hand as if to touch her mouth.

But something stopped her. From the door. "So you came back," a man said, his voice so deep, so sonorous that Houston felt it vibrate.

They whirled toward him in surprise.

Bellay stood in the open doorway, one hand on the doorjamb. He was well dressed as before, a brown suit this time, with a vest, the pants pressed neatly, the cut perfect. He watched them ironically, his eyebrows raised, his head cocked slightly, questioning. His short dark hair was neatly combed.

"Yesterday we meant to call you," Houston said. "I guess you know we didn't stay in town that night."

"Imagine my surprise." He stepped forward, his shoes clicking on the checkered floor. "At first I worried, but I went to the morgue, and when I didn't find you, I decided you were being careful. Anyway, if you were dead, there wasn't much I

110

could do to help you." His eyes gleamed with amusement. "I have questions."

"So do we. You lied to us," Houston said.

"Oh? How's that?"

"You told us you were stationed here. You're not. You came from Paris just to see us."

"Fascinating. And you know this for a fact?"

"We asked this policeman. He told us."

Fascination drained from Bellay's face. His eyes went dark. He scowled at the cop, who, cursing, struggled to type forms in triplicate. Bellay spoke curtly in what seemed to Houston gutter French.

The cop peered up. His face went red. He made a fist and twisted it obscenely.

Bellay gaped. The copy resumed his struggle with the carbon paper. Bellay laughed. He turned to Houston. "No respect."

"No secrets either."

"True, my friend. Except for you. Oh, you kept secrets, didn't you? I asked for information, and you told me tiny lies."

"No more than you did. Cut the shit! What's going on?"

For an instant Bellay's composure lapsed. Abruptly he stood straighter, and his eyes appeared amused again. "We'll trade," he said. "What I know for what you know. If you're ready to cooperate."

"Verlaine."

"That settles it. We talk." Bellay gestured toward the open doorway.

They went out, Simone following. The hall was gray. It needed painting. Two policemen left an office heading toward another. A detective went inside the men's room.

Bellay led them down the hall. He knocked on a frosted-glass door and, when he heard a voice, went in. He said three sentences in French. A man with weary eyes and sagging cheeks came out. He glanced at Houston, lingered on Simone. Reluctantly he left.

"They rushed me here," Bellay told Houston. "But they

didn't make arrangements for an office. Never mind. This place will do." With elegance, he motioned them inside.

Houston smelled the must of boxes, records, forms. A storage room. There was a table in the middle.

Bellay shut the door. The hallway sounds were muffled. "Have a chair please. This could take a while."

Simone obeyed.

But Houston didn't move. "Verlaine," he said. "Get on with it."

"No, that's not how this works. If you intend to swap, first you tell me."

"Okay, I'm leaving." Houston reached for the doorknob.

Bellay didn't try to stop him.

Houston stared down at his hand. He sighed and sat before the table. "Well, no harm in trying."

"No, indeed. But evidently you're more curious than I am." Bellay watched him. Then he seemed to make a choice and, imitating Houston, sighed. "In honesty," he admitted, "I'm so curious that I'd sell my mother's soul. Begin, please. Tell me everything that's happened to you. Leave out nothing. You don't know what might be important."

Houston lit a cigarette. He began, omitting no details, telling everything. "Verlaine," he concluded. "It all points to Verlaine."

"And St. Laurent, although I told the truth—the name is unfamiliar to me." Bellay paused and turned to Simone. "Do you have anything to add?"

"No. Peter's covered it all."

Bellay shifted his attention back to Houston. "Then your father may be still alive, involved in this. Or if he did die, nonetheless he was involved."

"In what? It's your turn. Keep your bargain."

"I'm not sure I can. Oh, I can tell you what I know. But I don't understand, so why should you?"

"For Christ's sake—"

"Listen carefully. I've worked on this too long. I've lost my objectivity. From your perspective, maybe you can see the pattern.''

Houston waited.

Bellay tapped his fingers on the table and began.

29

"I'm no policeman," Bellay told them. "I work for the government. Intelligence. What you would call a spy, though I prefer a less dramatic word.''

Simone leaned forward. Houston was only vaguely conscious of her.

''I won't name the agency I work for. It prefers to be anonymous, and anyway the name would have no meaning for you. Its mandate is essentially defensive not to interfere with foreign governments and not to ferret out their secrets. Quite the opposite. Our purpose is to stop a foreign government from interfering with our own. We are protectors. We defend. We seek out hostile foreign agents and discourage them.''

''Is that a synonym for kill?''

''I keep forgetting you're a novelist.''

''How did *you* know?''

Bellay smiled. ''We're efficient. Your own embassy is equally efficient. While you waited at Emergency, your file was being put together. And Simone's, of course. Don't be offended. These are necessary measures, and we keep that information confidential.''

''I've done nothing shameful,'' she said proudly.

''Yes, I know. I read your file.''

She look embarrassed, violated.

"Mr. Houston has no shameful secrets either. I'm convinced that your connection with Verlaine is inadvertent, innocent. You *have* become involved, though, and the question now is how to deal with that."

"You're telling me Verlaine's a front for foreign agents?"

Bellay studied him. "America is not the only country with a cancer at its soul. Drugs, crime, moral impotence. The evil is pervasive. France and England, Italy and Germany and—I don't need to give a list. The roster is endless. We are slowly dying, each of us, each nation."

Sermons? Houston thought. I ask for information, and he answers with a moral tract? "That isn't your concern," he said. "You're not a cop."

"Correct."

"Then—"

"Verlaine Enterprises is a front for drugs and fences, prostitution, gambling, hit men, loan sharks, counterfeiters. It owns buildings like the one in which you nearly died. It buys up failing businesses and uses them to hide illegal profits, making dirty money clean to satisfy the tax authorities. The lesson of your Al Capone was learned in France as well as in America. He didn't go to jail for murder but for tax evasion. You'll be amused that Verlaine, having no doubt blown that building up, is now demanding its insurance money."

"Jesus."

"In a way, I find their gall impressive. As you say, those crimes are not my business. But I do have other business with Verlaine. A year ago, policemen started hearing street talk. Not substantial. Rumors mostly. Not in Roncevaux, but in Paris and Marseilles. Large shipments of narcotics smuggled in without detection. I mean large amounts, ten times what normally comes in. Then twenty times. Then thirty. If these rumors were correct, that kind of traffic couldn't be achieved without wide payoffs, through organized corruption of officials. That alone made the rumors suspect. Such corruption surely wasn't possible. What's more, the rumors made no sense. Such massive shipments of narcotics would so glut the market that the price would be driven down. Why would gangsters want to damage profits? Why the massive shipments?"

Houston felt a surge of anger. "If you've set us up . . . If there's no answer . . ."

"There's an answer. Other rumors, not from street talk, but from reliable deep covers. It's no secret that détente has failed. Your president has made that clear. Your State Department treats the Soviets as if the Cold War never ended. The invasion of Afghanistan was proof of what the Soviets were planning. Poland, Cuba, South America, the Middle East, and Africa, of course. The pattern is consistent. But they know that there are many ways to conquer. From without and from within."

"What you said before—"

"You see now my connection with this matter. We can't prove, but we suspect that, losing patience finally, the Soviets are hastening the process of our dissolution. Verlaine Enterprises. It's a front for gangsters. But suppose the gangsters were a front as well. Suppose the Soviets controlled them as a silent hidden partner, keeping their involvement from the men whom they were using. Dirty money. Buy legitimate clean businesses. Control them from a distance. Bribe and gouge, corrupt and pander. Take advantage of the evils in our system. Cultivate those evils. Let the weeds spread. When at last we're so debased that we care only for our satisfactions, when the chaos overwhelms us, then the Soviets step in with ease."

"The Soviets control the mob?"

"And its equivalent in Italy, in England, in America. Use criminals to be unwitting foreign agents. Who would ever think it? But the rumors, Mr. Houston, they persist, and there are many of them. For the past nine months I've been investigating. I can't prove the link between the Soviets and Verlaine Enterprises. But the massive drug supplies, the drop in price—it makes no sense unless the object is to undermine this country's strength, to cause confusion."

Pete's anger did not lessen. "All I want to do is find Jan's murderer. I want to stop whoever wants to kill the two of us. *I want to live a normal life again.* If you know anything to help us, tell me. What's this got to do with us?''

''You tried to find your father's grave. In turn, you looked for St. Laurent. That led you to Verlaine. Beyond all that, we now must deal with nineteen forty-four. A missing squad of soldiers. St. Laurent's own disappearance. Something happened back then, and its repercussions continue. If we solve that mystery, we'll solve the others.''

''And my father's at the center of them,'' Houston said. His stomach dropped. ''Dear God, what kind of person was he? What was he involved in?''

''Is,'' Simone said.

''What?''

''Not *what* but *is*. It hasn't ended.''

Houston felt the room appear to darken.

Bellay nodded grimly.

''Tell me what to do,'' Houston said.

''There's nothing—''

''With you or without you, I intend to find him. Teach me,'' Houston said. ''I want to learn about Verlaine.''

30

Single-spaced, the list of Verlaine's holdings filled three pages. Businesses of every size and type. From laundries and importers and distributors and cinemas, to restaurants and office buildings and computers. Finance companies, conglomerates. Houston was appalled. He glanced up from the documents.

Bellay explained. ''On paper, Verlaine seems as innocent as

Christ's apostles. Everything looks legal, organized by skillful lawyers. It pays taxes. It donates to charities. It issues stocks. It pays a dividend to its investors. Everything it does seems so correct, so documented that we need our own lawyers to decipher all the paperwork. Beyond the labyrinth of facts and figures, though, it's vague as hell. If we investigate its principal investors, we find other corporations, which in turn are owned by other corporations, and the people who are listed as directors of those corporations don't exist. Their names are phony. In the end, we're not sure who supplies the money. That's on one side. On the other side, the businesses that Verlaine owns aren't strong enough to justify the profits they report."

"So the investments and the profits are probably illegal money from the syndicate," Pete said.

"Or from the Soviets, assuming I'm right."

Houston scanned the list of businesses again . . . and suddenly among the names he recognized one. So familiar, so astonishing he blanched.

"Pete, what's wrong?"

Alarmed, he turned to Simone. He studied each portion of her face, her exquisite hair, her perfectly proportioned chin and nose and cheeks. At last he settled on her searching eyes.

He couldn't bring himself to tell her. What if his suspicions weren't correct? He couldn't hurt her. Not till he was sure.

"It's just my ribs," he answered, fighting to sound natural. "They hurt. I tried to do too much."

"No wonder," Bellay told him, glancing at his watch. "It's after six. We all need rest. Would you accept my company at dinner?"

"No offense," Pete said, "but I need sleep instead of food. Another time?"

"Of course. Besides, I have some private matters to attend to. And, as well, we have a problem."

Houston frowned.

"You're still in danger. While you're learning, someone is still hunting you. The situation hasn't changed. We have to find a place for you to spend the night. And I agree with you. A hotel isn't safe."

"Then where?"

31

A hunting lodge. At least it seemed to be. It sat atop a treeless hill, slopes clear of brush, with woods on its perimeter. A chainlink fence circled it, the only indication that it was something more than a lodge. The low, wide building seemed innocuous. Its walls were formed of logs, its roof cedar shingles. It had a dingy porch, a woodshed, and a listing single-car garage.

To get there, Houston and Simone had left the Renault at the Roncevaux police station's underground garage. They'd made their exit in a police van, its driver turning down streets at random, wanting to lose a tail or, if that didn't work, at least to spot one. Houston and Simone were transferred to an unmarked car and driven out of town. Simone kept glancing toward him anxiously, as if desperate to ask a question. But she stayed in control. She clutched his hand. He felt her tension as he remembered what he'd seen in the Verlaine folder.

To distract himself he glanced out at the darkness, at the silhouettes of trees along this gently rising country road. The driver pressed a button on the dashboard. Houston almost asked him why, but then they angled off the road, climbing higher, this time on a bumpy rutted lane with bushes on each side so close they scraped along the car.

Then, past the dense gloom of the hulking trees, he saw the clearing on the hill. And at the top, shrouded by a haze of eerie moonlight, Houston saw the stark black outline of the hunting lodge. He shivered.

Once again the driver pressed a button on the dashboard. This time Houston felt no need to ask him why. The reason was self-evident. A metal gate swung open. They drove through the gap in the fence toward the building. Houston glanced back. The gate was swinging shut.

They stopped. The driver left the engine running but made no move to get out.

Pete leaned ahead. "We're waiting. Someone's coming for us?"

The driver turned, his face quizzical. Houston realized he spoke no English.

But Simone asked. She translated what the driver answered.

"We're expected. He's supposed to drive back for another job. He thought we were aware of this procedure."

"He's just going to leave us here?" Pete tensed with apprehension. "But the place is dark. We don't know where we are."

The driver spoke. Simone told Houston, "He wants us to get out. He's already late."

"The hell we will."

"He says that we'll be safe."

A sudden shadow loomed beside the car. Reflexively, Houston jerked backward, shielding Simone. His heart raced. Frantically he lunged to push the lock.

Too late. The door moved just before the lock clicked down. A man leaned in from the darkness. He was dressed in black from head to foot. He had a short black beard, a black beret, a thick black shoulder holster holding a massive black-gripped handgun. He was close to fifty, stern-eyed, and he squinted at Simone and Houston.

"Please," he said, his English heavily inflected. "It is safer if you come inside."

"You're from Bellay?" Houston said.

"We work together. Our employer is the same."

"This place—"

"Is your protection. Hurry, please. I can't defend you out here."

Houston looked for reassurance from Simone. She nodded. They stepped from the car.

At once the stranger shut the door. He tapped his knuckles on the roof. The driver steered away. As Houston walked behind the man, he heard the gate swing smoothly open, and he watched the headlights disappear. The engine's drone became inaudible. The gate closed with a whisper.

Then, except for footsteps on the dew-wet grass, except for the sound of flapping wings—a bat perhaps—the night was silent. Houston, conscious of Simone beside him, watched the broad muscled back he followed. The stranger carried his suitcase and Simone's.

"No one bothered to explain," Pete said. "What kind of place—"

"A refuge. Or a safe house for a meeting. Or a rest home. It has many uses. Sometimes for debriefing or interrogation. I am called Henri. No last name, if you please. I am your servant."

"And our bodyguard?"

They reached the steps up to the creaky porch.

"The word is too suggestive. In the old days I would be described as a retainer. My main purpose is your comfort and your security."

He opened the parched unpainted door. In semidarkness Houston saw another door, a solid metal one beside which Henri pushed some numbers on a console. Something whirred. The heavy door inched open.

"A precaution." Graciously Henri motioned them inside.

They entered blackness. Houston heard Henri touch something on the wall. When the door snicked shut, the lights came on. "They're automatic," Henri said. "They shut off when the door is open."

Houston blinked. The room was large, with wooden beams across the ceiling, rich dark panels on the walls, and thick deep rustic throw rugs on the floor. There was even a bearskin on the wall and an eight-point rack of antlers hung above the slate-framed fireplace.

But Houston's main astonishment was caused by the wide array of monitors—radios and multidialed devices—situated all along the right end of the room. They glowed and glinted. Needles wavered.

"All these gadgets," Houston said.

"They're sentries. Once the metal door is closed, this place is sealed. You'll notice there are no windows."

Houston glanced around the room. The walls were solid, with no openings.

Simone was puzzled. "Outside I saw windows, though, and they were dark. The place seemed vacant."

"That's how it's supposed to look. It's part of the illusion," Henri answered pleasantly. "The windows have their shades pulled down and then these walls behind them. The effect is that the occupants appear to want their privacy in daytime and to be away at night. No shadows on the blinds. No silhouettes for snipers. Safe, anonymous, and practical. This lodge is like a bunker. Metal shields behind the panels. Ample food and water."

"You designed it?"

"You're perceptive. It's my hobby. I'm fortunate because it's also my business. These devices put us into contact with our central bureau and its satellites. But more important, they guard the grounds. The fence, of course, is monitored. If anyone tries to cut it or climb over it, a signal is received here. And of course there are instruments surveying the woods as well. You may have noticed that the driver pressed a button on his dashboard as he left the main road coming toward the gate."

Pete nodded.

"That was to warn me he was coming. Otherwise the signals on these monitors would have alerted me. After sending an alarm, I would have braced myself for an attack."

Pete swallowed. "I could use a drink."

"Jack Daniel's, if I'm not mistaken. And the lady—"

"Dry martini."

"Oh? That isn't on your record." Henri seemed puzzled. "In that cabinet. I can't risk the side effects, but I take pleasure if my guests indulge."

Pete made the drinks. He gestured toward the many bottles on the bar. "Every one is sealed."

"My guests are careful."

"How is that?"

"They won't drink from an open bottle."

Houston gagged. The bourbon soured in his stomach. "It's not hard to drop the poison in and then put on a seal."

"There comes a time when they must trust."

As we are trusting, Houston thought.

"I have to talk to you," Simone said.

He had known that this was coming, though he'd hoped he could avoid it. All along, her eyes had followed him.

"Your room's through there," Henri said, pointing. "There's a bathroom with a shower. I'll serve dinner in an hour."

She went in before he'd finished talking. Houston grabbed their bags. The room was spacious, beamed, and paneled, with slick hardwood floors, a king-sized bed. She shut the door as soon as he came in. "The bathroom," she said.

"What?"

"You heard me." She walked swiftly toward another door and yanked it open. He saw the bright white tile. She stalked in. He set the bags down.

Frowning, he went after her. "What is it?"

But she didn't answer. She turned on the sink taps, then the shower faucets. In the noise, she faced him. "You're holding something back again."

"You think there's a microphone?"

"Of course I think so. I'd be stupid not to know this room was bugged. The truth! Quit hiding things from me."

The taps kept pouring water. "Tell me," she said.

He spoke reluctantly. "Bellay brought in the Verlaine folder. We were reading through the documents."

She nodded.

"I had the list of Verlaine's holdings, all the companies it owned. Simone, I didn't want to hurt you. That's the only reason I held back. I had to think about the implications. Halfway down the second sheet I saw the name of your father's hotel. Verlaine owns it."

She looked as if she'd been slapped. "My father works for Verlaine Enterprises?"

"Beneath the hotel's name I saw the right address. And then I saw your father's name."

"There's some mistake!"

"That's why I tried to hide it from you. Till I had a chance to learn the truth."

"Bellay must know."

"Of course."

"Then he's been testing us."

"That's why we're here. He's not protecting us. He's *watching* us."

"But if that's true"—her eyes were frantic—"if there isn't some mistake, that means my father—"

"Tried to stop me. That's how Jan got killed. That's how the man got in our room. And your room. He was trying to get even with your father."

"No. He didn't mention Father's name."

"It doesn't matter. All I know is that your father's name is on that list and—"

She charged from the bathroom.

"Hey!"

She whirled to face him. "No, I'll prove it to you. I refuse to let you think this. He's my *father*. Now you're telling me that I don't really know him, that he lied to us when he explained about Pierre de St. Laurent. The implication is that St. Laurent is still alive and that my father knows him, that they're partners, that . . . If I belived what you're suggesting, I'd go crazy. That my father tried to kill me!"

"I'm on your side. Keep your voice down, or that man out there will—"

"I don't care! I'm going to prove you're wrong! I'll prove it to Bellay! To everyone!"

123

"But *how?*"

"I'll phone him! Now! I'll tell him what we've learned! He wouldn't lie to me! I'll ask him!"

32

She grabbed at the door. Pete hurried toward her. Apparent-ly she feared that he wanted to stop her, for her movements now intensified. She yanked the door so hard that as she shoved it to one side it cracked against the wall. Pete rushed out behind her.

Past her shoulder, he saw Henri wheel around to face them, fumbling to remove the headphones he was listening to. His face was flustered, red above the short dark beard. "I only—" he began.

"I know what you were doing," Simone said. "You were listening! It doesn't matter! You know what I want! The phone! Where is it! Let me use it!"

"It's only for emergencies."

"And what the hell is this? You heard what we were saying! It's important!"

"Let me radio the agency to get permission."

She saw the phone between two monitors along the wall.

Henri stood to grab her.

Houston squeezed between them. Simone reached the phone and dialed.

"It's not allowed," Henri said.

"Relax," Pete answered. "If this works, you'll be com-mended. If it doesn't, you can say it was our fault."

Henri reached for his gun. But then his arm stopped, in sus-pension.

For Simone was speaking on the telephone. Her French was urgent. Houston only understood a few quick phrases.

Henri understood exactly, though. His eyes were narrow. He stood stiffly, lips taut, pinched together with such force they were pale and bloodless.

Without breathing, Houston turned to watch Simone. Her voice was louder now, her words more demanding.

Suddenly her tone changed from urgency to puzzlement, from certainty to confusion.

Houston looked at Henri, who now seemed sterner, nodding with grim resolve.

"What's she saying?" Houston's throat felt raw. His voice broke.

Henri raised his hand for silence, staring at Simone.

The phone slipped through her fingers, falling on its cradle. She studied it as if it were obscene.

She'd pulled her hair to one side. Houston saw the hackles on her neck. A ripple shuddered through him. She trembled, slowly turning, blinking through swollen eyes.

"What is it?" Houston said.

"My father," she said.

Houston walked to her and touched her shoulders. "What about your father? Tell me."

"He's gone," She started weeping.

Houston held her close, feeling her tears against his shirt. "He's on an errand."

"No." Her voice was blurred with tears. "He's gone. He left this morning. He took a suitcase."

"Where? I . . . This is crazy. Tell me what you heard."

"The desk clerk." She pushed back to face him, tear streaks on her cheeks. "This morning. No one knows what happened, but my father was nervous, talking to himself. He couldn't do his work. He told the staff to do their jobs without him—he'd be back in a few days, perhaps a week. He made some phone calls from his office. Then he packed his suitcase and he left."

The monitors kept humming. For the first time Pete was conscious of their sound. But then Simone began to weep, and he heard only her agony. He forced her to him, held her tightly, stroking at her hair. "It could mean nothing. Business problems."

"Don't you see the pattern? Don't you know what made him act that way?" He shook his head.

She pulled away from him. "My note. I told him I was leaving with you. I was helping you, I said. And helping me. I didn't have a choice, I said. I hoped he'd understand."

"My God. Last night."

"He wanted me to stay away from you. We thought he was only being fatherly, protective."

"But he wasn't. He knew what we faced. He's always known. Since he first heard I was looking for Pierre de St. Laurent."

"He didn't think they'd try to kill me too. He's gone to beg Verlaine. To plead with them to spare my life. Our fathers. Not just yours but mine. They're *both* involved in this."

"But he made phone calls," Henri said.

They turned, bewildered, as if he spoke neither French nor English but an arcane language.

"What?" Pete said.

"He made phone calls. From his office," Henri said.

"That's right," Simone replied.

"He packed a bag. He said he'd be gone for several days."

"What of it?" Houston said. "I don't see how that helps us."

"Think. He didn't stay in town. He traveled somewhere."

"I still don't—"

"The phone calls must have been long distance. They'll be billed. We'll get the numbers from the telephone computers," Henri said.

Houston gaped. The monitors began to wail.

33

Houston flinched as if a knife had struck him in the chest. He jerked abruptly toward the sound, a high-pitched strident shriek that rose and fell. "What is it?"

"The security alarm." Henri's eyes narrowed. He drew his handgun

The monitors kept wailing. Houston clutched at futile hope. "The system's malfunctioning."

"Impossible. I built it." Henri took three steps and reached the monitors.

Simone grabbed Houston's arm. He felt the pressure of her fingers.

"Someone's coming through the forest." Henri pointed toward one monitor. "The south." He gestured toward the farthest wall.

A band of light swept in a circle on the wide blue screen. A yellow dot crept upward from the bottom.

Henri aimed a finger toward a red spot in the middle of the screen. "That's us. The hilltop. Read the screen the way you would a map. The top is north, the bottom's south. The right and left are east and west."

The dot kept moving upward from the south. "An animal," Pete said.

"Impossible," Henri said. "All the sensors are adjusted to respond to size and weight and body heat. Especially to body heat. The only thing capable of triggering the sensors is a person."

"But whoever's in the forest doesn't have to be a threat," Simone insisted. "A camper or a hiker maybe."

"We'll soon know. The dot's at the fence."

"And if it's touched?"

"The metal is electrified."

"To stun?"

"To kill."

Simone's widened eyes revealed what Houston had been feeling. "But whoever's down there could be innocent," she said.

"We can't risk being wrong."

A second siren shrieked, louder than the first. Simone whirled in panic.

"There's your answer," Henri told them. "At the fence. Whoever's down there wasn't stopped."

"The dot was moving higher from the bottom.

"But you said the fence was charged."

"He came prepared. He knows precisely what he's doing."

Houston watched how Henri clutched the gun, his hand so tight his knuckles whitened. "Stop him," Houston said.

"Machine guns will shoot him the moment he gets halfway through the clearing toward the lodge. They're spaced so their line of fire intersects. The hill itself is mined, except for the driveway. He'll be stopped. Don't worry. There's no cover on that slope."

But Houston wondered why, if they shouldn't worry, Henri's breath was hoarse and rapid. When another siren started wailing, Houston had his answer. While they were protected in here, they were also trapped. The western sector of the screen now showed a second dot, also moving toward the center.

"Two of them!"

Houston grabbed the counter to control his trembling. There weren't two dots—there were three! The north now, moving inward!

And the east!

"Those sirens! I can't stand them any more!" Simone put her hands to her ears.

"The switch," Pete said.

Henri flicked it. The sirens stopped. But the silence was

worse than the noise. The air was like a vacuum. Numbness swept through Houston. And the four dots, having reached an equal distance from the lodge, now stopped.

The band of light kept circling on the screen. The dots stayed motionless, in perfect symmetry.

"What's happening?" Simone asked.

"If we had some windows, we could find out."

"Just be glad we don't have windows," Henri blurted. "Then we'd all be targets. Thank God for the metal walls."

"But aren't there television cameras?"

"Yes. But that screen. The static. Something's interfering with the image."

"I don't hear the machine guns," Pete said.

"Those men knew exactly where to stop. They haven't tripped the force field yet."

"They won't," Pete said.

"What makes you sure?"

"Because they've managed to outguess you this far. They're prepared. They knew what they'd be facing."

"That's impossible."

"You keep repeating that. It's not impossible. It's happened."

"Look!" Simone pointed toward the monitor.

The southern dot inched forward.

"What about the mines?"

"He must be on the driveway."

"Oh, that's swell. That's fucking great."

"But any second now."

"And what if they shut off the power?"

"Can't. The generator's underneath us."

"What the hell is that guy doing?"

Houston quickly learned. The southern dot stopped abruptly. The silence lengthened, and the door through which they'd entered blew apart.

34

It ruptured, tearing from its hinges toward the throw rugs on the floor. The stench of cordite, burning wood, and super-heated metal soared up Houston's nostrils. He coughed and found he'd fallen to his knees. For one disorienting instant, he thought he was back in Roncevaux, in the explosion at the office building.

But this wasn't any bomb. "A rocket!" Henri shouted. Houston couldn't see him in the smoke. "They didn't care about the guns! They never planned to come that far!" Henri's voice was a shout. "They'll just stand far back and blow this lodge apart! They'll—"

The second blast obscured all other sound. The western wall, where Houston earlier had poured the drinks, disintegrated, huge chunks of wood flying inward.

Simone began to scream. The eastern wall, where most of Henri's instruments were situated, blew apart. Houston fell back, hitting his skull hard on the floor, thrown down by flying rubble. It entangled him. He groped to climb above it, searching for Simone. Again the southern wall exploded.

"We can't stay here!" Henri shouted.

"We can't leave. They'll shoot us."

"There's a way." Henri's voice was so subdued, so controlled, that Houston stared at him, afraid that he'd gone crazy. "Help me!" Henri ordered, fumbling at the rubble.

Houston wiped his smoke-burned eyes. Confused, he watched Henri's frantic motions. In the smoke, Henri was like a demon, black clothes shrouded, black beard like a Satan's mask. Then Houston heard the stunning blast that walloped the bedroom. He heard something else, a whoosh of air. He felt heat. He turned and saw flames. The far side of the room was totally ablaze. The air was roaring like a hurricane, a fire storm.

"Help me!" Henri shouted.

Houston obeyed. He stumbled through the wreckage, legs pierced by the sharp-edged boards and shards of glass from broken monitors. A new explosion threw him forward. His ears were now so tortured he couldn't hear the crackle of the flames. But he could feel the swelling heat, much closer, more intense. The smoke obscured Simone. She coughed. Another blast. A flying piece of shrapnel sliced his shoulder.

Clear the rubble. Lift and throw. There had to be a trap door.

Henri pushed him backward, lunging toward the floor. The blow knocked Houston's wind out. As he fought to breathe, he inhaled smoke. His lungs revolted, and he retched.

But Henri had raised the trap door. Houston stared through swirling smoke at utter blackness. Instinct nagged him, warning. No, he told himself. He held back, repulsed by the obscene darkness.

Flames licked toward him, brilliant in the smoke. His clothes felt warm. His hair gave off an acrid odor.

"Hurry!" Henri told him.

Houston grabbed Simone. "Is there a ladder?" he shouted.

"Steps! A stairway!" Henri shouted back.

The next explosion settled any doubt. His arm around Simone, Houston eased down toward the darkness. Instantly he touched a step. Another as he moved his next foot lower. "It's all right!" he told Simone. "It's safe! Don't be afraid!"

Her hand was frenzied on his shoulder. Then he felt the hand relax as, groping down, she touched the steps. The flames were now so close above them that the darkness underneath was illuminated. Houston saw the earthen floor, the rough stone walls. He smelled a sour dampness, and he heard the the rumbling of an engine. Through the shadows, he squinted toward a corner where a bulky generator labored.

Henri charged down past them, flailing at his smoldering

clothes. He rolled insanely in the dirt, and Houston leapt to reach him. He wrapped his shirt around his hand and swatted smoke on Henri's clothes. And at last the smoke was gone. Henri groaned, forehead drenched with sweat.

"Are you all right?"

Henri said nothing, his eyes scrunched shut in pain. The odor from his flesh was sickening. He inhaled deeply. "There's no time." He struggled to his feet. When Houston moved to help him, Henri shrugged him off. "We can't wait. We have to hurry."

Glancing upward, Houston saw the flames that filled the entrance to the cellar. Air rushed past him toward the opening. The flames licked at the wooden steps. "We're going to suffocate down here."

"No, follow me." Henri pulled Houston's arm. He hurried toward the darkest corner of the cellar and yanked at a metal door. The door creaked open. They rushed forward.

"It's a tunnel. An escape route. It leads underneath the hill, the fence. It takes us to the forest."

They ran. Houston bumped against a moist dank wall. The stone scraped his shoulder. But he couldn't see where he was going. In a panic, he raced blindly on.

Simone lurched hard against him, reeling sideways. They entangled in the darkness, fell on earth so moist it was mud. They slid along their backs in muck. Pete's shoes were soaked, his pants cold and slimy. They struggled up. Behind him, Houston heard two more explosions, muffled by the distance. He felt shock waves.

He kept racing forward, sensing Henri and Simone beside him, hearing mud suck at his shoes, his panicked breath reverberating in the tunnel.

"They'll soon finish," Henri said, his voice strained. "They'll come up the driveway. They'll check through the wreckage. They'll see where we went."

Again, Pete's instinct nagged him, warning. There was something obvious, self-evident, but something he had overlooked. He couldn't isolate it, make it clear, but its insistence made him nervous. There was something wrong. Good Christ, what was it?

"Take it slowly," Henri ordered. He reached for them, fighting to restrain them. "Wait a minute."

Houston did what he was told. He held Simone. "Why?" he asked Henri.

"Ahead there'll be another door. We've almost reached it."

Houston felt Henri inch forward. Eight more steps. "It's here. I found it."

"Get us out of here," Simone said.

"Just a few more seconds."

Houston heard Henri shove at a bolt. It bit against the metal. Henri gasped and shoved again. "I've almost done it. There!" And Henri slumped against the wall. "We're safe now"

Houston's mind kept warning. Something's wrong. Beside him he felt Henri tug open the door. Pallid moonlight drifted through the gradually increasing crack. The air was fresh and sweet.

"Thank God," Simone said.

Houston felt exhilarated by the moonlight filtered through a crisscrossed obstacle of branches. Silhouetted, Henri stepped ahead to move the branches. Now the moonlight glinted brightly at them. Houston had never seen anything so wonderful. Still clutching Simone, he followed Henri from the tunnel, feeling liberated. A few more steps, and they would be completely safe. The trees loomed close before him.

Suddenly he found the warning thought, harsh and stark and urgent.

"Henri, wait. If they knew all about the lodge, about the current in the fence, about the mines and the machine guns, if they knew they needed rockets, then they'd know about—"

The gunshot from the forest interrupted Houston's sentence. He heard the bullet plow through Henri, felt the spattered blood. Henri arced, gasping. He convulsed and fell on Houston.

"Peter!" Simone screamed.

Houston couldn't speak. In horror, he scrambled from beneath the body. Mindlessly he grabbed the gun.

"Peter, talk to me!"

"He's dead."

"No!"

Houston pulled her down. Another bullet hit the door behind him, whining off the metal.

Houston saw the flash from out there in the trees. He heard the shot. Another shot. He saw a different muzzle flash. The two were separated, twenty yards away from one another.

Evidently they had counted on his running back inside the tunnel, on his hiding in there, while the other gunmen came down through the tunnel. They weren't shooting at clear targets. They were forcing Houston backward.

We can't go back, and sure as hell we can't stay here, he thought.

His rage welled up insanely. Panic changed to madness, desperation.

He saw another muzzle flash. He fired in return. He stood, leaping forward.

"Peter!"

But he didn't listen. He charged ahead, aiming where he'd seen the muzzle flash. He shot and heard a scream. He swerved. He saw a muzzle flash to his left, but he kept lunging toward the scream he'd heard. He leapt a stump, zigzagged past a tree. His fear had heightened every sense. He saw as if the night were day. His ears, despite the torture they'd endured, were perfectly attuned. A groan ahead of him. Some scrabbling in the brush. A stooping figure, clutching at a wounded arm. A disbelieving face. A young man, smooth-cheeked, begging.

Houston shot him in the skull.

The sound was awful, bursting flesh and bone, a hard sound, strangely liquid, the enormous gunblast swallowed by the impact.

Houston swung to one side, sickened, fell and hit and rolled. The second gunman fired. Houston heard the bullet wallop solidly against a tree. Bark flew, rattling on the dead leaves of the forest.

He kept rolling. Tumbled down a gully. Stopped.

He lay in water. His bare skin tightened from the wetness, from the cold.

"Peter!" Simone shouted. Her shouts would be distracting to the gunman. Don't stop shouting, he pled silently.

He squirmed along the stream, his noises blending with the sound of water bubbling over rocks and fallen branches.

Keep on shouting.

Fifteen yards. Then twenty. Chest cold, he wriggled up the bank and squinted through the darkness, through the maze of trees and bushes.

Mud clung to his chest. He clutched the gun. How many shots were left? He counted back and guessed at three.

He heard Simone shout, "Peter!" He saw movement near a tree. Not far ahead. A man who in distraction turned to watch Simone.

Houston aimed.

He held his breath, bracing his elbows on the ground. He gripped his right wrist, steadying the gun.

The barrel wavered.

No! He concentrated, squinting. No! He lost strength. His hand was drooping.

Sweat burned his eyes. His bare chest trembled against the ground.

The figure left the outline of the tree.

Houston pulled the trigger, jerking from the recoil. Deafened, he struggled to his feet. His shoes slipped on the leaves. He fell. He crawled. He scrambled.

The figure moved. Again Houston pulled the trigger. Metal clicked on metal. Nothing happened.

Oh, my God, I'm out of bullets!

But the man had been wounded. Houston reached him, rammed his head against the gunman's chest, and fell with him.

Houston punched him as hard as he could, lashed down with the empty handgun, beating him repeatedly. He cracked the handle of the gun down. Cracked it down again. He couldn't stop himself. He could not, did not want to restrain his rage.

But his body wearied sooner than his soul. His arm grew weak and heavy. The revolver fell from slackened fingers. He slumped across the body. And when he saw the gunman's face, when he discovered what he'd done to it, a moan escaped him, a deep nauseated wail. He threw up, clutching at his blood- and mud-specked face.

"Oh, Jesus," he whispered. "Forgive me."

35

"You're alive!" Simone rushed from the tunnel.

Houston staggered toward her in the darkness.

Sobbing, she embraced him. "I was so afraid you'd—"

Trembling, Houston kissed her.

"Are you hurt?" she said.

"My shoulder."

Blood dripped on the ground. "We have to get away from here," he said. "Those other men. They must have heard the shots."

He squinted above the tunnel toward the fire on the hill.

"They'll be here soon," he said. He pointed toward the forest. "Hurry."

In a panic, they began to run. His body ached. He crashed through bushes. Blackness loomed ahead of him.

The forest thickened.

"We have to find the road," she said.

Which way? he thought. He'd lost his sense of where they were. He couldn't calculate the road's direction. Somewhere on the far side of the hill, he guessed. They couldn't double back. The men would hear them. And for all he knew, the road was actually ahead of them.

He ran and heard the roar of water. A river, Houston saw as he came crashing from the bushes. He nearly lost his balance, falling. Simone held on to him. He squinted, breathing hoarsely, toward the moonlight glinting off the current.

"Oh, my God, we're trapped."

The river seethed, its white-capped blackness churning. Houston's stomach burned with fear. He clutched his chest.

"We'll have to run along the edge," she said. "But they'll split up. They'll go each way and cut us off."

He fought for his words. "We'll swim it," Houston forced himself to say.

She stared at him.

"Our only chance."

"The current's too strong. We'll drown," she said.

"They'll kill us if they find us. There's no other way."

She shook her head emphatically.

"We have to take the risk," he said.

"Your shoulder."

"Can't be helped. I'm losing too much blood."

Again she shook her head.

He fumbled to remove his belt. "Here, loop it tightly to your hand. I'll hold the other end. We have to stay together." Afraid, he scanned the river. "No more talking."

Belt taut, they scrambled down the bank. The current grabbed them, and they twisted in its violence. He gripped the belt, feeling its tension as Simone began to tumble sideways. He pulled at the belt to steady her. His face went under water. Coughing, he fought to the surface.

He'd never felt such numbing cold, such freezing pressure. Now he heard the river moan and howl, and then he realized that it was he himself who moaned as all around him chaos surged.

An object struck him, banging against his ribs. It nearly sucked him under. Houston saw it sweeping past him, saw the gnarled knobs of the tree limb, but too late he understood he could have used it to support him as a float. He stretched and strained for it, but it was gone, a murky heaving object in the darkness. Simone kicked next to him.

I'm going to die, he thought. And suddenly he was in his car again, fighting to get out the window, clawing toward the surface while his lungs expanded and his mind began to dim.

He no longer had the strength to fight. His injured shoulder failed him; he was carried by the current. Jan was dead. Soon he'd be dead as well. His hopes diminished, flickered, died. He gave up—and awakened as Simone pulled on the belt.

"Keep swimming," she told him.

"Can't. Too weak. Go on without me."

"No! We're almost there!"

He didn't think he'd heard correctly. "What?"

"The shore! We've almost reached it!"

Houston gaped stupidly. Black shapes. Hulking shadows. Silhouettes of trees and hills and—

"Jesus," he said. His new strength astounded him. His frantic need to live filled every portion of his body. He thrashed, kicking closer to the shore, and when he touched the mud beneath him, he began to shriek in triumph.

"We're here! We made it!"

He sloshed through the muddy water and flopped on the bank, staring toward the stars. He saw the moon. He worshiped it.

"We're safe," he told Simone, excitement warming his numb face. "They'll never find us. Even if they try to swim across, they won't know where we landed, how far down we drifted, not before we get away."

He tried to stand but didn't have the strength.

She told him, "Rest."

"We're cold and wet. If we don't find some shelter and dry clothes, we'll freeze to death."

He heard a far-off engine then, the motor of a truck. Behind him. Through the trees. He staggered to his feet, his breath hoarse. "Hurry," he said.

"There must be farms around here. We can reach a phone. We'll call Bellay."

He stiffened. "No. We can't."

"But he'll protect us."

"Will he? Someone knew! Bellay made the arrangements! He's the one who sent us here! Those men attacked the lodge as soon as we arrived!"

"He set a trap for us? Bellay did?"

"It's for damn sure someone did! Who knew where we were hiding?"

"But Bellay—I don't see why he'd—"

"If he works for them, if he's involved with them!"

She moaned. Her eyes were absolutely barren. "Tell me that's not true."

"What other answer is there? We were sent here to be killed!"

Her lips began to tremble. "Then there's no one who can help us. We don't have a chance."

He faced her, wet clothes clinging to him. He could feel her anguish, how totally she'd been demoralized. "No," he said. "There's still one man we can trust."

Part 4

36

"Something's wrong. He shouldn't be this late," Houston said.

The café got more crowded. Simone and he waited anxiously inside a corner booth with easy access to an exit in the rear. Uneasily they sipped their wine. They heard the drone of murmured conversations as the room filled up for lunch. At last, there wasn't any choice. Houston told Simone they had to leave.

"No, wait a little longer."

"But we can't afford the risk," he said. "Suppose his phone was tapped. Suppose he spoke to . . . All these people. What if one of them is here to kill us?"

"Now you sound like me last night."

"I don't understand."

"You said that if he's against us too we're finished. Once we feel no place is safe, then Verlaine's beaten us. We're paralyzed. We can't allow that. Wait and hope."

He studied her. "I don't know what I'd do without you."

"Hell, I don't know what you'd do without me either."

But the voice was not Simone's. It was a man's. Houston swung, alarmed.

Andrews loomed beside him at the table: short-haired, square-jawed, heavy-muscled. He stood rigidly, wearing a shirt with epaulets that made him look as if he was still in the military.

Houston slumped back. "Where'd you come from?"

"Through the back. That's why I'm late. I had to make sure no one followed me. I checked my phone, and it's not tapped."

143

His craggy face was troubled. Brooding, he set down a folder, pulled out a chair, and sat bolt-upright before the table. "You look awful. When you called last night, you didn't want to talk about it. What the hell happened?"

Houston told him.

He ended with the old man in the rusty truck who'd picked them up along the road. The old man had believed their lie about an accident and drove them to the nearest village, where as soon as the old man was out of sight, they paid a drunk to drive them to a village farther on.

"We found a doctor. We bought clothes. We spent a lot of time on trains and buses."

"After that, you still had nerve enough to want to meet me here? A public place?"

"We figured they wouldn't try to kill us in plain sight. Too many witnesses."

"From what you've told me, these guys aren't exactly bashful."

"Thanks. That's what I need. Encouragement."

"Verlaine and Charon? Something white?"

"I know. It doesn't make much sense."

"It's like a stone thrown in a pond. The ripples keep on spreading."

"Did you bring the numbers?" Houston asked.

Andrews studied him. "You're still determined to go on?"

"More than ever. What's the choice? We either run until they catch us, or we find the truth and fight."

Andrews sighed. "I've got the numbers." He reached for the folder he had set on the table.

But his fingers were reluctant. "It was difficult. I had to cancel favors that were owed me. I had to owe a lot of favors in return. I lost some friends at Army Intelligence. But finally I managed to persuade them. They were hesitant to get the numbers without asking for permission from . . . You still believe that you can't trust the French officials?"

"Would you trust them in my place? The local cops or Bellay's agency?"

"Considering what's happened, no."

"The numbers," Houston said.

Andrews squinted toward the folder. He debated, fingering the seal with apprehension. "Are you sure you wouldn't rather hide somewhere?" he asked. "Intelligence suggested—no, insisted—that you stay away while they investigated."

Houston reached to grab the folder.

Andrews broke the seal himself. He pulled out a sheet of paper. "Your father made three calls," Andrews told Simone. "Long distance, as you guessed. The numbers were recorded in the company's computer, so your father's hotel could be billed." He gave Simone the sheet of paper. "There they are. The numbers and the countries. I don't know who's at those numbers. But the places might have some significance. First France, then England, then America."

Pete felt a chill. "America?"

"Your father, possibly," Andrews said. "That's why I wondered if you really felt you had to know. The secrets of our childhood are best left that way."

"You're wrong," Pete said. "Without the truth, what else matters?"

"For your sake, I hope you're right. I can't help you any further. I've been ordered by Intelligence to stay away. From now, you're on your own. . . . And something else." Reluctantly Andrews reached inside the folder and withdrew the front page of a Paris newspaper. "Have you seen it?"

Houston nodded. "It's what happened at the hunting lodge. No mention of the two men I was forced to . . ." Houston swallowed something sour. "But the two of *us* are mentioned, and the cops believe we're responsible for killing a French undercover agent. They're out searching for us, thanks to Bellay. We weren't killed, and so he makes it look as if we caused what happened. If I get my hands around his . . ." Houston stiffened. "One more thing they've done to me."

"What's that?"

"They made me kill. They showed me something I don't want to know about myself."

"But self-defense . . ."

"*It doesn't make a difference,*" Houston told him. "I *killed* two men. I—" He saw that people turned to look at him. He glanced down at the circles his wine glass made on the table. Then the circles changed, became the ruined faces of the men he'd killed. He shuddered. "I'm not trained to kill," he went on, his voice low. "I responded on pure instinct. Oh, my books are violent in places, and I did some research for them, took some weapons classes, things like that. But this was real, and I was good at it. I won against professionals. I try to tell myself I was only lucky. But I *know* what I was feeling. I've got a *talent* for it. I don't like the *implications*."

Houston tensed. He felt Andrews clutch his hand.

"For what it's worth, I understand," Andrews said. "I was in Nam. There were some members of my unit who could kill and not be bothered. But it always gave me nightmares." Andrews paused as Houston had. He pursed his lips, remembering. "That's why I'm where I am. The cemetery. As a penance. All the same, I'll tell you this. A man who kills and isn't bothered, that man isn't worth a shit. But if he has to kill and doesn't, well, my friend, that man's as good as dead."

Pete concentrated on Andrews, considered, and then looked away. "The trouble is, I *want* to kill," he said. "I want to make them pay for what they did to me, to Janice, to Simone. That's why I'm bothered." He faced Andrews again. "I'm angry, and I'm scared. Because I killed two men, and maybe next time will be easier."

Andrews didn't move. He just kept staring. With assessment, new awareness. When he spoke at last, his voice was respectful. "Then maybe you've got a chance."

37

Pete set the phone back on its cradle and stepped from the
glassed-in booth. His hands were sweaty. In this massive, busy
room—a phone complex in Paris—all the walls were lined with
other booths. Behind a counter in the center of the room a group
of clerks received instructions from the many people, mostly
tourists, who had come here to make foreign calls. The room
was noisy, but that pleased Houston. He felt protected in the
chaos.

Once again he read the sheet of paper that the superintendent
had delivered to him. Three stark numbers. Telephones in
France and England and America. His hands kept shaking.
Next to him, he heard the rattle of an opening phone booth
door. Simone stepped out, her face tense and thoughtful.

"You got through?" he said. "You talked to someone?"

"Yes." Her voice was puzzled. "Not an office here in Paris.
It's a home. LeBlanc. François LeBlanc."

He couldn't hide the shock he felt. She stared at him.
"What's the matter?"

"I'll tell you in a second. It could mean nothing. What did he
say?"

"I didn't speak to him. He isn't there. A servant answered."

"Will LeBlanc be back soon?"

"No. Two days ago he left abruptly. For a business meeting
at his country home."

"Two days ago? That's when your father called him."

"Don't you think I know that?"

Houston studied her—the fear, the tension in her eyes. He

held her gently. "Take it easy. This is hard on you. It's hard on both of us. But we've got to find the answers."

"We've got to find my *father*. If he's trying to protect me, if he called LeBlanc to try to stop what's happening, then he's in danger. His employers will suspect his loyalty. He can't be faithful to Verlaine and to me."

"I think we're closer to him."

Anxiously she peered at him. "Your call?"

"The number was in London. Once again, a home. The name is Jules Fontaine. He isn't there. A secretary told me that two days ago he had to leave. An urgent business meeting."

"Here in France?"

"You guessed it."

"Then my father's with him! With LeBlanc!"

"Let's hope so," Houston said. "The puzzle's almost finished. One more piece."

The phone rang in the booth that Houston had just left. "America," he said. "I told the clerk to put the call through when I finished with the other one. New York." He stepped inside the booth, toward what he feared yet hoped would be the voice of his lost father.

"Hello," he said. The line crackled. Houston raised his voice, attempting to project it through the distance. "My name's Victor Corrigan," he said. "Somebody left a message and this number with my secretary. I'm supposed to call, but I'm not certain why. The message isn't clear." A woman's voice. Late middle age, distinctly upper class, refined, as if she'd been educated in a small exclusive college in New England. "Victor Corrigan? I'm sorry. I don't think I know the name." Her cadence was uncertain. Houston guessed that she apologized a lot.

"It's terribly embarrassing," he said. "My secretary's new. She's made mistakes all week. I might be forced to let her go."

"Oh, no, that's awful. Please, if this is business, I don't know enough to help you. It's my husband you should talk to."

"Is he there? Perhaps he knows what this is."

"No. He left two days ago. He's in the mountains."

Houston felt excitement rushing through him. "Then I'll wait and call again. I'm sorry to have—No, please, just a moment. One more question if you've got the time. My secretary's so disorganized. If you could tell me what your husband's name is, I could check my records. Maybe I could find a reason for—"

"Of course." She seemed relieved. "I seldom get the chance to help. His name is Paul Dassin."

"I should have recognized the number. Verlaine Enterprises."

"Not at all. I've never *heard* of Verlaine Enterprises. Hawthorne Imports."

Houston frowned. "My mistake. I sometimes mix them up. I won't keep you any longer. Give Paul my regards. The Rockies are especially attractive in the spring. With luck, he'll get a chance to do some skiing."

"Not the Rockies."

"Pardon me?"

"The Alps, young man. He's gone to France."

Houston feared that he'd be sick. He clutched the glass wall of the phone booth, thanking her, apologizing, fumbling to hang up. He pulled at the door. Simone stared at him, startled by the dazed expression on his face. "What is it?"

"I don't know. I . . ." Houston watched her face blur, seem to fade. "He left two days ago. The Alps. In France." The noises of the room echoed inside his head.

"They've got to be together," she said quickly. "All of them. My father."

"Paul Dassin." He gripped the booth's door for support.

"What?"

"That's his name. Like the other names—François LeBlanc and Jules Fontaine—it's French. We assumed they were the missing soldiers from my father's squad. But they wouldn't all be French descendants, wouldn't all have parents who were emigrants from France."

"They could have changed their names." Houston nodded.

"They could have assumed a new identity. It's possible. But why?"

"LeBlanc."

He frowned at her, bewildered.

"When I said his name—the first time—something happened to your face," she told him. "Your eyes changed."

"Since you're French, the name seems common to you, ordinary. But the language gives me trouble. Everything I hear in French, I automatically change into English."

"What's that got to do with—"

"Tell me what his last name means in English."

"What? LeBlanc? Well, *blanc* means—" She stopped abruptly, understanding.

"*Blanc* means white," he told her. "In your bedroom, when that man was dying, I thought he'd changed to speaking French, so I translated what he said. It made no sense of course. Because he wasn't speaking French. The man was giving me a name. He didn't say, 'the white.' He said 'LeBlanc.' "

"Verlaine and—"

"Now we know what those two mean. But who or what is Charon?"

38

Houston shivered on the busy Paris street. The sky was cloudy now, the light fading. A faint wind had started, chilly and damp. He pulled his sportcoat tight, fastening a button.

He was in a neighborhood of office buildings with boutiques at sidewalk level, some cafés. Late afternoon; the office workers had begun to swarm from buildings. Houston glanced across the street and saw a sign that told him LE MCDONALD'S, which he hoped was someone's notion of a joke.

He felt a drop of rain. And then another. Spots splashed darkly on the sidewalk. He felt rain on his nose, his hand, felt it soaking through his coat. If the storm was bad, he couldn't stand out in the open waiting for Simone. But if he ran for cover, she might drive by and not see him. He searched for some shelter where he would still be in sight. A canopy. A doorway.

We shouldn't have split up, he thought. We never should have separated.

To his left he saw a dark blue van half a block away. He squinted through the gusting rain to see the driver. He saw motion in the van and ran toward it, rain soaking his newly purchased shoes and socks.

Lightning flashed. Houston reached the van. He yanked open a door and scrambled in. "You had me worried," he said.

"One place didn't have a van for rent. Another place was closed." Simone wiped raindrops from his forehead.

"But you used your driver's license from America? You used your married name to rent the van?"

She nodded. "The police don't know about that name. They'll never trace this van to us."

He glanced behind her toward the rear compartment, "You've got the sleeping bags? The food?"

She nodded. "We're all set." She started the windshield wipers. Houston watched the cars ahead of them inch forward.

"Where, though?" she asked. "All we know is that they're in the Alps, a country home belonging to LeBlanc. We'll never find it."

Houston pulled a brochure from his pocket. "No. While you were at the rental agent, I was with a broker. I pretended I planned to buy some stock. Verlaine. The salesman gave me this." The brochure was an advertisement for Verlaine.

"Since LeBlanc claims he's in the Alps on business, I decided his country home is probably a Verlaine asset, not in his own name. That way he writes it off on taxes." He shrugged.

"So I called Verlaine. LeBlanc was gone, of course. His secretary said he was in the Alps on business. Naturally I didn't leave my name. But she was more specific than the servant at his home. He's at Verlaine's executive retreat."

"That doesn't help us."

"Yes, it does." He handed her the brochure. "Here." From a verdant valley, looking upward past thick stands of fir trees, they could see the turrets, parapets, and towers of a castle, ancient, gray against the snow on the mountains beyond it. Underneath the picture was a caption: Verlaine's training center, its executive retreat.

He told her, "There. That's where we'll find your father. And my own. And all our answers. In that castle in the Alps."

Simone steered toward a wider street, which led them out of Paris. Houston sensed her excitement.

"That's not all," he said. "Another coincidence. The broker said Verlaine began in nineteen fifty. That's the year the courthouse in your town was burned. The records were destroyed."

"You think it was arson?"

"To burn the death certificates. You said yourself, those soldiers must have taken new identities. They used the names of children who had died at St. Laurent. Your father found the names—no doubt from families who died in World War Two. That way no parents could object, 'You're not our sons. Our sons are dead.' Because those parents too were dead. Your father must have handled all the paperwork. He got the passports and the birth certificates, and then he burned the courthouse so no one could discover that those names belonged to children who were dead."

"God knows what else my father did for them."

"The main thing is that now we know why those men have French names."

"No. We know how," she said. "Not why. We still don't know what made them do it."

"Soon," he said. Grimly, he watched the storm.

39

"Ah, oui. Je le connais," *the young man at the gas pump* said, pleased that he could be of help. He wore mechanic's coveralls. The soft gray cloth showed evidence of recent cleaning, but the chest, the knees, and arms were stiff from oil and grit.

A service station near Grenoble. They had traveled through the night, exchanging places at the wheel from time to time, one napping while the other drove. Their only stops had been for fuel, take-out food, and a bathroom. They pursued a southeast line from Paris to Lyons and after that a road directly eastward toward the mountains. When the sun had risen, glinting far ahead of them, they'd guessed at first that they were seeing fleecy clouds along the skyline. Then they'd realized with shock that what they squinted at was bright snow on the mountaintops, a wondrous, soul-disturbing grandeur.

Throughout the morning they had stopped in fifteen different towns to ask about the photograph, but no one seemed to recognize the castle. As the mountains loomed closer, Houston—weary, cramped, and hungry—had at last become discouraged. He'd been certain that the castle was a landmark, well known to the people who lived near it. Now he doubted. "Hell, it's hopeless. I was wrong. We'll never find the place."

The young attendant's recognition of the photograph was like electric current.

"What?" he asked Simone. "He knows where to find it?"

The attendant's eyes were bright, delighted that he hadn't disappointed Houston. He grinned, gesturing beyond the

153

châteaux of Grenoble toward a faint dot in the tree line at the bottom of a far-off peak.

So near, so distant. Houston's mind began to trick him. His imagination magnified the dot. The tree line seemed to rush at him. To destroy the sickening illusion, he swung to face Simone. Her cheek was close beside him, thick hair hanging past her shoulders. Houston touched her, drawing fingers through her hair. "Just making sure you're beside me," Houston told her when she glanced at him, surprised. "For a second, I was doubtful. About everything."

"He's gone to get a road map. He can show us how to find the place."

"How far? It must be twenty-five kilometers."

"Or more. These mountains can fool you. They make the distance seem much shorter."

"That's exactly what I mean. If we can see the castle all the way from here, then how damned big is it? Up close, it must be huge."

They soon found out. The young man gave them directions and a map, and they drove eastward from Grenoble, higher into the mountains, crowding closely around him. As the van whined in low gear, they navigated switchback roads that angled up and down forbidding granite passes, fir trees thinning upward toward the gray rocks and the snow. The air got colder. They drove past cascading streams and swooping cliffs. They stared down toward the valley forests and what seemed a small-scale model of Grenoble in the distance. One wrong turn discouraged them, but they soon discovered their mistake, and finally they saw the castle they'd been searching for.

It lay above them, wedged between two mountains, black against a massive cliff, its spires rising high above the fir trees, its turrets and walkways clearly visible from this perspective.

The place was overwhelming, more impressive as they neared it. Houston studied the photograph, raising it so it blocked his vision through the windshield. On the page, the building seemed a childhood fantasy, a storybook depiction of a enchanted castle. He set the page down and saw the castle from the same perspective the photograph had shown, stunned by how much difference three dimensions made. The sheer expanse of what he stared at sent a shiver through him.

"It's like several buildings stacked on top of one another," he said. "It must have fifty rooms."

The road veered, skirting the estate. A private lane led toward a barred metal gate between high concrete walls.

"It's a fortress," Houston said.

Up close, the walls obscured his vision of the castle. Through the bars of the gate, he saw no guards beyond, no watch dogs, no activity at all, just wooded parkland and a gravel lane that curved until it disappeared. The grounds seemed rustic, innocent.

But among the sunbeams that filtered through the pastel forest, Houston knew there would be guards all right, security precautions, carefully prepared defenses.

As the van passed the massive gate, Houston had the strong sensation he was being studied from somewhere. Fighting to control the flutter in his stomach, he didn't turn to watch the gate recede behind him. Though he wanted to, he didn't scan the walls or try to locate what unnerved him. He peered forward, watching where the road climbed higher through the fir trees. He hoped that Simone and he seemed nothing more than unalarming tourists.

There had been a car ahead of them. He checked the sideview mirror on his door and saw another car approaching from behind. Granted, traffic wasn't frequent. All the same, there was enough that Houston didn't think this van would seem conspicuous. The wall came to a corner, merging with another wall that swept back from the road to reach a mountain. Houston turned to face Simone.

"As soon as we get up a little higher, find a place where we can stop."

She found a "scenic site" with a guardrail and a gravel parking surface off the road. There were picnic tables, benches, and a row of pay telescopes.

"Aim the back end of the van so it's pointed toward the castle," he told her, squinting toward the dizzy view of the majestic valley spread below them. "I'm sure they watch the traffic on this road," he went on. "They'll get suspicious if we stay too long. And while we're here, we have to seem like tourists. Get out, and go over to those telescopes. But keep your back turned to the castle. Act as if your single interest is the view toward the valley."

"Aren't you coming?"

"Not just yet."

"But if they watch the traffic on the road, they'll know there are two of us inside the van. They'll be suspicious if we don't both step out."

"I need five minutes."

Frowning, she opened her door and crossed the gravel toward the guardrail and the telescopes. The car that had been following them pulled up behind her. Houston tensed. But then he saw a man, a woman, and three children tumble out. Excitedly they scrambled near Simone, delighted by the vista. Good, he thought. They give her cover. With that car behind her, someone watching from the castle doesn't have an unobstructed view.

He crawled back to the rear compartment of the van and grabbed the binoculars he'd bought in Grenoble. Their eight-power lenses were the largest he could use without a tripod to control the tremors of his hands. He stayed back from the window to hide himself and, peering through the lenses, concentrated on the castle, which he judged to be a thousand meters away.

He scanned the edifice, a few small buildings near it, then the parkland and the wall enclosing the estate. At times, the image was so clear he felt he could almost touch the stone blocks of the castle or the smooth blue glinting surface of a Porsche that was parked beside a small peaked building—a carriage house or servants' quarters. Or a guardhouse.

Houston grabbed the picnic basket, pulled open the side door of the van and got out, hidden by the van from anyone who would be watching from the castle. He walked into view, showing his back and in particular the picnic basket that he held.

"Simone."

She stepped back from the telescope, as if reluctant to be leaving the perspective of the valley, and turned sideways toward a table. As she sat, the van was once again a barrier between the castle and themselves.

"It worked?" she said.

"I found out what we need to know."

Their breakfast had been hot croissants and coffee. They'd skipped lunch. His hunger was insistent as he reached inside the basket. Sausage, cheese, a strong red wine. He chewed and swallowed, mouth hot from the sausage.

"Guards with rifles," he said.

She stiffened.

"Five of them. Two German shepherds roaming freely. I assume there are more. The towers are equipped with searchlights." Houston heard the strangled noise in her throat. "The walls enclosing the estate hold television cameras. Even if we figured how to climb the walls and not be seen, we'd never get beyond the barbed wire at the top. Oh, we could cut the wire, but I'm guessing it's electrified, and once the current's interrupted, I'm assuming that alarms are triggered in the castle."

"Then it really is a fortress. There's no way to get inside."

He wiped his mouth, reluctant to suggest what he was thinking. "Maybe."

"Maybe nothing. It's impossible."

"No. Only difficult." He put the food and wine back in the basket.

"How?" she said.

He heard a door close, turned, and saw the man, woman, and their children get into their car. The engine started.

"We've stayed here long enough," he said. "When they pull out, we ought to go too. The view is great but not enough to make us hang around all day." He stood.

"I asked you how."

"We go in from behind the castle. From above it. No, don't turn around to look."

She stopped herself. "The back's a cliff! No, never mind a cliff! The sheer wall of a mountain!"

"So they won't expect visitors from there. They'll figure it's too dangerous."

"They'd be right! If you expect me to—"

"Just think about it. In the meantime, we've got errands."

She eyed him suspiciously.

"Equipment. From Grenoble."

40

"But I'm afraid of heights!" Simone said.

They struggled up the high-pitched rocky slope. Above, a ridge of fir trees beckoned. Houston's knapsack weighed against him, cutting at his shoulders. He was sweating, eyebrows scrunched together from his effort. Knees ached. Thighs objected. Underneath his knapsack, his thick shirt and sweater clung against his back, their wetness chilling him although his face felt feverish.

"Then don't look back," he answered.

Behind and below them, a maze of wooded draws and ridges fell abruptly toward the chasm of the valley. From this distance, he could not see where they'd left the van beside a hidden boarded-up chalet a hundred meters off the road. Nor could he see the disused weed-grown lane that led up to the building. He could see the main road through the mountains, though, a ribbon from this height, a random slender blackness on which isolated dots of traffic inched like insects.

"Don't look back?" she told him. "Don't look back? The shock would kill me. At the least, I'd wet my pants."

He had to laugh, although he didn't want to. If he lost his concentration, he would make mistakes, and while the slope was not a sheer drop, it was steep enough so that if he fell he'd hurt himself. Here, even minor injuries were deadly. Sprains and bruises would restrict his movements, causing other accidents until . . .

"You think that's funny?"

"No," he said. "It isn't. None of this is funny."

"Anyway, I don't mean now. If I get dizzy, there are rocks I can grab. But I mean later, with the ropes. I don't think I can do it."

He climbed toward her, staying to the right, so that if she dislodged a rock it would not hit him. "You're in shape. You jog. You used to do gymnastics."

"Physically I don't have any doubts. In principle I know I can use the ropes. But I'm not trained for them."

"I'll teach you."

"In one day?"

He didn't answer. To avoid the truth, he passed her, climbing higher.

"Even when I'm on a plane," she said "I can't look out the window. I get sick." Her voice was strained. He heard her boot soles scrape the rocks. "Besides, the sun is almost gone."

He squinted up. The sun was red and swollen, dipping low behind the mountains. "That can help," he said.

"I don't know how."

"Well, in the dark you won't see what's below you."

His hand gripped a rock. He braced a book on an outcrop of stone and heaved himself to the top. Relief spread through his muscles. Sweat dripped off his face. He quickly turned. Simone climbed near him. Offering his hand, he helped her up, and they peered past a narrow Alpine meadow toward a murky wall of fir trees and the craggy cliffs that soared beyond them.

Houston took no time to savor what he saw. The sun was lower. Hurriedly he left the slope's edge to prevent his silhouette being seen from below. Almost to the fir trees, standing on the soft grass of the meadow, he slipped off his knapsack, stretched, and rubbed his aching shoulders. Then he fumbled in the knapsack and pulled out a canteen and two chocolate bars. The bars were mushy from the heat of his exertion, but he peeled the wrappers and gave one bar to Simone and chewed on the other. His energy was so depleted that he couldn't taste the sweetness, but the bar was gone before he realized how fiercely he'd attacked it. He twisted off the cap of the canteen and swallowed warm metallic water.

Not too much, though. He'd get cramps.

Simone wiped chocolate from her mouth. "And now we rest, I hope."

"No, now we make sure we're not lost."

He pulled a map and compass from the knapsack. He spread the map on the grass and angled it so that the contour lines of slopes and ridges matched the terrain around them.

"Through these trees"—he pointed—"we'll reach another slope. Don't look like that. We're finished climbing. We head left along the base and pass two draws along the right. We reach a third draw—on the left. It takes us down. We'll come out on the cliff behind the castle."

"And how high is it?"

He checked the compass.

"Pete, the cliff. How high?"

"Don't ask."

"You really know what you're doing?"

"I told you the other day, to write a book I have to research special subjects. If there's shooting in my novels, I have to learn about the guns. I took a weapons course. In my second book, I had a hero who was chased up through some mountains. He knew all about survival. He could climb and use ropes and—well, I didn't have a clue about that stuff. I had to learn it so that I could be convincing. I can't make you any expert. But I'll keep you out of trouble."

Houston closed the map. He shoved the compass in his

pocket. "Let's get moving while we've still got light. I want to teach you how to use the ropes."

41

He stood behind her, watching her hold the rope. "That's good. Now keep your left arm straight ahead of you. No, not so high. Like this."

He stepped close, putting his arms around her, reaching in front to guide her hand.

The movement was instinctive. He didn't plan for what happened. Grief for Jan, combined with fear, had pushed the thought of sex completely from his mind. But as he held Simone, as he felt her body, he found he was suddenly kissing her. The smooth skin on her neck. The sweet smell of her hair. With a moan, she turned and embraced him. His impulse startled him. He tried to stop, to back away. She held him more tightly, kissed him again. As her tongue probed past his lips, he felt a flame surge through his body. Nothing mattered but his need.

He sank to the ground with her. He fumbled at her shirt. He touched her rising breasts. He kissed them, kissed her stomach. He was lost, his passion urgent, mindless. Everything around him disappeared—the sky, the air, the trees, the ground. Everything except Simone. He entered her, crying in total surrender. Gently, then with fury, slowly, deeply, quickly. Each instant became eternal. Smoothly *No! Yes!* His soul exploded, left his body, soaring.

She thrust upward, higher, tensing, shuddering. "Oooohhhh!"

The cool air made him conscious of the sweat on his back. He lay beside her holding her tightly, suddenly thinking of Jan.

"I'm not her rival," Simone said.

"I can't help it."

"You feel guilty? We did nothing shameful."

"Not because of this."

"Then why?"

"Because she's dead, but I'm alive. I shouldn't *feel* alive. It isn't right."

Simone gently touched his lips.

42

*In the darkness, with Simone beside him in his arms, he wak-*ened to a night bird's song. He gazed at the starry sky, the sickle moon on the horizon. Had he slept too long? How late was it? He checked his watch. The glowing dial showed him thirteen minutes after ten, and slumping back, reluctant to disturb Simone, he took advantage of these last few leisured moments. In the shelter of the boulders, near the soothing shadows of the forest, the fir trees giving off a pleasant resin scent, he felt the needle-matted earth beneath him and remembered the sweet love Simone and he had made before they slept.

He nudged her gently. Sleepily she looked at him. She smiled and put her hand against his cheek. "It's time," he said.

She nodded.

Something snapped among the trees. She sat up alarmed, her face tense toward the darkness.

"Just an animal," he said.

"How can you be sure?"

"The sounds are normal. Someone sneaking through those

trees, no matter how much care he took, would break more than one branch.''

It was a lie. A skillful hunter, taking time, could stalk his quarry silently in darkness. But he hoped to reassure her. More, if they had been discovered, there was nothing they could do about it. Someone with a sniperscope could see them in the dark, and they'd have no chance to defend themselves. He did have Henri's revolver and ten bullets he had taken from the body. But the gun was useless if he didn't have a target. Two quick, well-placed shots could kill them right now.

He couldn't let that worry him. There wasn't anything that he could do about it.

''We were cautious, and we did our best. That has to be enough. We have to hope.'' He held her tightly. Then he told himself he had to move, to face what he intended.

They crawled from the trees toward the cliff's edge. Houston tied a nylon sling around a tree and snapped a metal clip to it. He hooked the middle of his rope to the clip and knotted the rope's free ends.

''Why do it that way?'' Simone asked. ''Why not simply tie the rope around the tree?''

''Because when we get down there, we can't leave the rope in sight. Oh, sure, at night it can't be seen. But what if we're still down there in the morning? Someone's sure to see it. I'll untie the knotted ends. All I have to do is pull the one side of the rope. The other side will slip free from the clip and fall down toward me. There's no sign of us.''

''If the rope was looped around a tree, though, it might snag against the bark.''

He grinned, pretending bravado. ''We'd never get it down. You learn damn quickly.'' What he didn't say was that the friction of the rope against the tree might cause the rope to snap while they were climbing. The clip was smoother, safer.

Houston turned to face the cliff again. His heart raced as he peered down the abyss toward bright lights in the castle. He was troubled by the sickle moon behind him, by its glow and by the twinkling of the stars. But he was confident that no one below would see them. A faint cool wind had started. It might tug at them as they went down. He'd shown Simone what she should do, but she'd been awkward, nervous. Now he worried for her, hoping that as they climbed down together he'd be able to help her. He put on his leather gloves.

Her dark eyes burned. He sensed her terror. "Just stay close to me," he said. He threw the rope out from the cliff and listened to its hiss as it fell through the dark. It flopped against the rock face. He turned quickly toward the other rope.

Her hand on his shoulder stopped him. Had she heard another sound? Had something warned her? He spun urgently, on guard—and saw the sorrow in her eyes.

"Don't do it."

"What?"

"The other rope. Don't bother with it. I can't climb down there. I'm damn near paralyzed already. I'll stay here. I'll wait till you come back."

"Alone? But there's no food or shelter."

"Chocolate bars, two sandwiches. I'll make them last. The sky is clear. I doubt there'll be a storm."

"But you don't know for sure. If it starts snowing. Worse, if someone finds you . . ."

"Pete, I won't climb down that rope! I can't! I'm scared! Why won't you listen to me?"

He felt more than heard her desperation. "Okay," he told her. "We can talk about it."

"No." Her voice was tortured.

Houston held his breath, debating with himself. "All right." he told her softly.

"Pete, I'm sorry."

"Don't apologize. I know you'd do it if you could."

"You're not angry?"

"How can I be angry?"

Houston grinned. She sagged against him. But he felt the trembling in her shoulders—and understood how close they had come to absolute disaster.

"Hey, for all we know, I'll do it easier alone," he said.

"Just wait for me. If I'm not back by tomorrow night, then go down to the van."

"And then what? If you're hurt or if they've—"

"Make the cops come out here. Make them search for me."

"I'm frightened that I'll lose you. Don't go down there. Come with me. We'll reach the van. We'll run and—"

"No," he told her.

They stared at each other.

"We made love," he said. "I don't regret it. But it doesn't change a thing. It only complicates. My wife is dead, and I won't turn my back on what she meant to me. I'm going to find the man who killed her."

"And find your father. And my own."

"And save him. Save ourselves. We can't keep running."

She shrugged and smiled. "The answer I expected. Go." Her voice was bleak. "Before I try to stop you."

Houston kissed her. He stepped back from her and braced himself, then turned to face the cliff. The castle seemed distorted down there, far away yet close. Its lights were misted, and its towers had a ghostly haze. He felt as if he watched it from a former century.

He turned again and studied Simone's face for what was possibly the final time, memorizing it. His throat ached. With the double rope between his legs, he reached behind him, brought the rope around his right leg, looped it around his chest, and let it hang down his left shoulder. With his left hand clutching the part of the rope ahead of him, he dropped his right hand backward, gripping the portion of the rope that dangled down the cliff. The rope, thus wound around him, was supported by his right leg and his back. He said a prayer. He leaned down from the cliff top. Blood roared in his head. He felt the rope pinch where his leg and back supported it.

And slowly he started walking backward, downward.

165

43

Everything was off its center. Now the stars were not above him. Rather, they were straight ahead of him. The castle wasn't down from him; it was behind him. The illusion was that he walked backward on a horizontal surface. But the biting pressure of the rope against his leg and back, in tandem with the pressure in his stomach, contradicted that illusion. These sensations emphasized that he was moving on a vertical, instead of horizontal, plane. The different signals he was getting, incompatible with one another, made him nauseated. Ahead and yet above, Simone peered toward him from the cliff's edge. But her worried face got smaller as he played the rope out. Then she disappeared in darkness, and he saw only the murky rocks before him, then the speckled sky beyond.

He had to keep his knees straight while he bent his body forward from the hips. Otherwise his legs would rise above his head, and he would fall.

His motions were considered: slow and steady. He'd seen movies in which climbers swooped down cliffs, rebounding off the rocks and dropping twenty feet at once. But drops of twenty feet put too much strain on the rope and on its mooring. There was little chance of compensating for mistakes. And even if he had been tempted to be more aggressive he would not have tried it in the darkness; he could not see what was underneath him. Slow and steady, Houston told himself. Take care to do this right.

Despite his heavy gloves, he felt the friction of the rope. Heat soaked toward his hands. He inched the rope up, and the pressure burned his shoulder, chest, and leg. His stomach fluttered. He breathed quickly, gasping to stay calm.

His right hand touched the knot that held the two ends of the doubled rope. It warned him that he'd have to stop, to find a ledge, a place to stand. If he kept sliding downward, he'd run out of rope and fall.

His right hand pinched the rope against his side to stop him from descending any farther. He pressed waffle soles against the rock face, searching the craggy surface for a foothold. When he didn't find what he was groping for, he almost panicked. He had dreaded this. He'd been determined not to think about the hazards. If he didn't find a place to rest, he wouldn't have a chance to pull the rope down, anchor it once more, and then continue his descent. He'd be forced to climb back up or be stranded.

Houston dangled. The rope cut fiercely at his leg and chest, his shoulder and his back. His boots scrabbled at the cliff face; his heart thundered in his chest. He reached his boots down, testing. He leaned to the right, and then the left.

And Houston found it—a slight outcrop, wide enough for him to stand on. He swung himself toward it, reached with his left hand, gripped a jagged piece of rock, and pulled himself upright. He rested on the outcrop, gulping, sweat burning his eyes. He wiped his sleeve across his forehead; then he realized his arms were shaking. And his legs.

Don't think about it, Houston told himself. Don't think about the drop below you. Just be thankful you can't see it in the dark.

He clutched the rope with one hand while he slipped his knapsack from his shoulders. He took out a piton and a hammer, felt along the rock face, and found a solid crack. He wedged the piton in the crack, spreading a cloth across it to muffle sound. He hammered at it, wincing from the metallic noise the piton made despite the cloth. A dog barked from below him, near the castle.

He stiffened. The dog stopped barking. All the same, Houston waited, glancing through the darkness toward the castle. But he saw no guards, no sign of an alarm. The wind dried his forehead. He relaxed. He tested the piton, satisfied it would hold.

He put the hammer and the cloth inside the knapsack, pulled out a metal clip, snapped it through the hole inside the piton, and at last took off his gloves. With his fingers bare, he struggled with the knot that held the two ends of the doubled rope. His fingers shook. The knot refused to budge. He tried again, and as his breath burned in his throat, he felt the knot pull loose. The ends were free.

He was balanced on the outcrop, unsupported. He pulled on one side of the rope and watched the other side snake upward, imagining how the rope slid past Simone, then through the clip attached to the sling around the tree. Abruptly the rope had no weight; it slipped from the clip up there and streamed down the cliff. He clutched the end he held with all his might, felt the rope hiss past him. Then it jerked him forward, and he nearly lost his balance. Scrambling, he leaned back to compensate, bracing his boots against the outcrop. He pulled the rope up, tied its ends again, and hooked it through the clip inside the piton. All he had to do was put his gloves on, drop the rope, and he was ready to continue.

He pushed off, complacent; he didn't think to keep his knees straight. His legs jerked up, and he was upside down, dangling breathless from the rope that now constricted him. Dark turned to red, blood rushing to his brain. The pressure was like being under water. Houston's eyes began to bulge. His swollen cheeks sagged downward toward his forehead. Blood roared in his skull. The wind was stronger, scraping Houston's back against the cliff. His head cracked on a rock, and his hands went weak. He nearly dropped the rope. No! If he lost more balance, if his feet flipped outward, he'd be so entangled in the rope that he might hang himself. He twisted, scratching the side of the cliff with his boot soles, straining at the rope to pull his chest up even with his feet. He fought to bring his boots down as he raised himself, but now the pressure of the blood inside his brain had nearly rendered him unconscious. Houston gasped for air as if he were drowning. His arms were numb, their circulation cut off by the rope. Adrenaline insisted, burning. Fear created strength. He strained and heaved and scraped and pulled, and all at once the pressure in his brain diminished. He could breathe again. His cheeks no longer pressed down toward his eyes. His knees were straight, his body horizontal to the cliff. He leaned up and was safe again.

But he kept shaking, couldn't stop the spasms in his arms, his legs.

44

Thirty minutes later, exhausted, Houston finally touched bottom and collapsed inside the compound. Inside! He glanced behind him toward the fir trees. They were sighing in the wind. The air was colder. He pulled off his shredded gloves. His hands were blistered, bloody. With his swollen fingers he released the knot, tugged on the rope, and stumbled back. The rope hissed down, flopping heavily beside him. He took off his knapsack, packed the gloves and rope, withdrew the revolver, and slumped wearily against the stump of a tree. The revolver gave him confidence. Its smooth hard weight assured him. He caressed it.

He realized that he trembled more from fear than from exertion; he knew he had to move. It was almost midnight. There was too much to be done. He couldn't waste time resting, couldn't give himself a chance to reconsider.

He stood painfully and crammed his knapsack in a hole beneath the stump, covering it with rocks and fallen fir-tree needles. He rubbed dirt across his face to help his skin blend with the shadows. Nervously he started through the forest, boot soles silent on the spongy earth. He squinted forward through the spreading branches and saw the outline of the castle, saw the light-filled casement windows.

Fear was chilling. He had no thought beyond his plan to reach the castle. He would have to watch for guards and dogs, but if he reached the walls, then he could scale the ropelike vines that grew upon them. At the top, he could maneuver through the complex intersecting walkways to scout any portion of the castle. Errol Flynn, he thought. Sure, Douglas Fairbanks. What the hell is wrong with you? These people want to kill you.

He stood at the forest's edge, confronted by the lawn that he would have to cross to reach the inner wall of the castle. A spotlight glared down from the tower at each corner, but no sentries manned them, and the beam of one light did not extend to meet the other's beam. There was a shadowed section in the middle. Houston weighed the risk. He watched for dogs. He saw none—saw no guards.

He bolted toward a waist-high hedge that formed a square within which outdoor furniture had been arranged on landscape stones. He scurried past the hedge, then paused to catch his breath, to scan the grounds, before he hurried forward once again. His chest was pounding; he hunched beside the steps of a gazebo, peering through its trellis toward the shadow on the lawn between the searchlight beams. Despite the wind, the night was silent. He heard the shrill breath from his mouth. From this vantage, at the castle's rear, he saw the stables to his left, a seven-door garage, the bleak stone of the guardhouse.

Before he realized what he was doing, he had started running. Now or never! No guard here to see him. No dog close to scent him. In a minute, everything could change. For all he knew, the guards would soon emerge around a corner, checking this side, then continuing toward all the others in a constant, thorough pattern. Throat tight, Houston forced himself forward. His eyes misted from his effort. Searchlights threatened him on either side; he skirted their illumination. Frenzied, he rushed to the wall, and even as he glanced both ways to guarantee he'd not been seen, he shoved the revolver in his belt, then grabbed the thick vines on the wall. Their bark was dry, but their roots were solid, so enmeshed that they held firm. He wedged a boot among them, clawed up, wedged another boot, and was climbing. Half a minute later he was almost to the top.

Sounds below made him stop: gruff muttered voices and the click of metal. Panic made him hang there, frozen. Peering down, he saw two guards at the base of the wall. One lit a cigarette, and in a lighter's glow, Pete saw the other man unsling a rifle. Then he saw the German shepherd, and his breathing stopped.

Although the guards were underneath him, they were obviously not aware of him. The dog, though. That damn dog was sniffing at the grass, the wall, the vines. It tensed, whining, turning toward the open lawn and the intrusive scent of a stranger. No! Houston thought, and stared up at the short space he had yet to climb. He heard the men below him talking.

The vines he clutched were separating from the wall. He had to move, or else in seconds he would slip. He'd land on the guards. The dog would slash his throat. He raised a hand and found a better grip. The vines groaned. Now the dog was barking. Good. Its sounds obscured his own. He feared it was barking up at him but didn't dare to look down for confirmation. He just kept climbing—one hand, then the other—tensing for the bullet that would burst through his back and rupture his chest.

His trembling hand touched open air. The top! He'd reached the top! He slung his arm across the edge and squirmed down on a parapet.

He listened to the dog. A guard spoke sharply, and the barking stopped. He waited. Cautiously he raised his head to peer back down. The guards were walking, led by the dog. They crossed the shadowed space between the searchlights toward the steps of the gazebo. There the two men hesitated, frowned at the dog, and yanked its leash. The dog resisted. They yanked harder and continued their patrol.

Houston licked his cracked, cold lips. Relief that he had not been seen was followed by depression, the fatiguing aftermath of fear. Adrenaline stopped pulsing. He felt weak, lethargic.

High on the walkway, he crouched in darkness. Here, in ancient times, the shielded archers of the castle had faced outward toward the open ground below him, aiming crossbows toward intruders. There were notches in the parapet through which the soldiers would have shot their arrows.

Wind whistled past the black shape of the tower to his right. No guard stepped from its solid shadows to confront him. Nonetheless he drew the revolver from his belt, smelling the gun oil as he flicked off the safety catch. He gazed down at the courtyard in the middle of the castle walls. Deserted, it was bright from spotlights. Straight across from Houston, far below, a massive wooden barrier sealed off the entrance to the courtyard.

He crept to the walkway's edge and peered below him toward another walkway jutting out and, then below it, yet another walkway jutting farther out until like monstrous steps they reached the bottom. They were wide enough for Houston to assume that, in addition to providing access to the parapet, they were also the roofs of different levels in the castle.

But despite their semblance of order, Houston had the sense of labyrinths and mazes. Inside, he could wander aimlessly, he knew, losing direction until finally he was discovered.

No, don't think like that. Get moving.

Houston scurried soundlessly to the tower and found chiseled stairs. He scanned the corniced skyline of the castle, looking warily at what from this new angle was an overwhelming grandeur. Blocks of stone were taller than himself. Through canopied windows he saw rooms three times normal height. Most rooms were dark. The few that blazed with light from chandeliers and fireplaces drew his interest, made him study them.

These rooms were on the bottom level to his right, from where he crept along a lower walkway. Suddenly he stopped. Within the far right wall, beyond a huge, arched window—one of few without stained glass—he saw a man gesturing angrily, evidently berating someone unseen. Close to sixty, in a navy jacket, light-blue turtleneck, and dark-gray slacks, the man had short, neat sandy hair, a stern-eyed handsome face. But Houston couldn't see who else was in the room. He changed position, sprawling flat on stone, and now he saw much farther into the room.

He saw two other men, but not their faces. One wore a brown suit and a vest, the other slacks and a white shirt, its three top buttons open, revealing chest hair and a medallion dangling from a glinting chain.

These men were stiff, intense. With forceful movements, one man answered what the first man had been saying. Houston wished that he could hear. He crawled a little closer. And reflexively inhaled. Because from this new angle, seeing other portions of the room, he had a clear view of Monsard. The image sickened him.

The old man cowered in a deeply cushioned high-backed chair. He looked pathetic, shrunken, frightened—older than when Houston had last seen him. There were bruises on his face. His clothes were rumpled, bloody.

They had beaten him. That's something else they'll pay for! Houston thought. His anger seethed within him. He clutched the revolver harder, squeezing it with fury, I'll—!

He suddenly was rigid. In the room, two guards appeared; they flanked Monsard and jerked him to his feet. Monsard protested, face contorted by his fear.

From Houston's vantage on the walkway, he felt helpless. Rage was useless. He saw the guards drag Monsard backward, saw them leave the room.

He had to get inside—to save Monsard, to take him to Simone . . . and learn some answers, make the old man tell him what the hell was going on!

He trembled with the need for action. Even as he chose an entrance at the far end of the walkway, he imagined the stairs down which he'd hurry to subdue the guards. He didn't know how he would manage. All he knew was that he had to.

He was stopped before he entered. Below him, to his right, a door banged open. He heard muffled angry orders, heavy bootsteps, and a dragging, scraping sound, a whimpering.

He peered below the walkway's edge. The spotlights glared. He saw the two guards drag Monsard across the courtyard. They were huge, the old man frail between them, terrified, resisting. Houston strained to see which door they'd use. He'd follow. He would—

Blinding, blazing light shot out from all directions. Countless searchbeams intersected onto him. The night was day. The walkway was a stage, and he was the attraction. He felt totally exposed, completely naked in the piercing brilliance. He couldn't see. He raised his hands to shield his eyes. His body stiffened. Sphincter muscles gripped. On either side of him, guards scurried forward, rifles aimed, their faces grim. Above him, other guards appeared.

As Houston crouched defenseless, paralyzed in the sudden glare, a smooth, deep, resonant man's voice boomed from the speakers in the towers all around him.

"Welcome, Mr. Houston. We expected you."

Part 5

45

He dove.

He didn't plan to die or take time to calculate his chances or decide that any risk was worth the price of being captured. As the spotlights blazed on him, as his burning eyes strained through the brilliance toward the rifles pointed at him, he reacted with pure reflex.

He'd been facing toward his right. He pivoted toward the walkway's edge—in desperation plunged. The wind rushed past his cheeks. His stomach shifted. The cobbled courtyard zoomed to meet him; Houston aimed for one of the canopies he'd seen.

He struck the dark brown canvas with his shoulder, landing with bone-jarring suddenness. His breath exploded from him, He rebounded, struck the canopy again, and tumbled down its slope, his hands grotesquely clawing for a grip. His feet slid off the edge. He clutched the canvas border, hampered by the revolver in his hand. His legs kicked at air, and he lost his hold. He landed with a stunning wallop on the cobblestones.

He felt such pain his vision failed him. Clumsily, he forced his arms and legs to work. With sluggish, uncoordinated movements, he crawled to his knees. As he swayed in stupefaction to the rhythm of the dizziness inside his head, his vision cleared enough for him to see two guards in the courtyard. They let go of Monsard and charged toward him, faces pale above the barrels of their handguns. In his stupor, Houston thought their bootsteps sounded like thunder.

Though his body swayed, his arms refused to budge. His revolver seemed enormous. He lifted it with all his strength, and slowly it responded, as if by tomorrow he would raise it all the way. He tried to sight it, then remembered he hadn't cocked it. He groaned. The first guard reached him. Houston watched, completely helpless, as the guard's boot kicked at him with eye-blink speed, the steel toe battering his wrist. But Houston was already in so much pain that he barely felt the blow. He only felt his arm shift and his fingers loosen. Then he watched, perversely fascinated, as the revolver left his fingers, swerving through the air, cracking on the cobblestones.

As he clutched his wrist, he heard the scurry of more guards. They scrambled down the steps to reach him. Men shouted, breathing hoarsely, slings on rifles rattling. As they rushed at him, Houston felt the air constrict around him from the pressure of their bodies. Then he heard the latch snap on a huge door beneath the canopy directly facing him. The door swung open, banging against a wall inside.

His vision wavered; he didn't have strength to raise his eyes. He squinted toward the cobblestones at the bottom of the door and saw the gleaming black of patent leather, of expensive evening shoes step toward him. Then the shoes stopped, so near that, if he had wanted to, he could have touched them.

Houston slowly raised his eyes. Black formal trousers, a black dinner jacket, a black dinner tie. The man was almost sixty—tall and trim and handsome, full-lipped, with dark blazing eyes, strong cheeks, dark hair combed straight back from his sculptured forehead, skin so tanned that it was bronze. Pete blinked in awe.

"A foolish gesture, Mr. Houston," the man said.

"What would *you* have done?" Houston's angry words were muffled, as if spoken through cotton batting.

A moment's thought. A shrugging compliment, the eyes amused. "The same."

Now Houston recognized the voice. He'd heard it from the speakers in the towers just before he dove.

"Foolish all the same, You're hurt?" the man continued.

Houston didn't answer.

"You're late," the man explained. "We expected you sooner."

"You expected me?"

"Of course. But please, you can't continue kneeling. Help him up."

Two guards jerked Houston to his feet. He wavered.

"Hold him." The man considered him. "Yes. Surely you don't think you could have found this place without my help."

"I managed."

"Please. You've shown remarkable ability. But on occasion you've been helped. The calls you made to Paris, London, and New York, for instance. I began to doubt they'd be successful. I suspected you realized how easy I'd made things for you. All the little hints and clues you'd been given."

"I was led here? Those three people knew why I was calling?"

"Not exactly. But they had instructions. Though they didn't know the purpose, they did what was necessary."

"*Why?*"

"Because you hide too well. You run too quickly. I decided I'd never find you, so I changed the game. I felt it was easier if you instead found me. And as you see, I was right." He paused, smiling.

Houston raged, lunging at the man to punch the smirk off his face.

The guards yanked his arms behind his back.

The man seemed oblivious of the attempt. "I'd hoped you'd bring a guest. The invitation was for both of you. But I don't see Simone."

Houston shook. He sensed Monsard nearby, pushing through the guards.

"Simone?" the old man asked him, worried. "Is she with you?"

"I'm not foolish."

"Close perhaps?" the man in evening clothes asked.

"Hardly. But she knows I'm here, and if I don't return, she'll go to the police."

The man chuckled. "Really?"

Houston blurted, "Who the hell—Are you my father?"

But the man chuckled louder. "Dear me, Mr. Houston, no. Though I believe you've heard of me. Pierre de St. Laurent."

46

The man's eyes twinkled. Houston shuddered. After his long search, at last he'd been successful. But he felt no triumph, no satisfaction. He was sickened.

Something suddenly occurred to him. He swung to face Monsard. His scalp prickled. "You spoke English?"

"Qu'est-ce que c'est?"

"Just now. You asked if she was with me. *You spoke English.*"

But the old man raised his eyebrows, shrugging in confusion. *"Je ne comprends pas."*

"You're lying!"

The old man frowned, bewildered. Helplessly he glanced at St. Laurent.

But St. Laurent was more amused. "Jacques, it seems he found you out."

Monsard went rigid. Slowly he nodded. "Yes, it's true," he said.

"Simone?"

"She doesn't know. I don't speak English in the village. Years ago—the war was over—circumstances made me learn it."

"But why hide it?"

"To avoid attention. To remain a simple small-town Frenchman. Also, while Simone interpreted my conversations with you, I had time to think. Your difficulty with the language helped me to confuse you."

"I was misled from the start?"

The old man nodded.

Houston watched the old man's face. He realized another trick, another lie. "Your bruises." Monsard touched his swollen face. "They're phony. They're just makeup. You weren't beaten." In the spotlights, Houston saw how obvious the makeup was.

"Theatrical, I grant you, but effective," St. Laurent said. "Were you entertained? We lit the room as brightly as we could. The actors placed themselves conveniently so you'd see them through the window. We experimented with the makeup. If it wasn't thick, you never could have seen it from the walkway."

"I don't understand."

"Enticement. After all, we couldn't let you wander around the castle. If we'd sprung our trap too soon, you might have escaped. But this way, when we had you where we wanted you . . ." His one hand snared the other.

"Then you're not in danger?" Houston asked Monsard.

The old man shook his head.

"In strong disfavor," St. Laurent explained. "But for the moment, not in danger. He was foolish to have phoned us, to have run here with absurd demands about his daughter. As I thought about the problem, though, I realized he'd unwittingly done us a service. You'd escaped us at the hunting lodge. We didn't know where you were hiding. But your character's consistent. You're determined. I was sure you'd keep hunting us just as we kept hunting you. The phone calls he made. I was sure they'd eventually bring you to us."

"But you could have had me killed just now. Why capture me instead?"

"Because I need you. And Simone. I do wish you'd tell me where she is."

"Need us? As soon as you get both of us, we're finished."

"Such suspicion." St. Laurent clicked his tongue. "You must be tired. You need rest, food."

"What?"

St. Laurent passed Houston. The guards pushed Houston, forcing him to follow. Floodlights glistened off the cobblestones. Houston watched St. Laurent enter another huge door; next to it he saw the brilliant window he had studied from the walkway—the enormous fireplace, the chandelier, the paneling, the massive furniture.

He was shoved along; events controlled him. Through the door and down an arched stone corridor. The chill of night was replaced by dampness. To the left another corridor, but here the walls were wooden, painted. Then a complex hand-carved door, its detail fine. St. Laurent paused, glancing back at Houston, eyebrows raised ironically. He turned the doorknob.

Guided by the guards, Houston faced the opening and hesitantly entered. Nervous, stiff, in pain, he heard Monsard come in behind him. Then, as if on cue, one guard stepped out. The other shut the door. and snapped back to attention, weapon ready.

Houston gazed with wonder at the room—its warmth, its glow, its spendor. If there hadn't been electric lights, he would have sworn he'd tumbled through a hole in time. The suit of armor in one corner, the heraldic crest above the mantel, the crossed swords against one wall. *The Song of Roland*. Tristan, Lancelot, and Eleanor of Aquitaine. The splendor of medieval France.

He lost his breath.

But then his gaze reached St. Laurent, who smiled disarmingly at him. "Some coffee?" St. Laurent said. "A cordial? Brandy?"

Houston stopped himself from gaping, his concentration directed toward three men who stood beside a polished table in the far corner of the room. One man he'd seen completely from the walkway—close to sixty, sandy-haired, distinguished, in a light blue turtleneck and navy blazer. But the other two had been partially hidden. Now Houston saw that the man who wore the brown suit and the vest was close to sixty also—thin-haired, deep-eyed, gaunt, and haggard. Next to him, the man who wore the open-buttoned shirt with the medallion dangling on his chest was younger, maybe thirty, fierce-eyed, cruel-lipped, insolently handsome.

"But I've forgotten my manners," St. Laurent told Houston. "Let me introduce ourselves. You know me as François LeBlanc, of course. And these three gentlemen are Jules Fontaine from London . . ."

Fontaine (in the turtleneck and blazer) raised a half-full brandy snifter in salute.

"From New York, Paul Dassin . . ."

The haggard man nodded stiffly.

"His son, Charles," St. Laurent said.

White shirt and medallion. Absolutely no reaction. Haughty and aloof.

"But as you know, we once had other names."

"My father," Houston said, his voice so strong his muscles cramped his neck. They bulged like strands of swollen leather. "Which of you?" He glared from St. Laurent to them. "Who is it?"

Jules Fontaine? The man peered past his brandy snifter.

Paul Dassin? The man was rigid.

"Tell me!"

"I am," Paul Dassin told Houston, his eyes deep, darkly circled, voice reluctant, almost whispering. He cleared his throat as if he choked.

Houston didn't know he'd moved until he took three steps. Then, overwhelmed, he stopped and stared. He concentrated, studying. Was this pale, sickly man the ghost of all his boyhood fantasies? Was this the man whom he had once admired in his dreams and now had learned to hate? A haggard, thin, frail man inviting pity more than anger? Delicate, pathetic?

As his vision failed, his legs gave out. He stumbled toward a chair.

But never reached it. He collapsed.

47

"Are you alert enough to understand me?" St. Laurent asked.

Houston smelled the sharp fumes from the brandy snifter pressed against his lips. He shivered, nodding slightly, reaching for the glass. His back felt bruised. Movement gave him pain, but he was so intimidated that, despite his injuries, he wasn't groggy. Quite the opposite. He felt on edge, stimulated, fiercely wary.

"Excellent. Then we'll proceed to business. I'll be open with you." St. Laurent told Houston. "Totally direct."

"I don't see a need for this."

The voice was urgent, angry. Houston flinched, surprised, and turned abruptly toward the man who had objected. His half-brother, Charles, whose medallion trembled on his chest. "I don't agree. We shouldn't tell him. It's too risky. I say kill him and be done with it."

"We know," St. Laurent replied. "You've told us several times. Indeed you've tried to kill him several times. You weren't successful."

"There'll be no mistake this time."

"You killed my wife?" Houston said.

Charles squinted insolently.

"You?" Houston's voice rose louder as he set his glass down and rose from the satin chair. *"You drove that van?"*

"Of course not."

"But you gave the order? You're the man who murdered her?"

184

Houston stalked across the room, consumed by total burning hatred. He walked stiffly, one foot planted firmly, then the other, fists clenched at his sides, his vision narrowed so that all he saw was Charles.

He reached out. Charles stumbled to avoid him.

"Mr. Houston," St. Laurent insisted.

Houston took another step.

"I can't allow this," St. Laurent insisted.

Charles pivoted around a table. Houston took a further step and felt forceful hands restraining him.

A guard pressed the nerves behind Pete's ears. The pain was absolute, forcing him to his knees. He squirmed, so helpless he could not even moan. As quickly as it came, the pain was gone. The guard stepped back. Pete gasped and rubbed his injured neck. He slumped.

"Don't take advantage of my patience," St. Laurent warned Houston. "You're a guest here. Please behave like one."

Pete nodded, massaging his throbbing neck.

Charles scowled behind the table. "Now you see. The man's unstable. We'd be foolish if we trusted him."

"We made our choice. Abide by it."

"But—"

"No! Don't be disruptive!" This time it was Houston's father who objected. He'd been silent since admitting his identity. Throughout the argument, he hadn't moved. But now he took command. Despite his haggard face and body, he exuded confidence as he stepped toward the middle of the room. "We met to settle this. I speak for Jacques as well as for myself when I insist on an acceptable solution."

"All I care about is safety for my daughter," Monsard said. "I want her life protected." He trembled, pulling at the bruises on his face. The makeup peeled away in strips of grotesque supple rubber. Houston saw the worry in his eyes.

"He's right," Fontaine agreed. He reached inside his navy blazer and pulled out a silver cigarette case. "All this arguing is pointless." Fontaine lit a cigarette. "Proceed with our arrangement," he told St. Laurent, then turned to Houston, helping him to stand. "Here, take this cigarette. Sit down and listen. It concerns your future."

Drawing deeply on the cigarette, needing it, Houston walked back toward the chair. He didn't look at Charles, although he sensed Charles glaring at him.

"Everyone agrees?" St. Laurent asked.

No one spoke, Pete felt the tension.

"Very well then. Mr. Houston, you write stories. I shall tell you one. In nineteen forty-four, I was a double agent for the Germans."

"You admit this?"

"We'll accomplish nothing if I lie to you. I want you to believe in my good faith."

Houston gaped at his directness.

"I informed against the Allies. In exchange, the Germans paid me gold. From such beginnings, grand designs are born. I realized that if they had only a small amount of gold they wouldn't use it to reward me. So there had to be a lot of it. The Germans were retreating, grabbing everything of worth as they pulled back. They must have secret hoards, I thought, of wealth beyond belief. The trick was how to get it from them."

Houston sat bolt-upright. He leaned ahead. "That's what this is all about? You stole a treasure from the—"

"Don't anticipate my story. It's more intricate than you guess. I didn't steal the gold. I didn't have to. It was given to me."

Houston frowned.

"The German general was faced with a dilemna," St. Laurent continued. "He was sure the war would soon be over—that Germany would lose it. Hitler had gone crazy, stubbornly denying what was obvious, recalling all his armies, planning a heroic battle that would keep the Allies out of Germany. The Fatherland was bankrupt. But the treasures his retreating armies brought would finance new offensives."

"Madness."

"So this German general concluded. Needless further suffering. Cruel waste. The gold so many men had died for would be squandered so that still more men would die. And for no reason. But to disagree with Hitler was to risk your execution. What was more, the general had learned that Hitler wasn't honoring the bravery of his returning officers. Instead they were being punished for their failure. There was no sense in returning to the Fatherland. The general had learned that his two sons had died in combat, that his wife had killed herself from grief. What future did he have? He didn't trust his officers enough to ask them for their help. He needed someone without principle. Of course, he sent for me. 'Ten million dollars' worth of gold,' he said. 'It's yours. For helping me desert but without capture from the Allies.' South America, where, with his own share, he could live in splendor.''

"You agreed?"

"The hardest part was finding men to help me. I mistrusted my own countrymen. They were too loyal to the homeland, too unselfish. But I studied the Americans and found a squad I dared to trust. Young soldiers who were terrified by battles they had been through, who were eager to desert. Except they wouldn't have a future as deserters. They required some convincing. Several million dollars' worth.''

"The thought of all that money," Fontaine said. "More wealth than I could dream about or ever see. You don't know how it was. The fighting had been constant. D-Day. Landing on the beach, and then the . . . No one warned me I would be so frightened.''

Houston noticed his father didn't speak. "And then what?" he asked St. Laurent.

"I told the general the Americans would soon attack. He sent his soldiers to the front, including those who watched the gold. The move was logical. Who'd steal the gold while an attack was under way?''

"Confusion," Houston said. "Nine Allied soldiers sneak away. The Germans, looking for a major force from one direction, aren't prepared for such a small incursion from the opposite direction.''

"In particular when that flank isn't being watched. The gen-

187

eral made sure of that. He waited for us by the trucks that held the gold.''

''You took the trucks and you escaped?''

''Precisely. We were lucky. We were bold. And we were *rich*.''

''One problem. Wartime France. You had no way to leave the country with the gold. It was too bulky, and the Germans must have chased you.''

''Not before we hid the gold. We drove the trucks fifteen kilometers from where the gold was buried. Then we burned the trucks and fled. Our uniforms enabled us to cross through Allied lines.''

''The general—''

''—was dressed as one of us, of course. It took a month and every trick we could imagine. But we got to South America. We waited. When the war was over, other Germans wanted to escape the occupation. I don't mean that we helped maniacs. But many generals had been too zealous in their eagerness for Hitler's praise. They feared they'd go on trial in Nuremberg, so we arranged their disappearance, their safe trip to South America. And for our services, they paid us well.''

''But then in nineteen fifty you came back to France.''

''He knows,'' Fontaine said, startled.

''Let him tell it.''

''That's when you approached Monsard,'' Pete said. ''You'd thought it through while you were hiding. New identities. You wanted France as your home base, since this is where the gold was. Monsard had been your best friend in the old days. He was destitute. You bribed him with the hotel. He searched through the courthouse records, found the right identities, and took the risk of getting your new birth certificates and passports. Then he burned the courthouse, so no one could discover your names belonged to long-dead children.''

''You're resourceful.''

''What about the priest?''

''I had a moment's doubt. I took confession. It was superstitious, I admit, but I was young, and I was frightened. I told everything, relying on his vow of silence, hoping that if all else failed. I could negotiate for my salvation.''

"You depended on an honest man.''

"I knew he wouldn't tell.''

"And yet you had him killed.''

"Not true. Your brother did.''

"But why?''

"Ask him.''

"The priest was weakening,'' Charles said. "He would have told.''

"And you've been nervous lately,'' St. Laurent told Charles. "You make me nervous too. If I had known what you intended—''

"Someone has to cancel your mistakes.'' The two men stared at one another.

"Charon,'' Houston said.

They turned to him abruptly.

"Charon,'' he repeated.

"It's a pun we took from classical mythology. The boatman of the underworld. You pay him. He transports you. That's what we did for those Germans. Charon was our code name. We retained it as an all-inclusive term, uniting Verlaine and a dozen other corporations in as many different countries. Using the procedures we established to smuggle the Germans, we're now in what we like to call the import-export business.''

"Heroin?'' Houston said, remembering what Bellay had told him.

"Specifics seem vulgar.''

"Weapons?''

"No more questions, please. You have sufficient information for you to consider an offer we wish to make.'' St. Laurent stared at him. "Join us.''

Houston paled. He'd been wondering what St. Laurent was up to, why this conversation, why the explanation. He had come to no conclusion, but in all the possibilities, this proposal had never occurred to him. He wasn't prepared. His thoughts collided. "Join you?''

"Look around the room. As you know, in addition to myself there were nine American soldiers. After thirty-seven years, you see the remnants of the original group. Accident, sickness, suicide. Death has claimed our friends. Of course, we've delegated authority. Capable men are in charge of our various corporations, but their power is limited. One hand doesn't know what the other is doing. Only *we* have complete understanding, total knowledge of how Charon works. We share a bond, the secret of how we began. We've stubbornly kept our power, despite what death has done to our group. But now the dissension you've caused among us threatens to destroy us at last. My dear friend thinks we're a threat to him. And then, of course, your father. Though he's never known you, he is still related to you, and he feels an obligation. Less so than Monsard. Nonetheless an obligation. If we killed you, he would think about it, brood about it, finally resent it."

Houston turned to his father, studying those darkly circled, distraught eyes.

"The image is perhaps too vivid," St. Laurent continued. "But we desperately need new blood. I can't think of anyone more capable than the man who discovered our secret. The question is, Can you *keep* the secret? Certainly, if you accept our proposition, you'd not only give us needed strength. You'd also put an end to our dissension. We'd be in harmony again."

"Except for Charles."

"He knows what's best for us. He understands. He'll comply."

"But why should *I* comply?"

St. Laurent laughed. "I think your enticements are self-evident. If you don't agree, we'll kill you. And Simone, of course. Regardless of the bitterness it would cause among us. Think about Simone. If you feel fondness for her, make your choice with that in mind. And think about the wealth I offer."

"No amount of money—"

"—would be worth the wife you lost. Of course not. I don't intend to insult you. But I ask you to be practical. We have a problem. Tell us how to solve it."

"There's a flaw."

"Oh, really?"

"If I joined you, how could you feel confident enough to trust me? I'd be worrisome. A threat."

St. Laurent shook his head. "If there's a flaw, you haven't found it. Having lost your wife, you won't invite a second loss. If you betray us, then we'll kill Simone. If she betrays us, we'll kill you. That wouldn't save us, but if nothing else, revenge is sweet. I see you wonder how we'd get at you from prison. With a contract. Money held by someone whom you've never met, who'd pay an assassin. You've been running for your life. You know the fear, the desperation. Surely you don't want a repetition. For Simone or for yourself." The wind shrieked past the windows. "We've discussed this long enough."

"I need to talk about it with my father," Houston said. St. Laurent quit breathing. Houston's father stiffened, paling. "Just the two of us. Alone," Houston said. "There are some things I need to know."

Charles spoke with scorn. "A family reunion. Touching."

Houston's father turned. "He's your relation also."

"By an accident of birth," Charles said. "I don't acknowledge the relationship. I'll agree to what the group decides. I won't pretend to like it, though."

"There's no need to be jealous."

"Hardly, Father. Embarrassed for you. And disgusted. Since he's your mistake, you deal with him." Charles braced his shoulders. Scornfully he crossed the room and yanked the door open. He glanced dismissively at Houston and stepped out. And almost bumped against a guard who entered hurriedly.

"What is it?" St. Laurent said, frowning.

As the guard began to answer, he saw Houston, stopped, and nodded toward the hallway.

"Please excuse me." St. Laurent told Houston as he left. "Yes, discuss this with your father." He attempted to sound casual. "The three of you."

"What?"

"You, your father . . . and a guard."

48

The wind was cold. Houston paced the courtyard with his father while a guard watched from a parapet. He had the sense of other eyes watching from hidden vantages, but Houston didn't care. He felt as if he were both that abandoned boy whose dream had finally come true and that betrayed adult whose nightmares had been realized.

He watched the sickle moon. He thought about Simone and how she must be worried as she waited on the bluff. He saw the floodlights' glare reflecting off the cobblestones. Then Houston squinted, turning to confront his father. "*Why?*"

His father studied him. "I don't know what she said about me?"

"You were wonderful."

His father shrugged. "We didn't get along."

The courtyard seemed to tilt. "You're lying! To her death, she claimed to love you!"

Houston's father gaped. "You mean she's . . . Carol's *dead?*"

A block of ice sank in Houston's stomach.

"*When?*" his father said.

"Two months ago. A stroke."

"But she was only fifty-eight!"

"You still remember?"

"Certainly. I think about her all the time. I wondered what her life was like, what *you* were like, what you and she were doing."

"*But you said you didn't get along with her.*"

"That doesn't mean I didn't love her."

"I don't understand!"

"A special pain," his father said. "To love a person and to know that you in turn aren't loved. She didn't get along with *me* would be more accurate. You were an accident."

Houston paled.

"You didn't know?" his father said.

"I thought you wanted me."

"Please, understand. In those days, sex was not the easy thing that it became. And birth control was not as common. I had friends who carried contraceptives, but I wasn't either confident or cynical enough to have one. Both your mother and I agreed to wait, but one night passion overpowered us. That one time. Only once. You were the consequence. Abortion was unthinkable in those days. Morally and legally. The people who performed them could be butchers. We had planned to marry when I finished school. Instead we were married one month after Carol learned she was pregnant. For myself, I loved your mother so much our early marriage was a privilege. I was happy. But your mother was more sensitive to scandal, to the frowns of friends and neighbors and her parents. She had planned one kind of life, and now she had a different kind, less proper, less respectable. She blamed me for the pregnancy. Eventually she hated me."

"Then why did she describe you with such love?"

"To hide the truth. She could have taught you bitterness. She could have made you hate me. But she chose instead to teach you love, to make your origins seem good and decent."

"But I asked her why she didn't marry again. She said that, having known the best, she'd never find your equal. How could she be satisfied with someone less? she said."

"She hated sex. She lied to hide her bitterness."

Houston felt a freezing hollow in his stomach.

"Carol wanted a divorce. In those days that too was a scandal. But the military drafted me, and we agreed that when the war was over I wouldn't come back to her. The separation saved her from the scandal. I suppose I could have argued with the draft board, pointing out I'd soon be a father. But the war was getting worse. They needed every soldier they could get. And I doubted I would win. Your mother made me feel so worthless I let the Army take me. I sent letters, but your mother never answered them. If I survived the war, I hoped I could persuade her to think differently. But deep inside I knew she wouldn't change. When St. Laurent approached me, I felt so demoralized I took the chance he offered. See, I didn't have anything to lose. I thought if I was suddenly rich I could persuade her.''

"Did you try to get in touch with us?''

"I couldn't. Afterward, I realized I'd trapped myself with my own logic. St. Laurent insisted we stay in hiding. 'One mistake,' he told us, 'one step toward our former lives, a message sent to those we knew, and we'll all go to jail. The military will be watching all our relatives.' He vowed to kill whoever talked. From the moment we deserted, we were forced to realize that what we once had been was dead. Believe me, I was tempted to risk everything and try to contact Carol. Then I asked myself if she was worth the risk—a woman who repeatedly had done her best to let me know how much she hated me. In the end I was a coward.''

"She received a letter.''

"Yes. From St. Laurent. He sent one to each relative. A compromise to us. The military would have told them we were missing, but we didn't want them waiting, hoping we were still alive. The letter would have convinced them we were dead.''

"Suppose they took the letter to the War Department.''

"What harm could that do? The military couldn't prove the letter was a fake. For one thing, St. Laurent had disappeared —he couldn't answer questions. For another, in the chaos of the war, oversights occur, mistakes get made. The War Department would have concluded that its records had been wrong— those soldiers weren't just missing, they were dead. How else could there be graves for St. Laurent to tend? The War Department would have apologized and turned to more important matters.''

"Mother was convinced."

"It was convenient for her. No divorce. Instead the dignity of being a widow. She *wanted* to believe I was dead."

"And you remarried." Houston's voice was bitter.

"A good woman. But I never loved her as I loved your mother. All the same, the years go by. A lonely man accepts a compromise. I've lived in fear of being caught. I've lived by savoring my recollections of your mother. I've raised a son—you've seen what Charles is like—who isn't worthy of respect. Now I know my choice to go along with St. Laurent was foolish. I'd prefer to have your mother. I should have gone back to her and tried again to make her love me."

"And now what?"

"I want to save your life. You're everything I wish that Charles was. I can't be the father to you—it's too late for that—but I can treat you as the son I should have raised. I can protect you. Hate me as you will, but also trust me. Let me save your life."

"The Russians."

"What?"

"Your group works with the Russians."

"Utter nonsense. We're criminals. Not madmen. How could you conceive of such absurdity?"

"A man named Bellay told me."

"I don't know him."

"A French security official. He's convinced Verlaine is a front for Russian agents."

"Peter." For the first time, Houston's father said his name. Pete almost answered, "Father."

"We're not spies. We're old men who, having chosen to step outside the law, discovered we had to stay outside the law. Our crime caused other crimes. To sell the gold, we couldn't go through legal agencies. There would have been too many questions. We used fences, brokers for the mob. Their fee was half of what the gold was worth. At that, our gain was enormous. We were greedy, though. To recoup the half we'd lost, we needed to invest the money. But again we had the problem—

how to explain the money legally? Eventually we joined the mob. We learned how dirty money could be laundered and how crime was easier the second and third time, much more lucrative than legal business. Now the mob controls us. St. Laurent controls us too. We follow his direction. We are weaker than he is, afraid of the vengeance he'd take if we betrayed him.''

"But he's willing to accept Simone and me to keep Monsard and you content. That isn't logical.''

"A calculated risk. He needs our good intentions. Within limits, he appeases us. If we become divided, Verlaine crumbles. Charon is destroyed. And with it everything St. Laurent has worked for. Even now, he's afraid that Charles will split us. We're moderate, but Charles is vicious. Though I hate to say it of a son, the man is evil. Fight him. Use Verlaine to do some good.''

"Christ, you're as frightened of Charles as you are of St. Laurent.''

"Much more so. It's terrifying to discover that my flesh and blood can despise me as he does. If he's a danger to his father, who else would be safe from him? He has no restraints. He's absolutely ruthless.''

"So instead of fighting him, you give the job to me? You're doing it again. You wouldn't fight to save your marriage. You won't fight against your son. What *will* you fight for? Years ago, you turned to St. Laurent to tell you what to do. And now you turn to me. Christ, turn around and help yourself! Control your life! Take charge of it!''

"I am. I'm fighting for your life.''

Pete trembled in the wind. The floodlights glared but gave no warmth. They stung like shards of ice.

"You killed my wife!'' he screamed and grabbed his father, planning to destroy him. He would punch him, choke him, kill him! He would punish him! For everything!

Instead, he clutched his father, sobbing.

49

St. Laurent stepped from the shadows. Houston shuddered.
As the man came forward silently, his presence brought a chill.
He wore a pitch-black cape now, perfectly adapted to the darkness from which he'd emerged. The cape was lined with crimson, and in combination with his gleaming ruffled shirt, his
brilliant rigid smile, the colors seemed unnatural, grotesque.
His brooding eyes considered Houston, full lips pursed ironically.

"A gesture of agreement, Mr. Houston?"

No reply.

"I must admit your reluctance reassures me," St. Laurent
said.

Still Houston didn't answer.

"After all, if you joined us easily, I'd have to suspect your
motives," St. Laurent said. "All the same, perhaps another
guest can help convince you."

"Someone else?"

"Yes. Come with me, please."

St. Laurent clutched his cape and swung to face the darkness.
Houston squinted toward his back. Then St. Laurent stepped
forward. Houston blinked, for St. Laurent had disappeared.
The night absorbed him, seemed to swallow him. An eerie
shiver swept through Houston.

He felt chilled by something else. The Alpine wind continued gusting from the mountains, bringing with it glacier cold.
He crossed his arms and hugged his woolen jacket. Even so, the
freezing wind pierced through his jacket, gnawing. As the gale

tugged at his hair, he saw the rolling clouds obscure the moon. He'd warned Simone that in these mountains unexpected storms occurred with frightening abruptness. Now he thought about her waiting unprepared. He worried for her, cursing his stupidity, his error in allowing her to stay up there. She should have gone back to the van. If it began to snow. . .

"I'm waiting." St. Laurent's deep voice came seemingly from nowhere.

Houston felt a premonition. Then the wind stung fiercely. As he left the spotlight's glare, he suddenly felt colder. For a moment, while his eyes adjusted to the darkness, he was blind. He groped, afraid he'd bump against a wall. He shuffled on the cobblestones. His eyes tensed—light appeared before him, spilling from an opened door.

Houston saw St. Laurent, eyes gleaming as he gestured toward the door. The wind kept shrieking. Houston glanced back toward the courtyard, where large flecks of snow streaked on an angle, settling on the cobblestones.

He shuddered, going in. His father came behind him. St. Laurent came last and shut the door. The wind's shriek now was muffled.

Houston warily peered down an ornate hallway. His anxiety made the hallway seem to lengthen.

"No, not that way, Mr. Houston." St. Laurent inclined his head to indicate a stairwell to the right. The steps curved downward. Granite blocks formed contoured walls whose seams were perfectly aligned. The steps were steep. He had the dizzy sense of peering down a well.

He had to force himself forward. The contoured walls gave off an echo as he started down the spiral. He felt cold and damp as he went underground. The stairs wound farther than he had expected. Round and round. With every turn, he guessed he'd see the bottom. But the stairs went lower. He was so accustomed to the pattern that when at last he reached the bottom he turned in anticipation of more steps—and faced a corridor with dusty lights along the ceiling. Widely spaced, they barely touched the shadows on the walls.

The corridor smelled pungent. Moisture glimmered on the stones. As Houston glanced around, he saw two other corridors, identical. stretching right and left.

"It's this way," St. Laurent said.

To the right.

He walked, his father next to him, St. Laurent behind, their footsteps clattering. Houston felt the pressure in his chest. He wondered if he ought to take his chance—to overpower St. Laurent and try to get away.

But St. Laurent stepped past him, reaching for a massive iron door.

He pulled the latch, tugging at the door. It shifted, creaking. Light gleamed, growing as the door scraped open.

St. Laurent stepped back. Amused, he studied Houston's face.

Disbelief. Then shock and fright. A torture chamber. Racks and presses, chains and spikes. While Charles loomed in perverse delight, his eyes aglow with pleasure, Houston saw the figure struggling in a chair, the arms and legs bound tightly by thick leather straps, the head caught in a metal harness.

He stared at Simone. He gripped the doorjamb, groaning, struggling to control the paralyzing impotence that scalded him.

She should be on the bluff! She shouldn't be here! How in God's name did they find her? What in God's name had Charles done to her?

He saw her muscles tense against the straps. Her breasts heaved underneath her sweater. She twisted in a frenzy.

Houston suddenly had strength. His impotence changed to rage. He moved forward. "If you've hurt her, Charles . . ." His throat was so contorted his words came out as growls.

He reached his quarry, grabbing.

This time Charles did not step back. Insolent, he drew himself up straighter. "One more step, I'll yank the lever on this harness. It'll snap her neck."

Charles clutched the lever. Houston stopped. His lungs began to burn.

''She wasn't harmed.'' The voice belonged to St. Laurent, and Houston pivoted in accusation.

''Sure, that chair is for her posture! Therapy!''

''You have my word,'' St. Laurent told him.

''It's worth shit!''

''I mean exactly what I said. She wasn't harmed.''

Houston's father stood within the doorway, pale and troubled, glancing furtively from one man to the other.

''And you think I should join these people?'' Houston's face twisted with disgust.

His father wiped a handkerchief across his mouth. ''Just listen to him.''

Houston shook. He swallowed, frantically attempting to control himself. He leaned against a rack. Staring horrified at it, he managed to breathe more calmly, tensing his muscles to subdue his trembling. ''Tell me how you found her.''

''Process of elimination,'' St. Laurent replied. ''The outside walls are monitored. We know you didn't climb in that way, so you must have used the cliffs. The guards went up to search.''

''At night? Too dangerous. And anyway, they'd have taken longer going up and coming back.''

''If they were forced to climb, you'd be right. But there's a better way to reach the top.''

''A tunnel?''

''Much the same as your escape route from the hunting lodge. It's left over from the days when people were afraid of sieges. Food and water could be brought in through the hidden passage. Lords and ladies could escape. Simone was hiding, but the guards discovered her. To give her credit, she put up a fight. Don't get upset. She wasn't hurt. She saw the wisdom of surrender.''

''*Take that harness off.*''

''As soon as you relax.''

''If you don't take that—''

''Stalemate. Fine, I'll make the first move. Charles, take off the harness please.''

''But—''

"Do it!"

Charles reluctantly flicked the snaps on each side of the harness. Scowling, he pulled it off. Houston's stomach soured as he saw the imprints of the metal bands across her neck and forehead. He walked, trembling, toward her.

Awkwardly she moved her head from side to side. In pain, she worked her jaw. She massaged her neck. When she finally spoke, her voice was whispered, hoarse. "Pete . . ." She swallowed to put moisture in her throat.

He held her.

Then he swung toward St. Laurent. "If you don't plan to hurt us, tell me why —"

"I arranged this demonstration? It's quite simple. To show what'll happen if you don't cooperate. Believe me, if I meant to hurt her, I could arrange a much more vivid demonstration. It's a gesture of the guarantees I offer. Charles, release her arms and legs."

Charles' mouth went slack. But then the words appeared to register, and slowly, almost stupidly, he stooped to fumble at the straps.

Simone massaged her wrists and ankles. Too quickly, she tried standing. Weak, she lost her balance. Houston grabbed her.

"Mr. Houston, you said earlier I needed you to help me catch Simone, As soon as I had both of you. I'd kill you."

Houston nodded.

"An intelligent assumption. Wrong, however. My offer's legitimate. When I brought you here, I could have shown you her corpse—the last thing you'd ever see. Instead her freedom demonstrates my generosity. Which choice is more attractive? Death or safety? Torture or compliance? You're a man of conscience, granted. But a compromise is sometimes unavoidable. Remember, though, that if you agree but then betray us this room is your final destination."

"Listen to him," Houston's father said.

Charles mocked, "Yes, listen to him."

But the iron door had not been closed. From down the hall-way, footsteps clattered, rapidly approaching.

Houston turned to look.

Monsard burst in the room. His body seemed diminished, smaller, frailer. His face seemed older, eyes fierce. He gasped when he saw the room. "What have you done?" he said to St. Laurent.

"It's nothing that concerns you."

"She's my daughter!"

Houston's father flinched.

"If you didn't have children, we wouldn't be threatened! But God damn you, you're my friend! If I kill her, you won't for-give me! If I kill his son, he won't forgive me either! Every-thing I've worked for will be jeopardized! Convince them! Help me save their lives! And *your* lives!"

St. Laurent's angry shouts reverberated through the room, rebounding off the instruments of pain that were the conse-quence of Houston's failure to cooperate.

Monsard stared in pathetic anguish, pleading.

Houston turned to his own father, overcome with pity, sor-row, doubt. He didn't want to die. He didn't want *Simone* to die.

"All right," he said reluctantly. "I'll join you."

St. Laurent's eyes flashed triumphantly. "And what about Simone?"

She studied Houston's face.

He felt her tension.

Houston nodded to her, and she turned to St. Laurent. "I'll do what Peter says."

The tension slowly dissipated.

"Excellent. Now quickly. Who else knows about our secret? Who else was involved in your investigation?"

"What's that got to do with—"

"*Everything.* We have to be careful. Who else knows what you discovered?"

"You intend to kill them?"

"Absolutely not. Unlike your brother, I prefer more ordinary means. They can be bribed, confused. You can go to them and give them new, misleading information. *Who?*"

"A superintendent at the cemetery."

"Yes, we know. Who else?"

"The superintendent went to Army Intelligence."

"The names of the men?"

"He didn't tell me."

"We'll find out. We'll make it worth their while to stop investigating. One advantage of great wealth is that our bribes can be outrageous, far too generous to be declined."

"I called long distance to America, a man named Hutchinson."

"Yes, Fontaine's son."

"He seemed annoyed I'd bothered him."

"Unlike yourself, his interest in his father isn't an obsession. He'll forget."

Pete struggled to remember. "And Bellay, of course. But after all, he works for you."

"Excuse me?"

"Alfred Bellay. He's a French security official. He's the man who told you we were going to that hunting lodge."

"I never heard of this man!"

Houston felt a numbness in his chest. "But if he doesn't work for you, then how could you have known where we were hiding?"

"I used police informants. I don't know him either."

"He knows *you*," Pete said. "He claims that for a year he's been investigating you."

St. Laurent tensed. "That's what I was afraid of."

"I'll take care of it," Charles said.

"Yes, do it quickly." St. Laurent turned to Houston. "Please, excuse us. I regret I can't provide you better lodging."

"*What? You're going to leave us here?*"

"A necessary inconvenience. But I trust that with Simone you won't feel lonely."

Houston's father seemed embarrassed. "Pete, I'm sorry."

"It's a trick? You lied?"

"More civilized than torture," St. Laurent told Houston. "More effective."

Monsard shouted, "No!"

"My dear old friend, you disappoint me," St. Laurent said. "You make me sick. Your weakness threatens us. Your sentiment's a danger."

"Scum!" Monsard began to curse in French.

But St. Laurent just smiled. "Such language from one dear friend to another. Very well. You're so concerned about your daughter, I suspect you ought to stay here with her. Take the opportunity to search your conscience, to prepare yourself."

Monsard trembled. Making a fist, he swung at St. Laurent, who stood immobile, unconcerned, as if immune from harm. Indeed, he started laughing.

Houston suddenly knew why. As if by prearrangement, Charles stepped forward. While his right hand grabbed at Monsard's fist, his left hand swung a mace. It struck the old man's forehead, splitting Monsard's scalp and splashing his hair with blood that trickled down his face. The old man groaned. His knees gave out. He fell.

Pete gasped. Simone shrieked, rushing toward her father. Charles pivoted, debating whether he should strike her also. St. Laurent held up a hand to stop him. Two guards lunged inside the room.

Pete's anger deepened. "Charles, you're awfully brave with that thing."

"Care to test me?"

"Don't be stupid!" St. Laurent told Charles. "We don't have time for your amusement!"

"Maybe later," Charles told Houston. "Since I've waited this long. I can wait a little longer."

"Any comments?" St. Laurent asked Houston's father. "Care to join them?"

"I've been loyal to you," Houston's father said, standing straight with pride. "I don't deserve your accusation. I've done what you wanted. Always."

Houston raged. "You Goddamned—Everything we talked about! You made me think you wanted me! You used me!"

"We needed information," Houston's father said. "The people you'd involved in this. You had to tell us willingly, completely."

"What a fool I must have seemed. I don't know how you kept yourself from laughing."

"There were moments," St. Laurent agreed. "You played your part more willingly than we expected."

"I could kill you," Houston told his father.

"Temper," St. Laurent said. "You've only yourself to blame." He turned to leave.

Monsard groaned on the floor, his head on his daughter's lap. She wiped his blood and wept.

The iron door slammed shut, the three of them were all alone. Houston saw there were no windows; as he lunged to grab the door, he heard the lock scrape shut. He'd seen the light switch in the hall. He heard muffled contemptuous laughter, and although it was impossible, he swore he heard a click out there as suddenly the room fell into darkness.

50

Absolute. The darkness wasn't merely the absence of light. It was a positive oppression, an asphyxiating force that stifled Houston like a cloak. It was so full, so massively complete that Houston's other senses took control.

Monsard continued groaning. Houston's skin rose as Simone wailed, "Peter, help me!"

Every instinct shouted, *Light!* He tried to recollect the layout of the room, but only obscene objects came to him. He groped along a clammy wall, bumping hard against a sharp-edged metal object. Wincing, he rubbed his hip.

And touched a small box in his pants pocket. The guards had kicked away his gun. They'd searched him for other weapons. But they'd ignored the insignificant thing he needed most right now. His matches.

Houston pulled them out and, fingers trembling, lit one. The tiny flame dispelled a portion of the darkness. Flickering, pale, threatening to dwindle, die. But light. He turned to Simone and saw the fear in her eyes.

"The match is going out," he warned her. "I have to light another one."

All the same, he let the match burn down until it stung his fingers. He dropped it and quickly took out another to scrape it on the box. It flamed. He breathed, relaxing.

"Pete, you'll soon use all the matches." Her unspoken "Then what?" lingered in his mind.

He shuffled through the room, aiming the match to penetrate the darkness. Here an iron mask. And farther over branding irons.

Houston stumbled toward them. Branding irons! Fire!

He was frantic as he found the hearth, the wood stacked by the fireplace. He stooped. The match went out. He lit another. In its flicker, he ripped splinters from the wood. He crumbled them and built a tiny mount. He shoved two fingers in the mound to form a hollow.

But the match went out. He struck another, easing it toward the hollow. Bark crackled, sparking; flames began to grow. He gently blew on them. In thirty seconds, he slumped back. The flames spread. He smelled acrid smoke before the draft caught and the smoke swirled up the chimney. Smoke. The guards on the parapets will see it. They'll come down to put the fire out. Then Houston remembered the snow he'd seen falling outside. The snow would hide the smoke. He relaxed as trembling light groped through the room. It stretched until it reached Simone, but not beyond her toward the murky corners.

Houston's forehead dripped with sweat. He hurried toward Simone. "How is he?"

"I can't stop the bleeding!"

Houston fumbled in his jacket, yanking out a handkerchief. He pressed it on the old man's bloody forehead. Instantly the handkerchief was soaked. "A blow that hard. His skull must be fractured." Houston saw the way Simone reacted. "Hey," he said. "I could be wrong."

He gently shoved the old man's bloody hair aside. He saw the deep depression in the skull. Despite the fire's heat, he suddenly felt cold. His breath froze in his chest. The old man's eyelids fluttered.

"Pete, he's waking up!"

Or dying, Houston thought.

The old man blinked. His lips hung open. "Who—"

"Simone. I'm with you. Peter's with you."

"I can't see."

"You have to rest. Your head . . . Don't try to talk. You have to save your strength."

"But St. Laurent—"

"He locked us in. He plans to kill us," Houston said.

"I tried to warn you."

Houston watched, appalled. The old man's eyes rose whitely in their sockets.

"Tried to stop them too." The old man jerked. "To stop Verlaine."

"Pete, help me!"

Houston grabbed the old man's thrashing legs.

"He was my friend."

"Who? St. Laurent?"

"He wasn't worthy of my friendship." Then the old man blurted, "Charon."

"What?"

"The Russians pay us."

"But I asked my father. He *denied* you work for them."

"He had to lie or he'd be killed." The old man gagged. But when he cleared his throat he vomited.

Simone was frantic, wiping at her father's lips. "Don't talk."

"No time. You have to know. It started when they helped the Germans. First that general and then the maniacs who ran the concentration camps."

"But St. Laurent denied he helped war criminals."

"Lies. Always lies. After the war, he helped the Russians."

Houston tensed.

"And then the PLO. The Red Brigades. The Baader-Meinhof."

Terrorism, hate, insanity.

"The IRA. The Arabs and the Cubans and . . ." The old man spastically contorted. "All of them. They all use Charon."

"Why?" Pete said.

"A pipeline. An escape route. Charon is a network. It arranges safe ways in and out of countries."

"For assassins?"

"Passports, transportation, hiding places. Anything you want. The man who shot the Pope."

Simone clutched at her mouth.

"He hired us." The old man's body arched. "The hotel."

"What about it?" Houston said.

"A safe house for assassins. That's why Charon owns it. At this moment a killer waits there. He will shoot—" He paused, unable to go on. "You've seen him."

"*Who?*"

"He favors lilac talcum powder."

Houston gaped. Monsard shook uncontrollably. He thrashed.

"Pete, he's convulsing!"

Houston gripped him tightly, but the old man's strength was superhuman. Houston lost his hold and fell away. The old man kicked his stomach. Houston doubled over. He felt sickened by the old man's liquid choking sounds.

My God, his tongue! He's swallowing it!

Houston couldn't use his hand to reach the tongue. The old man's jaw's might snap together, biting his fingers off.

"Pete!"

Houston swung to face the room, to find a stick, a piece of metal. Anything!

He saw the fire in the hearth. He scrambled toward the wood beside it, grabbing a branch. He ran back toward Monsard.

The old man's face was dark. He pawed his throat, gagging.

Houston forced the wood between the old man's teeth. He probed and found the tongue where it had sunk back toward the throat, and as the old man's teeth gnawed on the branch, the tongue curved forward, pressed down by the wood.

The old man breathed. His hands slipped from his throat.

Houston stiffened; he heard a different sound. He stared at the iron door. Despite its thickness, he was sure he'd heard two muffled, dry metallic spits from out there in the hall.

"What is it?" Simone asked.

He didn't know. He stood in anger. If they'd come for him . . . He grabbed the mace that Charles had used, moving toward the wall so when the door was opened he would not be seen.

He heard the rattle of a key. The door cracked open. Houston saw a shadow enter. As he swung the mace, the figure lurched away. The mace cracked sharply on the granite wall.

His father.

The impact of the mace against the wall made Houston's hand sting. His shoulder swelled as if he'd been punched.

His father. Houston saw he was alone, dropped the mace, and lunged.

He froze when he saw the handgun. An automatic with a silencer.

His father shoved the barrel with its tubed extension forcibly toward Houston's face. "I've come to help you," he said. "Don't make me kill you."

Houston stared. Beyond his father, he saw bodies in the hallway, two guards lying limply in their blood.

"You shot them?" Houston said.

"You have to leave. St. Laurent has made arrangements. He's coming for you."

"Why?"

"Because you know too much, you Goddamnèd idiot!"

"That isn't what I mean. Why help me?"

"You're my son."

Pete glared. "That's what you told me in the courtyard. Then you changed your story. You told St. Laurent you didn't care."

"To keep my freedom. If I'd acted like Monsard, they would have locked me in here with you. I was lying to gain time. I planned to come back down."

"You're lying again."

"Those dead guards in the hallway—are they lies? I tell you St. Laurent is coming! Take your chance and get away!"

His father hurried toward Simone. He peered down at her father. "Leave him."

"No!" she said.

"But you can't help him. You can't take him with you."

"No! He needs me!"

"Then you'll die."

"I have to save him!"

"*Don't you understand? He's dead!*"

She flinched and jerked away. "But he was moving! No!" She nudged her father. "Show him you're alive!" She nudged him harder. "No! Dear God!"

Her father's hand flopped off his chest. His knuckles thudded on the floor. The stick protruded from his mouth.

"He isn't dead! He can't be!"

Houston pulled her up.

She slapped his face. He felt the sting.

"He isn't dead!" she wailed.

"You have to come with me."

Her hand flashed toward his face again. He caught her wrist and shook her. "No! I'm sorry he's dead! He was brave! He tried to help us! But dammit, listen to me! We have to leave!"

His father knelt by Monsard feeling for a pulse, shaking his head despondently.

"We're going with you," Houston said.

He forced Simone across the room. Her tearful eyes strained

toward her father. Grief made her awkward. She stumbled, bumping against the doorjamb.

Houston spun her toward the hall. When she saw the two dead guards, she retched.

51

Instead of vomiting, she ran—faster than both Houston and his father. In desperate panic, she raced blindly forward.

"This way!" Houston's father said and pointed.

They'd reached the intersection where the three halls met below the stairs. His father gestured toward the right, the middle hall. But Simone charged up the stairs. She disappeared beyond the lowest curve.

"They'll find her!"

Houston chased her up the stairs. He caught her sweater as she swung around another curve. The sweater tore, leaving a fragment in his hand. She toppled, sprawling onto Houston, both of them rolling to the bottom. Houston felt the sharp edge of the stairs against his spine. He groaned, pawing to stand. He grabbed Simone, pushing her down the middle hall.

They hurried through cobwebbed shadows, smelling dampness, passing bleak cold stones. They reached another intersection. His father chose the hall to the left this time, and soon another to the right, ignoring two others, lunging straight ahead. The maze became more complicated. Houston heard water dripping. He saw rats. He heard a scream and saw a huge-winged bat swoop toward Simone. Her hands flailed to protect her hair. And then with rodent squeaks the thing dove straight at Houston. It was brown and large, teeth bared. Houston didn't watch where he was going. When his stiff-soled boot caught on a crack, he fell. His face struck granite.

Someone picked him up—Simone, her face contorted, frantic. Houston crouched reflexively, afraid the bat would dive again.

"Are you all right?" she said.

He nodded, cheek raw, swollen. His father ran ahead; Houston hurried after him with Simone.

He didn't know where they were going, whether they faced toward the castle's front or toward its back. He sometimes thought the floor sloped down, but now for sure it angled up. His lungs burned as this hallway reached an end. The water dripped more loudly. He faced two big iron doors, their surfaces brown with scum. Cold moisture clung to them. He saw his frosty breath.

"Where are we?"

"At the back of the castle. This door"—his father pointed to the right—"leads toward the mountains. St. Laurent described a tunnel, you remember?"

"How the guards went up to catch Simone."

"That's how you get away from here. The blizzard will conceal you."

"It's still snowing?"

"More severely. Can you manage in the storm?"

"I'm trained for it. I'll show you how. We'll go as far as we have strength, and then we'll build a shelter."

"I'm not going."

"What?"

"My heart. I'd never stand the shock."

"But St. Laurent will kill you."

"If I go with you, I'll die out there. But this way I won't hold you back."

"I can't."

"Take this gift from me. When you were young, you needed me. I didn't come to help. Now let me make it up to you."

"But you're my father."

"And your father's giving you your life. You still haven't escaped. You could easily freeze out there, or they could find you, or . . . But if I go with you, I'll slow you down, and then you'll certainly die. For God's sake, think about Simone!''

His father's anguished pleading rumbled hollowly along the corridor. A rat stood on its hind legs, hissing.

"I don't know what to do.''

"Stop Charon. Do what I was too afraid to do.''

"I hear them,'' Simone said.

Houston glared along the hall. He heard the muffled far-off shouting. Boot soles clattered on the granite. Angry orders echoed through the murky distance.

"Quickly,'' his father said. "I'll give you time. I'll hold them off.'' He grabbed the slimy handle of the door.

But Houston frowned. Abruptly he recalled what had happened at the hunting lodge. How, as it burned, Henri had led them through the tunnel toward the forest. How the exit had been watched. How the escape had been a trap.

Now Houston searched his father's eyes—his frail, stooped, sickly father who'd abandoned Houston, who had never known his son but now would give his life to save him. Does it make sense, Pete thought, to trust a man you never saw before, who indirectly killed your wife, who works for Charon? Should you realize that this too is another trick, a lie? Your father claims he shot those guards, but did you make sure they were dead? They could be faking. You'll go up this tunnel and you'll find guards waiting for you. When the snow melts, the authorities will find two frozen campers fifty miles away from here. Another mountain accident.

His mind constricted in confusion. Safety had been offered, but suspicion took control. From the beginning of this nightmare, nothing had been what it seemed.

"You're lying,'' Houston said.

His father went pale. "They'll soon be here! Don't lose your chance!''

"My only chance is *this* way!'' Houston darted to the left. He grabbed the second door.

"That's wrong! It leads to the castle!''

"Where they won't expect us!"

"Trust me! Use the tunnel!"

Houston shouted, "No!" His shout was swallowed by a louder sound—a shrill excruciating siren amplified by the narrow confines of the tunnel. Houston clutched his ears. The noise was like a buzz-saw.

His father peered along the hallway, frightened. Houston yanked the gun away from him. He pulled the second door, feeling the slime on its handle.

The door held firm.

"It's locked!" He strained, his shoulder aching. "Help!"

Simone lunged next to him, grabbing the handle, tugging.

Suddenly the door gave way. They fell back. Houston scrambled to his feet. He saw a bolt on the door's far side, but it had not been locked.

He found a light switch on the wall beyond the door. When he flicked it, a faint bulb revealed a set of narrow, high-pitched stairs. The wood was rotten.

Houston couldn't bear the siren's wail. He pushed Simone ahead of him. His father squeezed past him, rushing up the stairs.

Pete tried to stop him. "No!"

"But you don't know the castle."

"I don't trust you."

"Then you'll have to kill me. I'm going with you."

His father didn't stay to argue. He ran up the stairs. The wood bent from his weight, groaning wet and muffled.

Houston turned to pull the door shut. Its metal bottom scraped along the granite, rumbling into place. As he heard his father and Simone race up the stairs, he shoved the bolt to lock the door, then started after them. His boot came down so hard the wood broke, capturing his ankle. Wincing, he leaned down to pry the splinters loose. His ankle wasn't sprained, but it felt tender. He climbed higher, worried that the other steps would not support him. The incline was so narrow that his shoulders scraped against the granite on each side. He nearly lost his balance. Behind him, the siren strained to pierce the door with its wail.

He reached a landing where the planks bent from his weight. The braces squeaked, pulling from the wall. He scrambled higher, staring at his father and Simone above him, frosty vapor panting from their mouths.

Another landing. His father and Simone abruptly stopped. They faced a polished wooden door. Houston hurried up.

"This door leads to the main rooms of the castle," his father said.

Mistrustful, Houston leaned against the door. He heard no voices.

Nodding, ready with the automatic. Houston twisted the knob. He pulled it. Blazing light flowed over him. He squinted, feeling the warmth of the castle.

He stared at a long, wide corridor. He saw a medieval painting on the wall—a man-sized lion at the feet of a woman in a purple robe. She wore a crown. She held a crucifix. He peered along the ornate carpet on the wall. He saw no guards. He sensed no danger.

"Hurry!"

52

Houston took the lead. He burst out from the door, glancing both ways along the corridor, swinging in anger toward his father.

"If you shout for help, I'll kill you. If you lie . . . How do we get to the parapets?"

"The guards will see you."

"In the blizzard? I don't think so. They're probably watching the tunnel. I got in this place by climbing. We'll get out that way."

"If you're determined. This way."

To the right.

"Then we'll go left."

"That's wrong. That's foolish. You're—"

The guard's appearance settled the debate; he came around the corner to the left. He sensed commotion, turned and stared, then raised his rifle.

Houston shot. The silencer made a spitting noise. The guard fell, rifle clattering, the gray of his uniform stained with blood.

The hallway had been silent. Now the siren without warning struck Pete's ears. He'd been hearing it below him, down the stairwell, through the door. But now it sounded through the castle. As his scalp rose, Houston went against his deep suspicions. Fearful that a second guard would enter from the left, he took his father's suggestion, darting toward the right.

Simone clutched his hand. They scurried past an intersection. As he glanced along another hall, he saw a man and fired.

Glass exploded. Houston flinched. The horror-stricken man he'd shot was his own image in a mirror!

Panicked, he ran on. He passed a door that opened so abruptly Houston faltered.

Jules Fontaine appeared. He wore pajamas, held a book. His features shrank when he saw Houston. Ducking back inside the room, he slammed the door.

The lock clicked. Houston shot, the silencer spitting faintly. As the bullet whunked against the door, the siren's shriek became Fontaine's shriek; Houston heard the muffled scream behind the splintered hole inside the door.

The hallway stretched before him. Other corridors led right and left. Every door became a threat. His heart swelled, pounding.

At the far end of the hall, the rush of footsteps blended with the wailing siren. Houston dropped to one knee, aiming with both hands, his arms straight, elbows locked. A guard careened around a corner, stumbling when he saw what faced him. Houston squeezed the trigger; recoil jolted him. The guard arched backward, forehead blown away.

The rifle, get the rifle! Houston thought. But the moment he began to scramble toward it, he heard other bootsteps pounding closer from the same direction that this guard had come.

"Get back!" he told Simone.

He scuttled after her. Shock drained him. From the other end of the hall, two guards ran into view. They saw their fallen comrade and angrily raised their rifles toward Houston, his father, and Simone.

From the remaining end of the hall, the bootsteps pounded nearer.

Trapped! No cover!

Houston lunged across the hall and fumbled at a doorknob, praying it wasn't locked. The door came open. Houston fell inside. His father and Simone rushed over him. He heard the shots. And then a scream out there, puzzling till he realized that, as the two guards shot from one end of the corridor, a different group of guards must have appeared down at this other end. The scream was from a guard caught in the cross fire.

Houston rolled, kicked the door shut, and jerked up to lock it. He scanned the room: magnificent, three stories high. A massive table stretched from one end to the other, high-backed chairs along it. Tapestries, a blazing fireplace. Light from the chandeliers was blinding. At the far end of the room, above what seemed to be a throne, a balcony stretched wall to wall.

No other doors. He heard the guards outside, cursing, pounding to break in.

But the door was thick; they couldn't smash it. Houston felt protected. Then he realized he'd trapped himself. He stared past Simone and his father toward the windows, high and narrow, recessed in a row along one wall.

He rushed across the hardwood floor and, careful not to show himself, peered out. The howling of the wind was louder than the siren. He saw gusting snow, so thick it cloaked the parapets, the courtyard, all the levels of the castle. Cold seeped through the wall, numbing the hand he held against it. Houston yanked the hand back, rubbing it.

The windows had hinges. Once he pulled the window toward him, he'd be able to squeeze out through the narrow space. The gusting snow died briefly, showing him a parapet. So this room was on an upper level; he was closer to the battlements than he'd suspected.

But a figure flashed across his snow-veiled vision. Soundless. Urgent. Houston gaped as if he'd seen a ghost. The figure had been absolutely white. It seemed to have no face or hands. A specter, it was gone before he realized what he had seen. It blended so completely with the snow he wasn't even sure that it had been there.

Houston trembled.

Then the gusts of snow died once again, and this time he saw farther—past the parapet, across the courtyard, toward the other parapets. He saw the murky shapes of two gray guards. They stiffened abruptly, aiming their rifles at something.

We're in *here*, though, Houston thought. Surely word was sent. The other guards must know we've been trapped in here.

What he saw next, he swore was a hallucination. Out of nowhere, two white shapes dropped on those guards. Now white and gray struggled with each other on the parapet beyond the courtyard. One white figure raised a metal object, striking at a guard. The second specter threw a guard out into space. The snow obscured the guard's contorted plummet toward the courtyard.

There was shooting outside—automatic weapons, rifles, handguns. Men screamed.

There was shooting from inside as well. The guards beyond the door had stopped their pounding. As the siren's shriek persisted, gunshots deafened him. Bullets splintered the door.

"They'll shoot the lock off!" Houston shouted. "Through the window! It's our only chance!" He frowned. "But something's happening outside!"

He heard more shots beyond the door. But these were different, quicker, louder—stuttered cracks from automatic weapons in the hallway. "*What is it?*" Houston said.

He couldn't think. He had to save Simone, to bring her to the window, get her out of here. She'd lost control. She moaned; her legs gave out; she sank.

He ran to her. The table blocked his way. He dodged around it.

Something jolted him, slicing his chest. He felt its sudden burning impact. Stunned, he couldn't breathe.

The gunshot echoed through the room. He felt the sticky warmth of blood flow down his chest and soak his pants. The bullet had grazed him as he dodged around the table toward Simone.

She pointed, lips wide. His father cringed. Houston spun.

The balcony! High above the far end of the room, a grinning figure aimed a revolver. Houston saw his gold medallion. Charles!

"So you brought friends!" Charles said.

"I don't know what you mean."

"The men in camouflage! The shock troops!"

Houston understood. The specters, all in white. He heard explosions, more staccato volleys, then two distant soul-disturbing disturbing screams.

Charles aimed.

Houston shot, the silencer spitting, the recoil jerking his arm. His bullet whocked against the railing of the balcony.

Charles laughed. "A silencer isn't accurate this far away!" he said.

Precisely as Charles pulled the trigger, Houston dove. The bullet pierced the high-backed chair he hid behind. The splitting whack reverberated through the room.

Simone crouched on her hands and knees. Whimpering, she scrambled out of sight beneath the table.

Houston fumbled to unscrew the silencer. The metal burned his hand. He winced, and then the silencer was off. Chest heaving, he glanced at his father, who stood in the open. "Get down! Get under the table!" Houston said.

His father didn't seem to hear. He stumbled toward the balcony. "Put down the gun, Charles," he said.

Houston didn't hear an answer. Hiding behind the chair, he slid the clip from the automatic's handle. *Empty.* Trembling, he pulled back the slide on top of the gun. A bullet in the chamber. His last chance.

He peered beyond the chair.

And instantly ducked back. Charles shot, hitting the chair. The shock wave rang in Houston's ears. A splinter fell on him.

He'll shoot through the chair till he hits me. One last bullet. I can't waste it, Houston thought, He sprinted from the chair.

Charles gaped, surprised.

As Houston shot, Charles disappeared.

Lungs swollen, Houston pressed his back against the wall and stared up at the balcony projecting over him.

From outside, in the storm, he heard more screams. And from inside, in the castle's maze. Beneath him, on the other levels, automatic weapons rattled. Houston flinched, afraid that bullets would burst up through the floor.

The siren stopped. Except for distant screams and gunfire, everything was silent.

No, not everything. The storm kept howling. Houston's ears rang. He couldn't control his strident breathing. Charles—if still alive—could hardly fail to hear it.

Houston heard the scrape of shoes. He whirled and saw his father stumbling toward this far end of the room. The old man clutched his chest in pain. His face had turned gray. He seemed more stooped, more weak and pale. His effort to take one step, then another, was alarming.

It's his heart! He's having chest pains!

His father's startled look was further evidence. A heart attack! The old man stiffened, standing straighter than seemed possible. Houston watched in horror, staring at the agony in his eyes.

Then Houston understood. The shock on his father's face came from something he had seen to Houston's left along the wall.

As Houston swung, he aimed his useless automatic, crouching to defend himself.

His brother wasn't on the balcony; he was down here facing Houston. How? The wall had no door, just tapestries and paintings. Worse, his brother wasn't wounded; Houston's shot had missed him.

"Go on," Charles said. "Pull the trigger."

Houston's heart froze. He peered helplessly at the gun.

"You're out of bullets," Charles said. "Otherwise you would have shot again."

Houston planned to throw the gun and lunge at Charles. He didn't see another way. But Charles aimed his gun, finger tensing on the trigger. Houston seemed to stand in neck-deep mud. His body wouldn't move.

"No! This must stop!"

The voice belonged to his father, who staggered forward, hands out, interceding, shielding Houston. "There's no sense! They've caught us! What's the point in killing him?"

"You damned old fart." Charles shot him.

Houston heard the liquid passage of the bullet through his father. Blood spattered.

His father didn't even groan. His spastic lifeless body shuddered back toward Houston, who reflexively pushed forward, and the corpse appeared to walk, to stalk mechanically toward Charles.

In disbelief, Charles screamed. The body lurched against him, throwing him off balance. As the corpse fell, Houston charged. He braced one foot before the other, crouched, and squeezed an angry fist.

His tight-drawn knuckles struck his brother viciously across the cheek, and Houston felt with teeth-clenched satisfaction how a bone cracked in his brother's face. Now Houston's fist became a stinging fury, knuckles crushed and burning, swelling. Houston moaned. He kicked the gun from Charles' hand. He punched again. And then again.

His brother's face contorted, wrenching to one side in misproportion. Charles was stupefied. He stumbled back, making no attempt to ward off Houston's blows.

Pursuing his advantage, Houston swung in closer.

He discovered his mistake. His brother had merely been waiting. With a savage straight-armed thrust, Charles struck at Houston's ribcage.

Houston gagged in pain. He felt as if a plank had hurtled into him. His speeding heart skipped several beats. His knees went weak.

Through swirling vision, he watched as Charles glanced toward his handgun on the floor. Instead of reaching for it, Charles assumed a martial arts pose, legs splayed, body crouched, his fingers wriggling like a nest of agitated serpents.

"This is better," Charles said through his swollen lips. "You've ruined everything. Before I'm caught, I'll make you wish you'd gone back home." He pointed toward where Houston massaged his ribs. "Don't worry, they're not broken. That's too soon, too easy. I don't want a splintered bone to lance your lungs." Blood foamed from his lips. He swallowed. "You'll be awake for every painful second. Toward the end, you'll beg for me to kill you or at least to knock you out. I won't though. When I let you die, you'll still be conscious, terribly aware of what I'm doing to you."

Houston's fear swept through him, cancelling his pain. He threw his gun, but Charles stepped sideways, and the gun soared past him, gouging the hardwood floor. Charles darted forward. Houston jumped on the table, vaulted past a chair, and dropped with knees bent on the other side. The jolt shot through his injured ribs and took his breath away.

Charles followed, leaping on the table, crouching like an animal.

From one distorted side of Houston's vision, he saw Simone crawl from beneath the table, running to avoid them toward the far side of the room.

Charles dove. He landed, poised to strike; Houston felt the crackling fireplace behind him. Heat licked at his clothing.

Houston whirled in search of something with which to defend himself. Along the wall, medieval weapons were displayed. He yanked a sword from its hooks, unprepared for the weight. The sword drooped in his hand. He had to clutch it with his other hand as well, and listing from his burden, Houston swung.

The sword sliced through the air. Charles jumped back, but even so, the sword's tip slashed his shirt, severing the chain on his medallion.

Charles bumped against a chair. He scowled at his medallion, which had fallen to the floor.

Houston swung the sword again.

Charles dodged in anger. "That's the way you want it?" Charles lunged toward the other weapons on display. "It's hardly sporting. I'm an expert."

He pulled down a ball and chain. The ball had spikes. He swung the ball so fast that Houston saw only a blur. The weapon hissed.

In panic, Houston fought the urge to run. He swung again.

The sword collided with the chain. The stunning impact jolted Houston off his balance, but the chain, instead of wrenching free, spun savagely around the sword, entangling it, jerking Houston forward.

Houston lost his grip. Charles yanked the chain. The sword spun through the air.

Charles grabbed it, dropping the chain. He needed only one hand to control the sword. He flashed it back and forth as he struck a fencer's pose, faced sideways, feet apart, left hand on his hip. He darted forward.

Houston tried to get away, but Charles aimed to the right and then the left, and Houston stumbled closer to the fire. Once again he felt the heat.

He blinked and saw a figure rising ghostlike from the far side of the room, stalking toward his brother's back. Simone!

Get the gun, Houston thought, then realized there wasn't time. He blanched as he saw her pull a dagger from the wall.

Charles didn't notice her. Even as he slashed the sword toward Houston, he did not suspect her presence until he saw that

Houston wasn't looking at him. Rather, Houston's eyes were directed past him toward the weapons on the wall.

Charles understood then, broke his movement, and began to turn. Not soon enough, however, for Simone had raised the dagger in both hands. She gritted her teeth as she brought the blade down, gasping from the impact.

Houston heard the muscle-rending stab. And worse, the scrape of metal over bone. Charles rose on his tiptoes, shuddering. He clawed at his back but couldn't reach the knife. He dropped the sword. His face went white. His mouth hung open in excruciating pain.

He bellowed, retrieving the sword. He shouted, "Bitch!" and in a rage he swung toward her.

The fire! Houston's clothes began to smoke. He snapped in panic from the flames, and on the mantel of the fireplace, he saw a lance hooked to the wall, its point lodged strangely in a cup.

Reflexively he grabbed the lance, yanking it from the cup and, spinning, shouted, "Charles!"

His brother sensed more danger and turned awkwardly, his sword raised.

Houston threw the lance, impaling Charles above the groin. The point projected out the other side.

Simone screamed, stumbling to avoid the falling body.

Charles dropped back on the knife. It pierced him to its hilt. His heels drummed. He was still.

Houston stumbled toward Simone and clutched her. Blood soaked his jacket and his pants. Fatigue took charge. He understood how much his wound had weakened him. He sagged against her.

"It's all right. It's over," she said, holding up his weight. She was wrong.

53

With a sudden roar, the door exploded. Planks and shrapnel flew. The shock wave knocked Simone and Houston backward.

Figures burst inside the room. In white. With automatic rifles. Their faces were hidden by ski masks as they aimed their rifles at the room.

As Houston stooped to grab the sword Charles had dropped, he knew he didn't have the strength to use it.

"Houston?" one man said. He reached his white gloves up to pull off his ski mask. Sweating, tense, Bellay's thin features contorted with relief. "I was afraid we were too late."

"You *are* too late," Houston told him bitterly, squinting toward his father's corpse.

"What? My God, you're bleeding!"

Houston peered down at his crimsom jacket. It clung to him, sticky, warm. "My penance."

"You're not making sense."

"Who's with you? *We*, you said."

"The best squad from our agency. We followed you from the time you met with Andrews."

"When he gave us those three numbers? At the café? He told you he was going to meet us?"

"It was cynical of me, but I decided we'd use you as a catalyst, to force Verlaine to make another move against you. This time we'd be ready, though."

"You tricked us? We were decoys?"

"You were under constant watch. You remember when you stopped outside the castle—at that scenic lookout?"

Houston glared at him.

"A car pulled up?" Bellay continued. "And a family got out? A man, a woman, and three kids? They work for us."

"If you were close, what took you so long getting in? You could have saved my father! And Simone's!"

Bellay was shaken. "You surprised us."

"What?"

"We never guessed you'd go inside. It seemed impossible for you. A man alone. The castle seemed too well protected. We assumed you'd try to make them come outside. Then, when we realized . . . We watched you at the cliff behind the castle. After you went down, the guards appeared and grabbed Simone. We mobilized as fast as we were able."

"Andrews?"

"I'm right here." Another man took off his ski mask. Andrews grinned with nervousness.

"You lied to me. You used me." Houston trembled, almost hitting him.

But Andrews held his hand out.

Houston stared at it, then told him, "Damn you," and shook hands reluctantly. He turned to Bellay, "At the hotel. There's an assassin. I can identify him."

Bellay frowned. "As soon as this is over. What about St. Laurent? We've searched the castle. We can't find him."

Houston blinked, dismayed.

He suddenly thought of the tunnel. His skin tingled as he swung to face the far end of the room—the balcony, the wall where Charles had appeared. The tapestries!

"What's wrong?" Bellay said.

Houston didn't answer. He ran toward the tapestries. There had to be a hidden door, a way for Charles to have come down here from the balcony. He yanked one tapestry and saw a wall. He yanked another; an archway.

"Here!"

Bellay and Andrews ran across the room. A stairway led up to the balcony. But straight ahead a corridor met other stairs, and these went down.

"This place is full of hidden passages," Houston said. "Below us there's a tunnel." He turned to Simone. "I have to do this."

"I'll go with you," she said.

"No. I need you too much. I don't want to lose you."

"What if I lose *you?*"

"I promise I'll be careful. If there's trouble, I'll make Andrews go ahead of me."

"Hey, thanks a lot," Andrews said.

"You owe me."

"Stay with her," Bellay told his men.

Houston ducked beneath the tapestry and ran along the hidden corridor with the superintendent and Bellay. They started down the stairs. It seemed their descent would never end.

But then they reached the bottom, in a cold dark granite tunnel sloping upward toward what seemed to be the castle's rear.

Bellay pulled out a flashlight from his snowsuit. The beam lanced up the tunnel; they crept forward. Andrews aimed his rifle. Soon the tunnel sloped much higher. Houston heard the howling wind. He felt the deeper cold.

"We must be heading toward the mountain. Toward the ridge above the castle." Houston's voice reverberated in the tunnel.

Through the flashlight's ghostly beam, he saw his frosty breath. They reached a corner. As they peered around it, Bellay aimed the light.

A door. They hurried forward. Cautiously they pulled the door. The shrieking darkness of the blizzard burst on them.

"There," Bellay said, pointing.

Houston raised his arms to protect his face from the storm. He peered toward where the flashlight showed half-filled footprints in the snow. A man, not far ahead of them, had run out toward the mountains.

Houston's cheeks felt frozen, numb. Despite the angry wind, he left the tunnel, following the footsteps.

"You won't find him," Bellay said.

"I have to try! I have to get my hands on him!"

"You'll freeze to death." Andrews tried to stop him. Houston pried his hands away and stumbled on.

"The storm will kill him for you," Bellay said. "He doesn't have a chance out here."

The footprints disappeared. As Houston stared in puzzlement, he feared he was hallucinating. The snow on the ground changed color. White became a vivid, splattered red.

Bellay groaned and fell, dropping his flashlight.

Houston crouched in fierce alarm. He'd heard a shot. From where? The wind played tricks, redirecting sound.

Andrews scrambled toward Bellay.

The blood had sprayed forward, Houston realized. Then the shot must have come from—

Houston swung to see what was behind him. He stared toward the tunnel's open door, but St. Laurent was not in sight. Was there a hiding place inside the tunnel from where St. Laurent had stalked them?

Frantically, Houston scanned the darkness. He saw a sudden crimson movement. Not inside the tunnel. Higher! On a ledge above the tunnel's exit! St. Laurent apparently had known he was being chased. Instead of racing forward through the blizzard, he'd walked backward on the footprints he had made. He'd climbed up to the ledge. He'd waited, planning to shoot the men who followed him.

Staring at the sudden crimson movement up there, freezing in the darkness. Houston understood that St. Laurent still wore his red-lined cape. The man had been in such a rush to get away he hadn't found outdoor clothing. There had been no time.

Now Houston saw the handgun St. Laurent was aiming. Something had gone wrong, however. St. Laurent could easily have shot them all and stripped a body for a snowsuit. What was stopping him?

The freezing wind that deadened Houston's cheeks. My God, his hand is bare! It's frozen to the gun! His fingers—he can't move them!

St. Laurent pawed desperately to free his fingers. He pried, wailing.

Houston had no weapon. "Andrews! Up behind you!"

But the warning came too late. In anguish, St. Laurent dove, arcing down. The crimson lining of the cape spread in the wind. The hurtling figure came from hell.

As Houston stumbled back, he felt the body strike him. He lurched backward, gasping from the blow. He fell, and St. Laurent lunged at him, pounding with the useless pistol frozen to his hand.

Andrews shouted. St. Laurent and Houston began to roll. They were on a slope. They tumbled downward through the snow.

Away from Andrews and the flashlight. He and St. Laurent were hidden by the chaos of the blizzard. They rolled in the darkness, punching ineffectually at each other. Houston's side scraped past a rock beneath the snow. His head glanced past a tree. He clawed at St. Laurent. He jabbed. He gouged.

And Houston suddenly felt weightless. Oh, my God, we're on a cliff! We're going off! His stomach rose. His breath ached from his lungs.

The two men twisted as they fell. The wind kept howling. Snow enshrouded them. They landed with a sickening abruptness. Houston felt the cold seep through him, numbing him as he fought.

His right leg dangled into open space. Though Houston couldn't see what was around him, he was sure they'd landed on an outcrop. In panic, he squirmed to escape.

But St. Laurent kept striking at him with the gun, and Houston's mind began to dim as if the snow were streaking through his brain. His strength diminished. He relaxed his grip from where he stabbed at eyes and tore at ears.

A shout from somewhere.

"Houston!"

Yes. Andrews searching for him. But too late.

I've reached my limit. I don't have the strength to fight. The cold. It's wonderful. I need to sleep. I have to rest.

The flashlight's beam probed through the blizzard.

"Houston!"

Coming closer.

St. Laurent was frantic. Striking once more with the gun, he scrambled to his feet. He seemed to realize he couldn't fight both Houston and Andrews. He glanced around in search of somewhere he could run and hide.

He rushed away.

The wrong way.

Toward the cliff's edge, which he couldn't see. And for a moment Houston thought his eyes played tricks. The cape spread. St. Laurent appeared to fly.

Then St. Laurent was screaming. He fell, twisting. Red and black, then red and black. Then only white.

And he was gone.

Andrews struggled down a snowy slope. He hunkered anxiously near Houston. "Are you hurt?"

"Don't know. . . . Bellay?"

"He's only wounded. . . . St. Laurent?"

"Went off the cliff."

"Come on, you'll freeze to death," Andrews said. "I've got to take you back."

The swirling snow became a swirling in Pete's head.

To what? he thought. You've got to take me back to what?

His wife was dead. And his father.

The swirling blizzard seemed to part, and in his spinning mind he thought he saw a figure beckoning. A woman. She offered him salvation and the future.

Yes, he thought. Yes, take me back to her. *Simone.*

Andrews helped him up, turned him, and led him through the snow. But long before they reached the tunnel's mouth, a different tunnel opened, and it swallowed him. Unconsciousness was merciful, an end to pain and sorrow.

When he wakened, she was waiting for him.

About The Author

David Morrell is a professor of American Literature at the University of Iowa.